DATE DUE

MR 25 '95			
JUL 21 '97			
FEB 6 '98			
MAR 1 0 1998			

Demco, Inc. 38-293

White Jade

White Jade.

WILLO DAVIS ROBERTS

PUBLISHED FOR THE CRIME CLUB BY

DOUBLEDAY & COMPANY, INC.

GARDEN CITY, NEW YORK

1975

All the characters in this book are
fictitious, and any resemblance to actual
persons, living or dead, is purely
coincidental.

Library of Congress Cataloging in Publication Data

Roberts, Willo Davis.
  White jade.

  I. Title.
PZ4.R648Wh [PS3568.02478] 813'.5'4
ISBN 0-385-09966-5
Library of Congress Catalog Card Number: 74-14383

I cannot see the Golden Gate
Securely hidden by heavy folds
That hang between my West
And the mysterious Orient,
But mist, nor ocean, nor man
Can limit the passage of my mind,
China-bound on carven ivory bark.

Tenderly I fondle the white jade—
From ancient times the symbol
Of all that sage Confucius called "good,"
And upon which my dream ship stands,
Daring time, space, and dark water.

Through the veil of imagery
I see patient fingers, long dead,
Fashioning intricate dragons
To guard me, in centuries yet to come,
From looming dangers before which my household gods
Are as nothing more than gray firecrackers
Popping through their red paper packs—
Or an angry sun, stabbing its enemy, fog.

By Helen Fletcher Collins

Reprinted by permission of the author and
Pacific Publishing Company

White Jade

"Over there, Sissy! As soon as the tug comes out we'll be going through into the Bay, and we'll be home at last!" Christopher leaned forward, hands gripping the arms of his chair, as if to project himself closer to the distant shore.

I stared with him, as eager as he to establish a new home, yet far less trusting that we would find what we sought. The sea rose and fell, but it was not the pitching deck beneath my feet that was responsible for my inward churning.

My brother twisted suddenly in the chair-conveyance that had imprisoned him for two of his twelve years. His face, so like my own with the wind-blown dark curls around it, showed a mercurial flash of apprehension.

"What if Grandfather doesn't like us?"

"How could he not?" I countered, forcing a smile that went no further than my mouth.

For a moment his green eyes met mine, and then he laughed. "Yes, how could he not? When you are so beautiful and I am so clever . . . !"

"And our mother was his only beloved daughter. That's more to the point." I had pinned his chair between myself and the ship's rail, where we took our share of the salt spray; now it lurched so that it took all my strength to keep it from escaping me. I might have failed had not a pair of strong, rough hands placed themselves over mine and helped me to maneuver to a safer position.

It was one of the sailors, a man named Rufus. He looked at me disapprovingly. "It's a dangerous contraption, that chair, on the deck of a ship, miss. He'd be safer inside the cabin."

"But I want to be out here, where I can see!" Christopher told him. "And Sissy always lets me do what I want, don't you, Sissy?"

The sailor was not impressed by my lack of common sense. "A poor habit with a young-'un, if you don't mind my sayin' so, miss. It may be some time before we go across the bar, and there's trouble enough doin' that without havin' to fish a crippled boy out of the sea into the bargain!"

He strode away about his business, having washed the pleasure out of my brother's face. It wasn't the first time Chris had been referred to as a cripple, and it wouldn't be the last, but it hurt him, as always.

"It's a difficult bar to cross," I reminded him gently. "One of the worst on the California coast, the captain said. I suppose it makes everyone nervous."

"I'm not nervous," Chris said. "What if we're scalped by Indians before we get to Grandfather's house, Sissy?"

"I shouldn't think it likely."

"But there was a terrible massacre, two hundred and fifty Indians killed, and it set off new Indian wars." Anticipation had already returned to his features, and I could almost believe he would have welcomed such a diversion upon our landing.

"That was in 1860. In twenty-five years I'm sure the wars are all over, and the Indians—if there are any around—are no longer hostile," I assured him. I leaned my full weight against the handles of his chair; even wedged as it was, it rolled with the vessel.

"Surely the Indians aren't all gone! They won't be, do you think? We'll see some real, live Indians . . ."

"Perhaps. Look, is that the tug, coming out to meet us?"

He chattered on, as was his way—very talkative or very silent, highly excited or deeply depressed. There was little middle ground with Christopher.

I scarcely heard his words. My eyes were on the forested shore, but my mind was not. Somewhere inside that harbor in the town of Eureka, where our mother had been raised, lived our only remaining relative, Grandfather Robards. We had written to him to say that we were coming, but in the year 1885 mail delivery was uncertain; there was no way of knowing for sure that he'd received the letter.

I put down the prick of tears that still rose when I thought about Mama. It had been her dearest dream to see her father again, but it was not to be. Almost a year, now, she had lain beneath the alien Chinese earth; and when my missionary father realized that he, too, would be buried on the back side of the world, he had told us what to do.

"Go to your grandfather. He'll take care of you, Cecilia. You've been too long away from him. Go to Eureka."

I hadn't wanted to go to Eureka, but what else could we do? There was no money to support us, no prospect of a marriage with a fellow Caucasian if I remained in China. The day after my father was put to his final resting place, we boarded the ship for the United States. That was some four and a half months ago. We had touched at the islands of the dusky-skinned people, at the equally alien San Francisco, and now, within a matter of hours, we were to disembark on our native but totally unknown soil.

I was curious about my grandfather, but I wondered more about my own future in this land. There would be men here, I knew. Always more men than there were women to match them, my mother had said. Who could blame me if, at the age of almost twenty, the idea excited me? The fact that I would undoubtedly be responsible, for the rest of our lives, for my brother gave me only a little pause. Surely any man whom I could love would also come to love Chris!

The tug approached slowly, so slowly, disappearing in a trough, then breasting the next wave. My eyes glazed, watching its progress. Two years of my stay in China had been spent at the school for Christian Young Ladies in Peking, under the auspices of the Reverend Timothy Wingate. I had nothing against Reverend Wingate, but he hadn't had the warmth and personality of my father, and we'd never established a personal relationship. For a time I had had a good friend there, Grace Sheffield, whose father was some sort of adventurer and who could hardly have been called a Christian young lady; together we'd kept life on a tolerable level, until her father decided to return to his native England and Grace had gone with him. After that, somehow, I never managed to find rapport with any of the other girls and had wanted only to go home.

Home, of course, meant to my parents. Not to this isolated place, to an unknown grandfather.

He'd be an old man now, Alexander Robards would. In his seventies. What if he, too, had died since the last we'd heard from him? What if we landed in this strange place and found no one, no one at all, to take us in or befriend us?

Oh, please, I prayed, let Grandfather have gotten the letter, let him meet us at the dock! Let him welcome us and make no comment on Christopher's confinement to the chair! Let him make us safe and restore to us some measure of happiness!

Crossing the bar was an experience I hoped never to endure again. Not for nothing had the entrance to Humboldt Bay earned its reputation. There was now no question of remaining on the deck; we should have been washed overboard in the green water that poured through the scuppers over the deck between cabin and wheelhouse.

The motion of the sea was more distressing here than it had been outside. I'd never been particularly susceptible to seasickness, but by the time we'd crossed over the treacherous bar I was feeling distinctly unwell. Chris watched from the cabin windows, but I could not; it looked too much as if each moment might be our last.

And then we were in calm waters, and the sailors were hurrying, and I heard the captain shouting orders as we glided to a safe berth at the wharf.

There was no one there who looked as if he might be meeting us. It would be some time before our baggage was set ashore; recklessly, I decided to leave it, except for the small cases we carried. Two sailors got Christopher and his chair down the gangway onto the dock, and I was left with him while the mists that rose off the water enveloped us.

"This is as good as a London fog, I'll bet," Chris observed cheerily. "What are we going to do now, Sissy?"

"We're going to find a carriage . . . or something . . . and get a ride to somewhere we can rest and eat . . . and get warm." Although it was nearly the end of May, there was no hint of summer in the late afternoon air; indeed, the sun had vanished and the fog was cold and alarming. Which was foolish, of course. It couldn't change anything; it was simply a natural phenomenon.

"To Grandfather's house?"

"I don't know. There's no telling how far away it is."

"What if nobody's ever heard of him?"

Having been struggling with the same unpleasant thought, I made a sharp reply. "Don't be silly. Of course they'll have heard of him, he's lived here for thirty years, and it isn't all that big a place."

"How can you tell? It's like trying to look through cotton wool. I'm hungry, Sissy."

"Well, sit where you are—and I mean *exactly* where you are, so you don't fall into the water—until I find some sort of conveyance."

I left him there, moving toward land, with the planks sounding hollowly beneath my feet. God helps those who help themselves, and if I was quaking inwardly, at least I gave the appearance of self-reliance on the outside.

There was some sort of tavern shrouded in the fog, from which issued voices and laughter. Hesitantly, for I'd heard all my life of the evils of such a place, I pushed open the door and entered.

I nearly retreated without finding the help I needed. The smell of spirits, the rowdy male voices, combined to intimidate. Only the thought of Christopher, abandoned there on the wharf, spurred me on to approach the long counter.

"Yes, miss?" The man was fat, with a long, curling mustache decorating his upper lip; he leaned toward me, appreciation obvious in his eyes. "Can I help you?"

"Yes, please. I'm looking for a . . . a carriage, to take my brother and myself to . . . to a hotel or to my grandfather's house, if it's not too far away. Could you tell me how to go about finding one?"

"Yes, certainly. Hi, there, Willie, this young lady's needing a lift. Run out and find someone, will you? Probably Shiftly's about somewhere, if there's a ship in."

A seedy-looking young man moved obediently, and I felt dozens of eyes turn in my direction. I was conscious of my mussed clothes, the dark hair straggling around my face after the buffeting by the wind and the spray. I couldn't stand here to be inspected as if I were a slave to be marketed; I withdrew after the helpful Willie, to stand outside in the mist, thanking God that we'd arrived before full dark.

"Hello, there, missy. You waitin' for someone?"

I spun, startled, knowing without knowing how I knew that the man was drunk. My back was pressed to the rough, unpainted siding of the building, my heart hammering in the hope that Willie would be quick.

"Come along inside, I'll buy you a drink," the man offered. He was unshaven, his breath was incredible, and the way he licked his lips made my stomach churn more than the rough sea had done. He put a hand on my arm and I felt my flesh crawl as if with vermin.

"No, thank you. I'm waiting for my brother and a carriage." He didn't have to know how small and how helpless my brother was.

But he wasn't frightened off by the existence of a supposed protector. "That's all right, we'll have time for a drink, won't we? Raw day, a little rum will warm you up, missy."

"No, thank you." I tried to pull away, but the grip was tenacious.

"Aw, come along. No need to be standoffish, you know."

A man came out of the fog, his boots making a welcome clatter on the planks that formed the walk. I didn't see much of him at first, only noting that he was tall and dressed in work clothes.

He stopped, peering down at us, assessing the situation.

"I think I heard the young lady decline your invitation. On your way, then," the newcomer said crisply.

"Aw, what's it to you, gov'ner? I don't mean her any harm; she needs a warmin' drink."

"If she does she'll choose her own company, then." A large hand came out, shoving the man aside, and then the newcomer looked directly into my face. "Are you being met?"

"A . . . a young man has gone to fetch a carriage. My brother's waiting out there on the dock; we're on our way to our grandfather's house," I offered, reassured by the fact that this one, at least, was sober.

Something shifted, changed, in his face. It was an unusual face. Not conventionally handsome, but one that would draw attention with its strength and air of authority. The hair that surmounted it was as dark as my own, while the eyes were brown and sharp, overhung by thick, heavy brows, and the nose was high-bridged and prominent.

"And who would your grandfather be?"

"Alexander Robards. Do you know him?" I met his gaze eagerly.

For a moment more he scrutinized my face, as if memorizing every feature. His mouth was wide and rather thin-lipped, a mouth that could be expressive when he allowed it to be. Right now, however, he wasn't allowing anything.

"So you did get here, after all." He said it thoughtfully and perhaps with regret, I thought, although why should that be? "You're Charlotte's daughter."

Relief flooded through me. The letter had reached its destination, and we were expected!

I opened my mouth to inquire his own identity, since he hadn't offered the information himself, but he was already moving away from me.

"Stay put; I'll bring the wagon around."

The man who had accosted me had gone on into the tavern, leaving me alone amidst the swirling fog that grew thicker by the moment. I hesitated, trying without success to make out Christopher's form out there on the wharf. I had already left him to his own devices longer than I liked; he could propel the chair himself, after a fashion, but not with any degree of safety.

"Chris?" My first call was so wavering that I felt compelled to try again, to put some strength into it. He wasn't, after all, so very far away, only out of sight.

"I'm here. Hurry up, Sissy, it's cold!"

"It'll only be a little longer! I've met"—whom had I met?—"someone who's gone for a wagon, and he knows Grandfather."

The one called Willie and my hawk-visaged rescuer returned together; Willie was notably subservient, although there was nothing about their dress to distinguish them from one another, both being in rough work clothes. The unknown one, however, did have an air of authority, gesturing with one hand for a wagon to stop before me. The driver was an old man who sprang down and hurried around the horses to reach for my satchel.

"There'll be more luggage than that, no doubt, Ames, and there's a brother somewhere. Where is he?"

The dark eyes raked across my face in an almost tangible way; I felt as if he'd touched me, and could not have said whether the touch was to my liking or not, only that it stirred me.

"He's on the dock. He . . . he can't walk; he's in a wheeled chair."

"Will you be wanting any help, Mr. Shea?" Willie asked.

So his name was Shea. I was obscurely pleased to be able to put a tag on this man.

"No, thanks. Up you go, missy." He swept me up easily into the seat of the wagon, in a flurry of long skirts that must have revealed more ankle than my mother would have approved. Not that he appeared to be looking in that direction; he was already taking off into the mists for Chris.

I heard their voices, although I couldn't make out the exchange of words, and then the rumble of the chair wheels on the planks as they moved toward us. Ames had disappeared, too, to run down the luggage, no doubt. Already I felt warmer, for it was clear there was no need for panic. We had been met; we would be cared for.

Christopher was handled as easily as I, hoisted into the wagon beside me. Mr. Shea grunted audibly as he hauled the chair up behind us.

"That's an unwieldy piece of stuff if I ever saw one," he said, although its weight didn't prevent his handling it alone; I knew how heavy the chair was, and observed to myself that there were muscles under the blue chambray of his shirt. "Homemade, isn't it?"

"Yes, my father built it." Chris was animated, smiling. "Before he figured out how to do it, I couldn't get around at all."

Mr. Shea stood beside us, looking at my brother's twisted foot. "What happened to you?"

"I had an accident with a runaway carriage. My foot was crushed." I was shrinking from the necessary questions, but it never affected Christopher that way. He only objected to being called a cripple. "Two years ago. I'm used to it, now."

"Does it hurt?" The brown eyes swept upward, probing Chris's.

"No, not any more. I just can't walk on it, is all."

Mr. Shea grunted again, turning away toward the sounds of approaching footsteps on the dock, and it was only then I saw that he, too, had an injured foot or leg. His limp was not especially prominent, but there was no question that our benefactor had at some time suffered his own accident.

He was back with our driver, Ames, and the two trunks and assorted boxes and parcels which made up all that remained of our worldly goods. It was not much to bring to a new life.

They loaded it all into the back of the wagon, and Ames sprang up beside us, gathering up the reins. I leaned past Christopher to speak to the man who was obviously not going with us.

"Please . . . let me thank you for your help. We're most grateful. I don't even know who you are."

It was an open invitation, one that I urgently wanted a reply to. The reply, however, was totally unexpected.

The man addressed as "Mr. Shea" smiled for the first time. It was a curious smile, because I wasn't sure it denoted amusement, although I couldn't have said what else it might have meant.

"Why, I'm your cousin, Shea Robards," he said. "I'll be seeing you about, Miss Cummings. Take them on home, Ames."

My cousin? I stared after him as the wagon began to move; already he was being blotted out by the cottony fog, but I thought he was going into the tavern.

My cousin. It wouldn't do to continue to peer after him when the wagon had been turned around, but my thoughts remained with him. My cousin. I'd never thought of the possibility of relatives other than my grandfather. Mother had never mentioned cousins. But of course she might not have known of them; while she had no living brothers or sisters, she might easily have had cousins, and this man would have been no more than a very small child when she left Eureka all those years ago.

As we jolted along the street, I scarcely noticed what sort of town Eureka was except that large and imposing buildings loomed around us, veiled by the fog. I was absorbed in remembering Shea Robards. If we were related we would be seeing more of one another, surely. And while he had, after that first intense scrutiny, no more than glanced at me (and no wonder, considering my bedraggled appearance) it was possible that when he saw me in . . . in my moss-green silk . . . he might be more impressed.

"If this is summer," Christopher said, his teeth chattering, "I won't be looking forward to winter."

Ames, flapping the reins to urge a little more speed out of his horses, spat expertly over the edge of the wagon. "Not much difference, winter or summer. More fog in the summer, when it gets hot over the hills in the inland valleys. Rains in the winter, but it don't get much colder than this." He rolled his eyes in our direction. "The old man know you're coming, does he?"

"The old man? My grandfather, you mean?"

"Aye, Mr. Robards. He's your grandfather?"

"Yes. My mother's father." A wheel dropped into a chuckhole, making the wagon lurch so that I almost lost my seat. "We sent a letter, so I hope he knows. Mr. . . . Shea, he seemed to know . . ."

"Aye, then the old man knows," Ames said, and spat again.

But in this, it seemed, we were jumping to conclusions, for when we arrived at our journey's end we were greeted with blank-faced surprise. If our letter had preceded us, it had not reached the hands for which it had been intended. My grandfather knew nothing of us at all.

2

I knew from my mother's tales of her childhood that, while she had never suffered deprivation, she had certainly not been raised in affluence.

My father used to remark upon the wisdom of the Almighty in this instance, since from the time she was twenty she had been a minister's wife and she had not had to get unused to having luxuries and material things.

So it was that I had no idea what to expect my grandfather's financial situation to be. I wouldn't have been terribly surprised if Ames had delivered us to a log cabin in this land of incredible trees said to tower as much as three hundred feet in the air.

When the wagon jolted to a halt and I realized that this was my grandfather's house, my first thought was that an edifice of such size and magnificence must have required a number of those enormous trees.

I had seen a few stylish American houses, during the three days we'd spent in San Francisco waiting for the ship to take us on the final lap of our journey. None of them had impressed me as this one did.

It rose three full stories into the air, a somewhat narrow house in the manner of the Victorian; it extended so far back that I couldn't make out where the other end of it was. But the size alone was not what was so striking, although that was impressive enough.

The carved decorations . . . what I learned was called "gingerbread" . . . must have taken hundreds of hours to make and affix. The house was painted white, and all those knobs and flowers and leaves and vines and curlicues were delicately touched in two shades of blue and more of the white . . . we stared as entranced as children on the threshold of fairyland.

A high wrought-iron fence, as elaborate in workmanship as the house, enclosed parklike grounds. Ames climbed down and reached up to assist me.

"I think I'll get another pair of hands to unload the chair before we bring down your brother," he said. "And the luggage is heavy, too, for an old man."

He moved off toward the house, leaving the gate ajar behind him, and when I turned to look up at Chris, he was gaping at our new home.

"Look at the stained-glass windows! Sissy, we've died and gone to heaven!"

"Don't be blasphemous," I said automatically, but without much heat, for I had somewhat the same feeling myself. "At least we won't be putting a financial burden on Grandfather, from the look of it. He isn't a poor man."

"I guess not! Lord, I hope they hurry; I'm cold, and hungry enough to eat my own chair if they don't come up with something else right away."

"Christopher, don't take the name of the Lord in vain."

"I didn't, I only . . ." He stopped as the front door opened and a woman appeared beyond the figure of our driver. She was middle-aged and heavy-set; I couldn't hear the words exchanged, but her face expressed what I thought was shock.

I didn't think too much of it, for after all, she had the look of a servant . . . naturally anyone with a house the size of this one would have servants . . . and one needn't tell one's servants the contents of one's letters. Not that I knew anything about servants, so far as that went; even in China, where help was comparatively cheap, my mother had done almost everything for our household herself.

The woman vanished into the dusky interior, and Ames returned to start unloading the lighter pieces. A minute or two later a boy came out to help, a lanky, towheaded youth who looked at us with silent curiosity. The chair came down, not without difficulty, and then Christopher was lowered into it. The problem of stairs remained, for the house was set high up off the ground; at home we had been accustomed to ramps that simplified entry and exit.

Ames had given some thought to this, however, for he and the boy, who was addressed as Ned, each took an arm of the chair and proceeded up the walk with it, leaving me to follow.

Excitement and anxiety warred within me. Grandfather was a complete stranger to us, but he had loved my mother; would it follow that he would love us, too, that he would be happy to have us?

We passed into the entry hall where, with the housekeeper, we made quite a crowd. We were being inspected as avidly as we returned the stares.

"This is Mrs. Dutton, she'll see to you," Ames informed us, and gave the boy a clout to send him back for the trunks.

Mrs. Dutton, whom I rightly took to be the housekeeper, was making an effort to pull herself together. "I didn't know they was to be anybody coming," she said several times, while I let myself be dazzled by white and gold wallpaper in an elegant pattern and a crystal chandelier that, even unlighted, was a thing of magnificence, indeed.

"But . . . surely my grandfather got the letter, saying we were on our way. It was sent from China, ever so long ago, and well ahead of us."

"China?" I might as well have said "the moon," for all her comprehension of it. "I've had no orders, you understand, miss. No orders at all."

"Well, then, until you do, surely it's possible for us to get warm and rest a little," I suggested.

"And have something to eat," Christopher added. His green eyes were unnaturally bright; he eased his chair forward to peer through the doorway to our right. "Look, Sissy, there's a picture of Mother, there on the wall!"

Mrs. Dutton worked her hands together over an ample bosom. "Yes, I s'pose that would be all right. I'll see to it."

She started to move away, past the foot of the stairway that rose on one side of the hall, its posts and railing intricately carved in a fascinating variety of flowers, vines, and small creatures that would captivate my brother once he noticed them. A wide hall ran deep into the house, with closed doors on either side and an open one at the end which revealed a dining room.

"Mrs. Dutton!" I took a step after her, one hand lifted as if to hold her back. "My grandfather—has he been told we're here?"

She shook her head with emphasis. "He hasn't been told nothing, nor likely to be, at the moment!"

My hand fell back at my side. "I'm afraid I don't understand."

"He's ill, that's why. Ill in bed. He's an old man, you know. Past seventy, this Christmastime."

She turned once more, trotting on her way as if her feet hurt, as well they might considering how fat she was.

"Sissy, look! There's more books than Father had, even with the ones that burned in Peking!" My brother rolled his chair laboriously through a doorway only just wide enough to permit its passage; I stepped to the door of this room, which opened under the stairs, to caution him.

"Don't touch anything, Chris. And don't . . . don't go poking around; remember everything belongs to someone else."

"Don't be silly, it's Grandfather's and we're going to live with him, aren't we?" He pulled a volume from one of the shelves and opened it, reading aloud the title. *"The Practical Family Doctor . . .* Aiee! Sissy, look at the pictures . . ."

A brief glimpse was enough to know the book had not been intended for twelve-year-old boys. I took it out of his hand and replaced it on the shelf.

"I mean it, Chris, don't move in and take over as if someone had given the place to you. Remember your manners, or they may turn us out on the street."

"Why would they do that? I think I'm going to like living here, if the food's any good. Look at that, do you think it came from China?"

"That" was a vase on a low table, which I knew at once for valuable jade. It was intricately carved, showing a Chinese temple and tiny pilgrims wending their way toward it, up a mountainside.

"Yes. Maybe Mother sent it to him. Chris, don't *touch* it!"

He rolled his eyes, expressing without words his opinion of my female notions, but he replaced the vase undamaged. "It's a big house, isn't it? I wonder if they'll have private rooms for us? Do you think very many people live here, besides Grandfather?" He ran a finger over the soft blue velvet chair cover, savoring its luxury. "Did you notice, Sissy? There's a lot of velvet, and across the hall there's yellow brocade. I wonder if anyone is allowed to sit on those chairs?"

I was wondering that myself, and thinking uneasily that the place didn't look as if it had been planned to accommodate a young boy, even one confined to a wheeled chair.

"I wish I had something to draw with. Do you suppose there's a chance Grandfather will let me get some paper, and something to draw with?"

"I'm sure I don't know. And for heaven's sake, don't ask him!"

"Not ever?"

"Well, not at once, at any rate. There's no telling how the people in the household will react to our arrival; don't make the situation more difficult by being rude or curious or too outspoken."

"Miss?"

The voice, young and lively with interest, brought me around to face the hallway. The girl was my own age, with a wild flurry of reddish-brown hair and bright eyes of a vivid blue; she wore a simple cotton frock with an apron over it. The only thing that saved her from real prettiness was the freckles, and I wasn't sure even they were such a detraction, really, for all that freckles were supposed to be undesirable.

"I'm Annie. Mrs. Dutton says if you'll come back to the dining room, she'll bring something to eat." She was looking me over very thoroughly and once more I was conscious of my disheveled state. "She hopes you won't mind if it's very simple . . . regular supper isn't for over two hours yet, and the meat is still cooking, you see."

"Anything at all will be fine," I said quickly, and stepped to take the handles on Chris's chair.

She led the way into the spacious room with more elegant wallpaper, this time a mural in blue and white, where a hooked blue and white rug covered most of the polished floor. The table was long and shining, and if the chairs around it were simply fashioned they, too, were brought to a high gloss with wax and rubbing. As in all of the house, the windows were very high, and these were hung with lace curtains through which we could see little more than dense fog.

It was a pleasant room . . . no, a beautiful one. Annie indicated two chairs at one end of the table. "Sit, and I'll bring something." She made as if to go, but couldn't quite bring herself to do it. "She said . . . you'd come all the way from *China?* My, you must be very tired!"

Christopher's grin came easily. "Well, we didn't do it all today, you know! It takes months."

"Were you . . . seasick?"

"No. Well, Sissy was, a little, right at first when we ran into a storm, but after that not. You're not our cousin or anything, are you?"

Now it was Annie's turn to show amusement. "Lord, no! I'm Annie Crumley; I work in, days. Not for too much longer, though, maybe." Her smile deepened. "More than like I won't be scrubbing and fetching for the Robardses much longer."

Something about the way she phrased that last sentence made me wonder if she found "fetching for the Robardses" to be an unpleasant task. I wouldn't have asked, of course, but Christopher had no such reticence.

"Don't you like working here?"

Belatedly, Annie remembered that we were of the family, too. "Oh, it's all right, but it's not the same as doing for your own, is it?"

"Is . . . is there a large family? Others besides my grandfather?" I asked. Surely that wouldn't be considered a discourteous query.

"Big enough," was the ambiguous reply. "I'll bring your supper."

Supper may have been simple by Robards standards, but we found it ample and filling. Freshly baked bread and butter, a thick and tasty soup, and bowls of stewed fruit accompanied by small cakes, all disappeared in short order. I had hoped that Annie might linger and talk to us while we ate, thereby providing a source of information, but she did not.

There were voices from the back part of the house, Annie's and

Mrs. Dutton's and then a male voice which I recognized with a quickening heartbeat. Did Shea Robards live in this house, too?

I was later appalled at my own actions, but at the time it seemed the practical thing to do. I rose quickly from the table, smoothing down my hair, and stepped to the doorway that opened onto the kitchen passage.

Chris watched me, not commenting; I pretended to examine a pair of small paintings on the wall while my ears were strained to make out the words.

"Aye, they're here, and all," Mrs. Dutton was saying. "What am I s'posed to do with 'em?"

"Well, from a humanitarian point of view, you might try feeding them and finding them beds. I expect they're worn out; the girl certainly looked to be."

"But where am I to put 'em?" Mrs. Dutton demanded, in the tone of one driven beyond her endurance. "The boy in that great cumbersome chair . . . how's he to be got up and down the stairs? *I* can't be expected to help haul him up and down, not with my back, I can't!"

"Find him a space down here, then," my cousin advised. "He's only a boy, not a very big one, he'll fit into a corner somewhere."

"What corner, may I ask? There's no empty rooms, Mr. Shea, you know that! If there was, we'd have Annie living in, 'stead of getting here late every morning because she can't get herself up and on foot at a decent hour! Ned's got the little corner room, and Cook the big one, and even if we shipped Ned up to the third floor his little cubby ain't fit for a member of the family!"

Shea's voice was patient. "Then ship Ned up, as you say, and shift Cook over to his room, and give hers to the boy. Or better yet, maybe he'd want to share it with Ned . . . he can't walk, he might enjoy having another boy in there with him to give him a hand. It's plenty large enough for two half-grown boys, isn't it?"

I heard what I interpreted to be a moan. "And who's to tell Cook she's to squeeze herself and her belongin's into the cubby? She wouldn't have room to turn around!"

"Might be reason enough to lose fifty pounds," my cousin said. He sounded as if his mouth were full, and I wondered if he had sampled the meat that was roasting, for its odor was rich and fragrant. "Oh, don't make such a problem out of it, Mrs. Dutton! Tell Cook she can move into the cubby or up onto the third floor, take her choice! If she doesn't like it, she can move out altogether."

"And leave me with only Annie to run the house and do the cooking, too?"

"She won't move out, Mrs. Dutton. Take my word for it, she won't move out. This is very good. I can't be here for supper tonight; let's have a bit of it now, eh?"

"If you like it half-raw, help yoursel'. And what about the young lady? She don't look like she's used to sleeping in cubbies, neither. For all it's a big house, it ain't the bloomin' Buckingham Palace! Where am I s'posed to put *her?*"

"Well, that's easily solved. Put her in the green room. How about a slice of bread to go with this?"

I was close enough to hear her indrawn breath, and perhaps a second reaction, too, from Annie. "The green room, Mr. Shea? But that has a connecting door with . . ."

"I know what it has a connecting door with, Mrs. Dutton. Nevertheless, it's empty, it's suitable, put her there. Oh, and I wouldn't bother the old man with the newcomers tonight; wait until tomorrow, when he'll be stronger."

"Did you know they was coming?" Mrs. Dutton said, and her tone had an accusatory note.

"Yes. There was a letter, arrived over a month ago."

"But you didn't tell Mr. Robards."

"No. In his condition, we considered it unwise to do so. After all, he's lost everyone he has in the world . . . except for those of us here, and this pair of youngsters. They're Charlotte's children, which will make them important to him. A sea voyage from China . . . God Almighty, all the things that could have happened to them on such a journey! What if we'd told him they were coming, and then had to report that they'd been shipwrecked, drowned, set upon by bandits, whatever? Wouldn't that be harder on his heart than not knowing about them at all?"

Her grudging assent seemed to satisfy him, if indeed he cared about that. "You're sure, then? You want me to put the young lady in the green room?"

"I'm sure. Cut me just one more sliver of that roast, will you? I'll eat it here and then be off. I don't suppose Edward's been around?"

"Haven't seen him since he ate six eggs and half a loaf of bread for breakfast at six."

"Well, if he comes in, tell him I'm meeting Styver at the mill in an hour. He can come along if he likes."

I heard footsteps approaching and I drew quickly away from the doorway, slipping into my chair not a moment too soon. Annie was there to collect our empty dishes, and there was something new in her face. Speculation, perhaps?

I wanted to ask her about the green room, but of course I could not. A connecting door with—what? My cheeks felt hot, and my hands trembled with what could only be weariness. Whose room would mine connect with?

Annie whisked up the plates and bowls; the moment she left the room Christopher leaned toward me, whispering, "What was it? What did you hear?"

"Oh, nothing in particular. They were discussing where to put us . . . it's a big house, but it seems most of the rooms are full, and it's a problem to know how to manage your chair on the stairs. But they've figured it out."

He didn't press me, although I don't think he believed me, either. He was eager to be moving about, seeing the rest of the place, poking into those books, making himself acquainted.

As for me, I was very tired, and somewhat upset into the bargain. My grandfather must be very ill, if they couldn't tell him of our arrival. Ill, and old . . . and no longer in control of his own household, from the sound of it. What differences would this make to us, to Christopher and me?

Still, my cousin Shea had given orders, which had been accepted, and he appeared to bear us no ill will. Certainly he had taken it for granted that we were to be assimilated into the household.

Why, then, did I struggle with a growing sense of dread as I followed the housekeeper up the stairs?

3

The green room was on the second floor, about halfway back. Mrs. Dutton went about turning up the gas lights, which I had previously seen only briefly in the hotel in San Francisco.

"This is it. There's a bathroom down the hall . . . it's the narrower door, and it's left open unless there's someone in there. I expect you're tired and will want to rest now."

"My brother . . ."

"We'll see to quarters for him on the first floor, where it's easier to get him about in that chair-thing." She paused, curiosity molding her fleshy face. "What happened to him, anyway? Was he born that way?"

"No. He was trampled by a runaway horse and a carriage, two years ago."

"I see. He can't walk at all?"

"No. But he can move himself from bed to chair and back, by balancing on the good foot. He won't be any extra work to you, I promise," I said, thinking I saw the reason for her restless air. "I'll take care of anything he can't do for himself."

"More than like *he* thinks you died, years ago out there in that heathen land," she observed. "I heard sommat about grandchildren dying, out in some foreign place."

I stood ramrod-straight in my crumpled, old-fashioned gown, fighting the unwarranted emotion that threatened me. I sensed no friendliness or welcome in this woman, and there was nothing I needed more desperately at this stage of my life than a welcome, a home, a friend. "My two sisters died, and my little brother, in the cholera epidemic in 1883."

"Oh, that would be it, then." Not a word of sympathy. "Well, I hope it won't be too hard on the old man, hearing you're still alive."

A trace of tartness crept into my voice, for all that I tried to keep it out. "I hardly think it will upset him more than hearing that we had died."

"Oh, they prob'ly wouldn't have told him, if you'd died. No sense upsetting him any more, poor man." She turned once more to go. "There's no maid stays in the house at night, only Cook and me. She don't get up the stairs and I sleep up there," she gestured with a thumb toward the floor above, "so if there's sommat you want at night there's no one to fetch it."

"I'm sure I'll manage nicely," I told her, and was glad when she had gone, for I did not want her to see me shaking. I moved to the door to see if it was possible to lock it, but it was not. It was a foolish thought, anyway, simply a childish way of striking back at one I resented.

I could almost hear my mother's quiet voice, speaking as she had so many times during one of my rages. "Come now, Cecilia, what right have you to resent the woman? She runs the house, you're an added burden, and you've done nothing at all to ingratiate yourself with her; why should she be welcoming you with open arms, after all?"

Still, my hurt didn't ease. I was recently orphaned, responsible for a crippled younger brother, almost penniless, without a friend on this side of the ocean. I had counted so heavily on finding a loving grandfather, and now they didn't want me to see him right away . . . it wouldn't do even to tell him we were still alive! . . . and there was nowhere at all to turn if things didn't work out here . . .

Things *had* to work out here, simply because there *was* nowhere else. I tried to pull myself together, and inspected the room to which I had been ushered.

In itself, it was reassuring, for it was large and light, with high ceilings decorated in the bas-relief carvings I would find in the plaster throughout the house; in my room, there were cupids and flowers in a circular pattern around the light fixture. The carpeting underfoot was a luxurious one of pale beige with multicolor flowers worked in an intricate design, and the walls were papered in pale green.

Everything in the room had been designed for comfort and beauty. Besides the large bed with the heavily carved headboard, there were a dresser, a wardrobe, a dressing table, a desk, a bookcase full of books, and two chairs, both covered in white brocade that matched the spread. I had had the thought of flinging myself across the bed in a releasing flood of tears, but it was too elegant to be subjected to such mundane action, so I contented myself with opening drawers and examining the objects atop the dresser.

It had been a woman's room; there were toilet articles set out as if ready for use, and when I turned over the hairbrush with the gold back, a single long blond hair was still caught in it.

Whose hair was it? Whose room had this been? Why had the housekeeper and the hired girl drawn in their breath when my cousin suggested it for my use? And of course, this brought me back, full circle, to the puzzling question of what (or whom) this room connected with.

There was the door in question, a multipaneled, varnished door, the only other exit from the room besides the way we had entered from the hall. I stood before it, curiosity devouring me. So far as I could tell, it was no more lockable than the other one, which meant that I could simply turn the knob and see what lay next door.

I thought about it, and knew I hadn't the nerve. What if I walked into someone's bedroom while the occupant was there? It might even be my grandfather's room. I stooped to peer into the keyhole, but the adjoining room was dark.

Just as well, no doubt, I thought guiltily. My parents hadn't reared me to peer through keyholes.

My luggage had been brought up and I turned to opening it and shaking out crumpled garments. There were a few books (we had dared to salvage so few of them, because of the expense of shipping them halfway around the world) and the jade.

I took it out, unwrapping each piece and setting it on the night table beside the bed. There was not a great deal of it, but the items were all fine and rare. There was the figurine my mother had intended to send to my grandfather, and a miniature replica of a Chinese temple, and the jewelry. My father, though a genial and far from narrow-minded man, had not approved of his women adorning themselves with jewels. Not that jewelry was considered evil in itself, but he felt that anything of value was an extravagance few of us could afford, and that there were better places to put one's money than into something so frivolous.

In this one instance my mother had won out, however, for like me she was fascinated by jade; so fascinated that she had included it in my name, over my father's mild protests. I had never seen her wear the brooch or the earrings or the single, oddly shaped stone that hung as a pendant from a thin gold chain; nor had I ever been allowed to wear them.

They were, Mama had said, my dowry. Someday they could be sold when I went to a man in marriage. We had come by all the pieces in odd ways, as when the figurine of the old man had been pressed upon my mother when she tended a dying old Chinese. I had no idea of the value of any of the things, only a vague notion that they might be sold to keep us from going hungry if things should reach such a desperate state.

I fingered the stone of the pendant, liking the cool smoothness of it, and the pale green color. I didn't want to sell it. I wanted, I thought suddenly, to wear it.

I turned toward the mirror over the dressing table, holding it against my throat.

It was absurd, of course. The girl who stared back from the mirror needed her face washed and her hair combed, and the stone was incongruous against the coarse black material of my crumpled dress.

What the pendant needed was a dress with a neckline that exposed my throat and bosom, a beautiful gown of some soft, shimmering fabric. There was nothing in the wardrobe of a missionary's daughter that answered the description, and I put the jewelry down, turning away from the revealing image of myself.

I thought I was reasonably pretty. My father had always referred to us as his beauties, and Chris said I was pretty, but family opinions scarcely counted. My friend Grace, at the school in Peking, had told me I was passable. I was grateful for this accolade, coming as it did from one who was known as a raving beauty.

I had known so few American girls, and literally no young American men at all. Yet it was here, among *these* men, that I would seek and, I hoped, find a husband. Would I seem attractive to them? My cousin Shea had found me looking all worn out, but he could hardly have seen me more at a disadvantage.

For all that I was tired, I had no inclination to go to bed. It was still early evening; I knew the family had not yet had dinner. I wanted very much to meet them, to discover who my "family" was, yet it had been made clear to me that for this evening, at least, I was not to be included in their activity.

Still, they were quartering Christopher downstairs; it would be natural for me to be concerned about him and to go down to check on him, wouldn't it?

I whipped a brush through my dark hair, drawing it severely back in a bun and holding it with combs. I knew, from the women I had seen in San Francisco, that the style of it was long out of the mode, but I had no idea what to do to achieve the more desirable effect. There was water in the pitcher on the stand, and I poured enough of it into the basin to quickly wash my face. Then I would see how my brother was faring; if he were up to his usual standards he had probably taken over the ground floor.

There was a gas jet burning at each end of the long corridor. I glanced at the door next to mine . . . the room which connected with my own . . . ; it was blank and unrevealing.

As I started down the stairs a clock began to chime, and I halted before it on the landing, entranced as it counted out the hour of six. How my mother would have loved that, I thought, and turned to continue on my way when I was suddenly grabbed from behind by a pair of strong masculine hands.

"Well, what have we here! A delicious young female, indeed!"

The hands rested familiarly on my waist, above my hips, and I struggled to withdraw from them with an indignant protest.

The tone of voice changed to one of genuine admiration. "Well, and well again . . . a beauty! What's your name, young lady?"

The speaker stood two steps below me on the stairs; he did allow me to draw back enough to face him. He was very tall, and very broad in the chest and shoulders; if I hadn't been so angry with him I'd have thought him exceedingly good-looking in a dark, overpowering sort of way.

I drew myself up to my fullest height, adjusting my clothing, although he hadn't done much damage to it.

"I'm Cecilia Cummings. May I ask who you are?"

He forgot he was on the stairs and stepped back, nearly falling; it was only then, from the odor on his breath, that I realized he'd been drinking. One large hand closed around the rail before he went down more than a step or two.

"The little granddaughter from China. I beg your pardon, I thought you were a new hired girl." Embarrassment flashed across his countenance and was gone. "Welcome to Eureka, Cousin."

"You still have the advantage of me," I reminded, wondering if he customarily greeted serving girls with such familiarity. Was this what Annie had meant about the Robardses?

"Oh, certainly, I have to introduce myself, don't I? I'm Edward Robards. Your cousin."

His conduct verged on the deplorable, but he was, after all, a member of the family I would have to live with. I couldn't quite manage a smile but I did manage civility, which was as much as he deserved.

"How do you do? I met your brother earlier, I believe."

"Lawrie? Good old Lawrie." He said it in such a way as to suggest that meeting Lawrie had been a waste of time.

Puzzled, I corrected the impression I had given. "No, Shea."

Again there was a change in tone, and this time I was sure I detected hostility. "Oh. Shea's my cousin, not my brother. Trust Shea to be the first to meet a pretty female. Have you met the old man, too, then?" His gaze went beyond me, as if Grandfather might be standing at the top of the stairs.

"No. They said he was too ill to see us tonight."

Edward nodded. "Yes. 's right. You're coming down to dinner?"

"No. We had a meal when we arrived."

"There are more of you?" I could see him trying to remember what he knew about us. "Oh, the other one's a brother, right?"

I didn't feel able to withstand much more of his alcoholic breath, and I moved to go around him. "I'm on my way down to check on him, now."

"Let me go with you. I'll show you around."

I did want to look around, but I didn't especially want an intoxicated cousin for a guide. "No, thank you. Excuse me, Cousin Edward."

He did not, however, let me pass him on the stairs. One sturdy arm barred my passage, put out so as to make contact with my midsection in a way that quickened my breathing in an odd mixture of alarm and excitement.

"We've only just met. You can't walk off and leave me."

"Why can't she?" This voice was softer, without the booming resonance of Edward's. The speaker came down the stairs from behind me, reaching out with one well-kept hand to brush aside the offending arm.

Not that he could have done it if Edward had decided to be stubborn, for he was a smaller man, slight of stature, and far less muscular. This one, too, (another cousin?) was good-looking; it seemed to run in the Robards family.

The newcomer smiled at me. "I'm Lawrie, and I assume you're Cecilia."

"Yes." Had they all known we were coming, all the cousins, yet kept it to themselves? It seemed odd to me that they hadn't so much as warned the housekeeper that sleeping space would be needed.

"Get out of the way, Edward, and let us go down. I apologize for my brother, Cecilia; he's been drinking, I'm afraid. He's not quite such a boor when he's sober. I hope he didn't frighten you."

Edward scowled at being called a boor, but he moved aside now to let us pass. My spirits were beginning to rise again. Three cousins, at least, in this house. All of them young, all attractive . . . in all fairness, even Edward was attractive, except for the actions brought on by alcohol.

"Mrs. Dutton told me you'd arrived. I'm sorry none of the family was here to welcome you," Lawrie said as we gained the lower hallway.

"Your . . . Cousin Shea met us at the dock, luckily, and found a wagon to send us home. But he had a . . . a meeting, or something."

Lawrie grimaced. "Shea always has a meeting. It's business, business with that one. If it doesn't have to do with lumber, he isn't aware of it. Did I hear you say you'd already eaten? That's too bad, but no doubt you're very tired. I hope you were adequately fed?"

"Very adequately," I assured him, already beginning to thaw under the first friendly overtures I had encountered in this house.

Once more we made our way down the long corridor, through the dining room, and into the passageway that led to a kitchen, a pantry, and several smaller rooms, including the one where Christopher had been established.

I knew at once that it was the room previously claimed by the cook, for it certainly didn't qualify as the "cubby." The second of our trunks stood open and Christopher was nearly falling into it from his chair, reaching for something.

He came erect as we entered, his face flushed, triumphantly clutching the chessboard. "Oh, it's you, Sissy! I thought it was Ned coming back; I'm going to teach him to play chess!"

My eyes wandered around the room, to the furnishings that were nearly as elegant as those in my quarters upstairs. There was no sign of the cook's occupancy; I hoped she wasn't too bitter at having been turned out so hastily.

"Very good. Chris, this is our cousin Lawrie."

Lawrie advanced to shake hands as if Chris were an adult; he lingered to admire the chessboard.

"It's a beautiful thing . . . what sort of wood is it?"

"It's teak and mahogany," Chris told him, relinquishing it for closer inspection. "My father got the wood for me, and I cut the pieces and fitted them together. I carved some of the chessmen, too. They're in the trunk but I can't reach them."

Helpfully, Lawrie probed the innards of the trunk, and when he came up with the chessmen he was as impressed as Chris had known he would be. If the jade was my dowry, the chess set was Chris's treasure.

"This old man . . . he was a friend of my father's . . . he was carving the chessmen," Chris was explaining as I familiarized myself with the room. "He died before they were finished, but his daughter said that he wanted me to have them. They're quite valuable, so for a while I was afraid Father wouldn't let me keep them, but the daughter insisted. The black queen and one of the pawns were unfinished, so

I did them the best I could. The black queen isn't as nice as the white queen, but I did fairly well, I think."

His words had an arrogant and unbecoming sound, but were in fact so truthful that it was difficult for me to remonstrate. The chessmen were exquisitely formed, and even the ones Chris had completed were objects of rare beauty.

I turned to watch their faces as Lawrie admired and held the pieces up to the light. I saw then that we had another observer, as well, for Shea had come quietly to the doorway and was standing there.

"Well, you're settling in, I see," he greeted us, and this time there was a faint smile on that wide mouth, a smile that sent a premonitory tingle through me.

Lawrie extended the black queen for inspection. "The boy's a craftsman, Shea."

"It was partly done when I got it," Chris admitted, but his face reflected the pleasure he felt at the praise.

Shea took the piece, but his glance at it was no more than perfunctory. He was looking, instead, at me. "You find your room comfortable, I hope."

"Yes, very much so. The entire house is . . . somewhat overwhelming."

Both cousins laughed. "It is, isn't it? The old man wanted the finest house in Eureka, and I think maybe he built it," Shea said. "Since we were all raised in shacks and shanties, it's taken some getting used to."

"Do you play chess?" Chris demanded, glancing from one face to the other.

Shea shook his head, turning away, but Lawrie was smiling. "I've always wanted to learn."

Chris was all for giving a lesson at once. I watched the other cousin, the hawk-visaged one, as he moved restlessly around the room, touching an object here, one there, and finally coming up with the Bible that had been given to me on the occasion of my twelfth birthday. He stood with it in his hands—hands quite different from Lawrie's, in that he obviously did hard manual labor with them—and looked into my face.

"He calls you Sissy."

"It's sort of a combination of Cecilia and Sister, I suppose. I don't remember how it got started." For no reason I could think of, my face felt warm.

For a moment his eyes touched mine, then dropped to the book in his hands as he opened the leather cover. "I don't think I'm going to call you Sissy," he said, and although I sensed a depth in meaning I could not determine what it was.

He read aloud the inscription on the flyleaf. "To Cecilia Jade Cummings on her twelfth birthday, June seventeenth, 1877." The dark eyes again sought mine, this time so penetrating that I almost fell back before them. "Cecilia *Jade?*"

Now I knew the flush on my cheeks was visible. "My mother had a poetic turn of mind, and she was . . . she thought jade was very beautiful."

"Jade. Yes, that's what I'll call you. It's much more appropriate than Cecilia, or Sissy."

There was no misunderstanding that statement, surely. Color flooded my face at the compliment.

Shea closed the Bible and put it aside. "Your father was a missionary. You were a very strictly brought-up young lady."

"I suppose so. I have nothing to compare with," I confessed, wondering if my upbringing was a detriment in the eyes of this man. Detriment to what, I hadn't yet put into words.

His smile was warmer, though still casual and impersonal. "Have you had a tour of the ground floor, yet, to help you get your bearings?"

"No, we only came back here to see how her brother was doing," Lawrie answered for me, speaking over his shoulder. They had closed the trunk and were setting out the chessmen on the board atop it. "Unfortunately, she met Edward before she met me."

A shadow passed across the dark face. "I suppose he was drunk."

"Well . . . on Saturday night, you know, he'd had one or two."

Shea grimaced. "Good old Edward. I hope he didn't pinch you or back you into a corner. Edward fancies himself a ladies' man, but unfortunately the ladies sometimes find him too crude for their tastes."

I murmured something noncommittal, speculating on how lucky I had been that Lawrie came along when he did. Although of course by that time I had explained who I was, and Edward had already apologized. I would take care, however, to avoid Edward on Saturday nights.

"Would you like the tour?" Shea asked, and I nodded acquiescence, glad to leave the subject of Edward.

We were not too welcome in the kitchen, for the final meal preparations were under way; I met Cook (I was never to know her by any other name than that) who was even fatter than the housekeeper and who fixed me with a rather unfriendly glare, and glimpsed the oversized range where both Mrs. Dutton and Annie were assisting, and then I was swept out and away.

Shea touched my elbow, lightly but firmly, to steer me in the direction he wanted me to go. The touch, though only momentary, was even more tingle-producing than his smile. His limp was more pronounced than it had been earlier, perhaps because he was tired, but it did nothing to detract from his masculine magnetism. I was beginning to worry that he might possibly be married, although there had so far been no mention of women in this house other than servants.

"This is the back parlor. It's the one we're allowed to sit in," Shea said dryly. What it lacked in elegance, it made up in comfort, I saw, for there were cushions and rocking chairs and a long settle of some dark carved wood and thick upholstering. I remarked on the number of books everywhere.

"Yes. The old man has always been a reader, and he instilled that in all of us, as well, except for Edward. Edward is not a scholar."

"Have you lived with Grandfather all your life, then?" I asked, twisting to look up into his face. Already I was admitting to myself how pleasurable it was, to look up into this man's face.

"Oh, no. I've been with him since I was fifteen—half my lifetime, nearly. He took me in when *my* grandfather died—he'd had me and my mother from the time my own father was killed in a logging accident three years earlier."

"Logging?"

"Yes, that's what the Robards family fortune is built on, didn't you know? Lumber. There's more lumber in this north coast area than can be used in hundreds of years—a single tree can build two houses!" He glanced down at his own feet, moving the left one into prominent view. "That's where I got this, too. In the woods. I was seventeen, and careless. A chain slipped and I was pinned beneath a ton of logs. Luckily the earth was soft after a rain; even so, the foot was crushed badly enough so that they wanted to cut it off."

I ran my tongue over my lips, remembering when Chris had been hurt. The agony of it remained vividly, even after two years.

"But . . . someone . . . didn't let them."

"*I* didn't let them. I fought against it until Uncle Alex told them to leave off, to let me be. Who was to say whether dying was so much worse than living a cripple? But I didn't die, and as you see, I'm not crippled so badly that I'm less than a man."

Was there a challenge in the look he gave me? Did he, perhaps, want to know if *I felt him to be less than a whole man?* Confused, uncertain, I didn't know what to say. I did not want to embarrass us both by reading more into his words than he intended; neither could I let him think I found his injury repugnant to me.

I groped for words slowly, praying they would be all right. "I was there when Christopher was . . . hurt. It was so . . . terrible. But now . . . you see him, now, even though he's confined to the chair . . . he's bright, and quick, and a thoroughly delightful person . . ."

Shea nodded, moving on to the next room, and I couldn't tell how he'd interpreted my words.

"These are the front parlors . . . there's a set of sliding doors between them, so they can be joined for a large party. Not that we do all that much partying, with no young women in the house any more." The impact of that was sufficient so that I lost a bit of what he was saying. The parlors were matching rooms, with gold and white papered walls, buttery yellow brocaded chairs and sofas in the Victorian style, an elaborately carved white fireplace at one end, a massive semicircular window of colored glass at the other. The marble-topped tables with their bowls and vases of wildflowers and roses swam before my eyes, and I struggled to come back to whatever my companion was saying.

"A man likes a place he can put his feet up," registered quite out of context and I attempted a suitable reply.

"Not on yellow brocade, naturally."

"And on the other side of the hall is the library . . ."

"Yes, I've . . . Christopher is enchanted with that; he's a reader, too."

"You've seen it? The last room, then, is the music room."

He stood aside for me to precede him; my arm brushed his and I swayed a little so that he put out a hand to steady me. Was I succumbing to some sort of female vapors (I'd never been subject to them before!) or was I simply so worn out that my strength was uncertain?

I moved on, so that he relinquished my arm, although that was not what I wanted him to do. What did I want? Only half an hour ago

I had been indignant when Edward dared to put his hands on me. My confusion increased, but fortunately there was something to draw forth an exclamation of genuine interest and pleasure.

"An organ! You have an organ!"

The music room, like the family parlor, was a homey, used-looking room, for there were comfortable chairs as well as the primary piece of furniture, the organ. It was a massive, ornately carved instrument, and I moved to touch the keys.

"Do you play?" He was smiling, as if pleased at my childish delight.

"A little. My mother was teaching me when . . . Will it be all right if I practice here? Or . . ."

"Of course you may practice. Lawrie plays, but there'll be plenty of times when no one's using it. The old man never learned to play, but he loves to listen. Go ahead, play something."

Suddenly shy, I withdrew. "No, not now. I'm only an amateur, and I don't have any familiar music. Besides, I only know hymns."

"Befitting to a missionary's daughter," he said, but the smile remained, and I didn't think he was holding that against me.

The voice behind us was unexpected, sharp, and unquestionably female. "Shea! Is it true, is . . ."

He had been standing so that he shielded me from view; as we both spun around to face the newcomer, I saw shock and dismay written clearly across the woman's countenance.

She was a big woman, not fat, but big. She was dark and there was a hint of facial hair across her upper lip; she wore a rich dark dress with a cameo at the throat, and a ring with a flashing stone on her left hand. At the moment the hand was at her throat, working the crepy, loose skin.

When Shea said there were no young women in the house, I had taken it for granted there were *no* women at all. It was impossible not to reveal my own surprise, and I think I took an involuntary step toward my cousin, for this woman's anger seemed directed at me.

She was in her middle fifties and might have passed for younger had it not been for the sagging flesh at her throat. She had an air of authority that informed me of her superior position in this household; for a matter of seconds her dark eyes raked across me in an almost physical way, and then I watched as she began to draw herself under control.

Shea didn't act as if anything was wrong, although I thought I detected a lack of warmth in his response to her.

"Good evening, Aunt Hesper. I'm showing our new cousin over the house. Jade, this is our Aunt Hesper . . . Lawrie and Edward's mother. Her late husband was Uncle Alex's nephew . . . my father's brother."

It was a few seconds before I realized that "Uncle Alex" was my grandfather. The woman's manner was intimidating, and it was all I could do to murmur an acknowledgment of the introduction.

However, when she spoke again some of the animosity seemed gone. "Jade? What an extraordinary name."

"It's actually Cecilia Jade, but the family always called me Sissy." I was immediately sorry I had added that last, for I couldn't imagine this woman ever addressing me as "Sissy."

She managed a wintry smile, perhaps at some effort. "Cecilia. Yes, I remember now. Mrs. Dutton told me"—the dark eyes, which seemed to be so cold, swung to Shea—"that she's been established in Anthea's room."

I shifted my eyes quickly, to catch any changing expression from Shea: who was Anthea?

His face was closed. I'd never thought that about a person's face, before, but that's what it was, as if he'd closed a door so that no one could see into him in any way.

"Yes, that's right. It seemed the logical place for her." Was there a hint of challenge there? Good grief, I was reading significance into everything, whether it was there or not.

Aunt Hesper stared at me a moment longer; when she inhaled her magnificent bosom rose, carrying the cameo on a gentle tide. "I believe dinner is to be served momentarily," she said.

"I ate earlier, but I've worn most of it off; I think I'll go around again," Shea said. "How about you, Cousin Jade?"

I was feeling upset and anything but at ease; the strain of the weeks of travel had caught up with me, and I felt it in my legs, which wanted to collapse. I shook my head.

"Thank you, no. I believe I'll retire now. Good night."

I scarcely heard their murmured "good nights"; I could feel eyes on my back as I made my way to the stairs, but couldn't tell which of them it was until I'd reached the landing and looked down. Shea stood there, smiling; he lifted one hand in a little salute, and then went on toward the dining room.

I was positive that when Aunt Hesper had burst into the music room to demand information of Shea, it had been of me that she spoke. "Is it true . . . ?" that Christopher and I had arrived? Was that what she had meant to ask?

Who was Anthea? Why did it bother everyone that I was in her room? And to whose room did it connect?

4

For all my shaking limbs, I couldn't sit down and rest. I paced the floor, then opened all the drawers and doors, looking for any clue to the former occupant of this room. I found nothing. Whoever Anthea was, whatever she had kept in these storage places, no signs remained.

They were all downstairs, now. Eating. No one would know if I opened the door to the connecting bedroom.

The brazen idea didn't seem quite so outrageous the second time around. My father had had very strict ideas about how one acts in another's house, and for the most part I agreed with him. But surely these were exceptional circumstances?

Aunt Hesper, at least, resented and disliked me. For all her quick cover-up, I was sure of that. The servants were still an unknown quantity . . . it was only natural that they should be perturbed when their routine was upset, their living arrangements overturned. But why did Aunt Hesper resent me?

I was too inexperienced, too naïve, to come up with much in the way of explanations. If only I could meet with my grandfather and be sure that he, at least, welcomed us and offered his protection!

My grandfather. I paused in mid-stride, skirts swirling out around my ankles. *He* wasn't eating, at least not downstairs with the rest of them.

Was he really so ill that seeing me, learning I was alive, would be dangerously upsetting to him? I found that entire idea unlikely; I should think it would be the other way around, that his joy in seeing us at last would make him better, not worse.

I went to my own door and would have opened it except that I heard footsteps in the corridor outside. Aunt Hesper, I thought, for I could hear the rustle of taffeta petticoats. She passed on toward the back of the house, and somewhere in the distance I heard the closing of a door.

Well, she hadn't entered next door. Dared I open up that room?

Feeling so daring and so wicked that my breathing was almost cut off, I crossed to the mysterious door and turned the knob before I had time to reconsider.

The room beyond, where a kerosene lamp had been left burning low, was a disappointment. Not that it wasn't large and as lavishly furnished as the rest of the house; but it was only a bedroom, a room that gave no more clue than my own to its occupant.

I stood looking around in chagrin. What had I expected, that there would be a sign over the bed proclaiming, "I am so-and-so's room"?

And then I realized that there were clues, of a sort, at least to the sex of the person who lived here. For there were no feminine fripperies; certainly Aunt Hesper had had no hand in the decorating.

A man's room . . . currently lived in, for the light was lit and there were a few masculine toilet articles atop the dresser, and an open book on the night table.

Not Edward, for Edward wasn't a reader, Shea had said. I was just as pleased that it wasn't Edward.

I was beginning to be familiar with the fine tremor of excitement that touched me when I thought about Shea. Already, in so short a time, I was drawn to Shea. Was this Shea's room?

I couldn't bring myself to poke about in the wardrobe and drawers to ascertain anything further. Already I had transgressed the rules of good manners so far that my parents would have been horrified. I withdrew, and was about to try the door again, when there were more footsteps. Heavy ones, this time. Perhaps Edward?

They, too, passed on down the hall, and I heard a door close. Well, I thought, wasn't there supposed to be a bathroom down there that was for the use of everyone? Surely no one would think anything of it if I went to the bathroom.

So easily I justified my snooping in this house, for of course that's what I intended. I let myself out of my room and strode briskly— but quietly—toward the promised bath.

I couldn't tell which rooms were now occupied; toward the far end I slowed down and listened. No voices. No sounds of movement. There was nothing for it but to enter the bathroom.

I had seen one once before, in the hotel in San Francisco, but it hadn't been as elegantly equipped as this. At another time I would have been fascinated with the great, clawfooted tub and the marvelous water closet, but right now I wanted some reassurances about the members of this household.

If I had walked into an atmosphere of hostility I must do something to overcome it. My small supply of jade could scarcely be expected to sustain us for long if we had to leave, and living in a household of open animosity was so far outside my understanding that it was beyond contemplating.

I hesitated in the doorway, wondering which room was my grandfather's. Surely the others would be going down soon, if dinner was to be served momentarily.

And then the clue came—Aunt Hesper's voice, sounding much more amiable than when she had been speaking to me.

"Is there anything else, then, Alex? Or shall I run along to dinner?"

Grandfather! I pressed myself to the wall, listening, ready to move back into the bathroom if anyone opened a door. I was just across the hall from the chamber where Aunt Hesper was, and I waited eagerly for the sound of the old man's voice.

It was strong and slightly querulous, not at all like a sick old man.

"Yes, yes, go on, Hesper, I don't need a thing, except some peace and quiet. People tromping in and out all the time, it's like a circus."

Hesper gave a throaty chuckle. "I'm sure no one means to disturb you, Alex. It's only that we're all concerned about you."

"Well, don't be. When it's time to die, I'll die, but I haven't reached that point yet, I assure you. Tell Shea I'd like a bit of brandy before he goes to bed; it'll help me sleep."

"I'm not sure Shea's here," Hesper said, with an urbanity I found despicable, since I knew she was lying. "But perhaps Edward . . ."

"Saturday night, ain't it? He'll be reeking like a pig, if I know Edward. Last time he was in here he tripped over my stool and nearly went through a window. Where's Shea?"

"I don't know, I'm sure. But if he comes in, I'll tell him. I'll look in on you again before I go to bed, Alex."

"Don't bother," the old man said.

Although I was poised for instant action, she opened the door before I could move. Displeasure was written strongly across her face, and she pulled the door shut behind her at once, but not before I had seen into the room. The old man—I had only a glimpse of him—was not even in bed; he sat in a chair with a robe over his knees.

"Were you looking for something?"

Her voice was very low, calculated not to carry to my grandfather's ears, and her bulk was so menacing that I withdrew against the woodwork. I would have liked to raise my voice enough to make him hear me, but it didn't come out that way.

"No, just . . . the bathroom."

Her smile was cool and didn't touch anything but the corners of her mouth. "I see. Well, we try not to make any noise that will annoy poor Alex; he's not at all well, you know."

There was nothing for me to do except return to my room, feeling angry and awkward and helpless. But if they didn't take me in to see him tomorrow I'd go in by myself, no matter what they said!

I got ready for bed in a haphazard fashion, brushing out my hair and tying it back with a ribbon, putting a warm robe nearby in case I needed it during the night. It wasn't late, but it had been a long time since I'd caught up on my rest—not since I'd left China, really, for the pitching of a ship was not always conducive to the best sleep.

I said my prayers and got into the big bed; it was comfortable and I needed the blanket, nearly summer or not. What had Ames said, that it didn't get much warmer or colder, no matter what the time of year? That was hard to believe, but the climate was the least of my worries.

For all my exhaustion, I could not immediately sleep. The house was so constructed that very little sound carried up from the first floor; I did hear the others as they came up to their rooms, however.

It was possible to identify the opening of the door next to mine, and I rolled over, holding my breath, wondering which of them it was. Shea? Was it Shea? And if so, why did his room connect with that of someone called Anthea?

Ordinarily, I decided, one wouldn't expect connecting doors between the rooms of a man and a woman unless they were married. I didn't want Shea to be married. Already I was sure of that. But he had said there were no young women in the house, he hadn't mentioned a wife . . . perhaps she had been his wife, and she was now . . . where? Gone? Dead?

The house made the usual cooling-off sounds. For a short time I heard someone moving around next door, and then all was quiet. I wished I could go to sleep.

After listening to the clock on the landing strike out the hours of ten, and then eleven, I gave up and groped on the table beside me for matches. I didn't know how to work the gas fixture . . . I hadn't paid attention when Mrs. Dutton did it . . . but I was familiar with kerosene lamps, and I lit that.

I would go downstairs and find a book; perhaps reading would take my mind off everything else so that I could fall asleep.

I was glad my robe was a heavy one for the house had grown cold. I had no slippers, but the floors were all carpeted except the lower hall, and I wasn't susceptible to chills.

The trip downstairs was uneventful; I had taken my own lamp, as the gas jets were all extinguished, and I chose a book of poetry. Book in one hand, lamp in the other, I prepared to mount the stairs as the quarter hour struck. Perhaps its chiming covered the sounds of a door opening above; at any rate, I didn't hear it and had no way of knowing whose door it was.

I heard the girl, though. She was running, and she didn't expect to encounter anyone in the darkened house. From the speed with which she moved I could conclude that she knew her way about even in the dark, although that didn't occur to me until later.

We met at the foot of the stairs and for a moment she was poised in her flight, one hand touching the carved rail, the dark cloud of her hair framing an angry, weeping face. Her eyes went wide upon seeing me; we stared at one another, too startled to speak.

She was young, younger than I by several years, and pretty. Her clothes were simple and inexpensive ones, and she clutched a knitted shawl around her throat, caught there with a tiny gold cross on a fine chain that had become entangled with her fingers.

Her distress was evident, and I gave way before it, stepping to one side. She bounded past me without a word, although I heard a choked sob, and then she was gone, out the double front doors with their colored glass panes.

A moment longer I stood, then moved to close the doors, for she had left them standing open. I waited, thinking someone might come to call after her, yet nothing happened.

But of course, anyone on the second floor could tell that I was down here with a lamp. If he didn't want anyone to know he'd been receiving late-night callers, he'd hardly give himself away by appearing.

There were three men up there, excluding Grandfather. Which of them was entertaining so clandestinely?

It was none of my business, of course. But when has that ever stopped anyone from speculating?

In the year 1885 few parents offered their daughters much in the way of sex education, it being thought improper to do so. A young woman was introduced into the mysteries of the marital relationship by a tender and loving husband during the honeymoon. Still, any reasonably observant girl kept her eyes and ears open and put two and two together to make three, or five, or perhaps even four.

I made my own immediate conclusions as to why the girl was here in this house in the middle of the night. It made me feel very strange, and I was not at all in the mood for reading poetry when I regained my room.

The morning was glorious.

I woke late but refreshed and determined. I would meet my grandfather today, and establish my place in this household. On such a beautiful day how could it be other than that I would be accepted as if I were his own beloved daughter?

I was still in mourning, but my supply of black frocks was so limited, and they were so worn and crumpled, that I justified choosing instead a simple dress of gray cotton with a lace collar and cuffs. For a tempting moment I held the jade pendant against it, then regretfully replaced it on the dresser.

Somewhere out there in the sunny city I heard church bells chiming. I wondered if there would be a carriage available to take me to services, and hoped that there would be breakfast served before I went, for I was ravenous. The fare on board ship, where I had spent so many weeks, didn't compare to the meal we had been served last night.

I found Christopher in the dining room, devouring ham and eggs and thick slices of hot bread dripping with butter and jam. He greeted me with elation.

"Sissy, this place is going to be elegant! Do you know there's an organ?"

"Yes, I saw it. Have you met any of the family this morning?"

"Only someone named Aunt Hesper." He made a face to indicate his reaction to her. "She reminds me of the ogre from Grimms'. Why doesn't she like me?"

"I suspect she doesn't like anyone very much. Chris, you really shouldn't talk about the other people in this house."

"Why not? Sissy, sometimes you're a regular dolt. How can I not talk about the people I'm going to live with?"

There was enough logic in this so that I had to smile. "Well, all right, but be discreet. At least make sure you can't be overheard when you do it."

"Nobody can hear me now. Ned's already had breakfast and he's gone out to do something with the horses. Cook's busy, and Mrs. Dutton has gone to get ready for church. I told her we wouldn't be going today."

"Why ever not? We always go to church on Sunday, when it's possible."

"Well, I thought we were both too tired," Christopher offered glibly, exuding vitality from every pore. "Did you know I'm to have Ned for a roommate? They brought in a cot for him, and he's to help me dress and everything."

"You don't need any help dressing."

"No, well, they don't know that, and Ned says it'll be easier than some of the other things they're always wanting him to do. Ned says they've put you into one of the nicest rooms in the house, Anthea's room."

I couldn't help myself; I leaned forward, blurting out the question. "Who is Anthea?"

"She was Shea's wife. She's been dead for over a year, now. She was drowned. They found her on the beach, in a white nightgown, and nobody knew how she got there or what happened." He took half a glass of milk in one long swallow. "She was very pretty, and very young. There were bruises on her throat and it was suspected she was murdered but there was never any evidence; they couldn't prove anything."

I stared at him, wondering how much to believe. "Ned talks quite a bit, doesn't he?"

"He's lived here since he was fourteen. He's fifteen now. He has to empty all the slops and things like that. He says Cook is grouchy, but she makes wonderful pies, and she's never stingy with the food."

"Does Ned say anything about Grandfather?" My touch of sarcasm passed unnoticed.

"He says Grandfather has a bad heart, and he can't run the mills any more, so the cousins do that. Mostly it's Shea who runs things, but Edward wants to. Lawrie doesn't care anything about the mills. Did you know Lawrie is an artist? He painted most of the pictures in the house. I beat him playing chess last night."

"That's not surprising, since he didn't know how to play. Does Ned think Grandfather is very seriously ill, then?"

Christopher shrugged. "I don't know. He says the doctor comes to see him, so I suppose he is. Lawrie says he'll give me some paper and things to sketch with, and maybe after a while I'll get good enough so he'll let me have some paints, too."

He chattered on after my own meal was served; I half listened, seeing that "Ned says" was going to be a major part of my brother's vocabulary from now on. Still, it was good that there was another boy in the house to keep him company, and Ned might be a welcome source of information, if he proved to be truthful.

So Anthea had been Shea's wife, and that meant that it *was* Shea in the room next to mine. I felt much better, knowing it wasn't Edward. I remembered, then, the girl I had met on the stairs before midnight. Whose room had *she* been in? I wondered if Ned could have told me *that*.

Annie, her flaming hair caught back with a blue ribbon, appeared in the doorway. "If you please, miss, Mr. Shea says will you come upstairs when you've finished?"

I pushed back my chair. "Are we going to meet Grandfather, do you know?"

Annie shrugged. "I couldn't say. If you're not needing anything else, I'll go on, then. Sunday I have the afternoon off."

I smiled my thanks, and though she bobbed her head politely I didn't have the feeling that Annie was interested in becoming my friend or confidante. There must be other girls in Eureka, though, who could become my friends. I wondered how to go about meeting them.

"Am I to go upstairs, too?" Chris demanded.

"I don't know—I'll have to ask," I said, but it turned out not to be necessary. Shea and Edward appeared a few minutes later, each to take one side of the heavy chair, and Chris was transported to the second floor.

"My God, that thing weighs a ton," Edward complained. Even the months at sea with rough-speaking sailors hadn't hardened me enough to keep me from wincing at this casual use of the Lord's name.

"Yes. We'll have to see about something lighter," Shea said. He paused to look down at Christopher's useless foot. "You can't stand on it at all?"

"No. The bones are all crushed."

"Why didn't they put you on crutches?"

"Crutches?" Christopher lifted his face to me. "What are crutches? You mean like that thing you put under your arm to prop you up?"

"Yes. Why didn't they give you one of those—or a pair of them?"

I shook my head. "I don't know. For a long time he was in such pain that he couldn't leave his bed, and we thought they would have to remove his foot. The doctors said he would die if they didn't take it, because of the poisons in his system; he ran terrible fevers and was out of his head for weeks at a time. During the whole thing he begged them not to take his foot, and Father didn't allow them to do it. He believed there were better things in store for us after death, and that Chris had the right to make his own decision about the foot, even though he was so young.

"Of course he didn't die, although he was so very ill for such a long time that he was too weak to do anything but lie in bed. By the time he began to regain his strength somewhat my mother had become ill, and Father's attention was all for her. Perhaps after her death he might have tried something beyond the wheeled chair, but by the time Chris might have been ready for crutches Father had been injured, himself. If the doctors suggested crutches I didn't know about it, but it was a very difficult time for us . . . for Father, for Chris and me . . . so many things to do . . ."

I didn't mention that there had been so little to do it on, and how crushed my father had been after Mother's death, how little able to cope with the problems of daily living when his grief was coupled with his own physical pain.

No more was said, and it looked as if there was a gathering of the clan for the announcement to Grandfather of our presence. Lawrie was there, smiling encouragement, and so was Aunt Hesper. It made me considerably more nervous than I had expected to be about the meeting.

"Perhaps we'd better break the news to Alex, first," Hesper said uneasily. "Before they go in."

"Why? The shock isn't going to kill him," Edward said impatiently.

"How do you know? He's been very ill." Her nostrils flared and I saw why Christopher had compared her to an ogre; one almost expected to see flames and smoke emerge.

"Edward's right; there won't be that much shock in *good* news, and Uncle Alex seems better this morning." It was Shea who made the decision, and urged us on down the corridor. It was he, too, who entered ahead of us and broke the news even as he drew me forward, with Chris trundling his chair behind.

"Uncle Alex, we have a surprise for you. Charlotte's children are here, come all the way from China." My hand was cold in his as Shea laid it in the old man's. For a moment we both trembled, and then the papery old hand closed around mine, cool and firm.

"Sissy? Is it Sissy? And little Christopher?" The eyes were my mother's eyes, my eyes, a clear green under tufted white brows, and his voice was strong. "Child, child, let me look at you . . ." He did, a scrutiny so intense that I could not break the locking of our eyes, and then he broke into a slow smile. "Aye, Charlotte's daughter, indeed, I'd need no proof of that! You're the spitting image of her! Oh, a lovely lass she was, my Charlotte! And the boy . . . not so little, after all, eh? How old are you now, boy?"

He relinquished my hand to reach for Christopher's, and I stepped aside for my brother to roll his chair up close. In so doing I faced all the others, who stood about us in a small semicircle.

I might have expected them to be smiling, for was not their beloved "old man" greeting with joy his only remaining grandchildren? Yet, curiously, that was not what I read at all.

They were all fixed upon Grandfather, for the moment unaware of my examination, and not a single face revealed any pleasure. Aunt Hesper was positively grim in her attention. The others were less transparent, but I knew with a chilling certainty that whatever they felt, it was not delight in our coming. Even Shea stood in what might have been cynical speculation.

"Ah, such a long journey! Such a terrible journey! Why didn't you let me know you were coming?"

I wet my lips, uncertain what reply to make, but Shea saved me that much.

"They did write, Uncle Alex, but the letter didn't precede them by much, and since you were ill we thought it better to wait until they actually arrived. I wouldn't have wanted to be the one to break bad news if they had failed to cross the ocean."

My grandfather accepted this, nodding, smiling, squeezing Christopher's hand.

"I got the letter from your father about Charlotte," he said at last, the smile fading but lingering still around the wide mouth that was, I saw, much like Shea's. "Somehow I knew when she went away to that heathen country that I'd never see her again. But she's come back to me after all, hasn't she, in this lovely miss? And your father, what of him . . . ?"

"He died," I said against the hard lump in my throat. "He was injured in a fall; his back was broken. We stayed with him, until—until the end. He told us to come to you."

"Of course he told you to come to me! What else should my grandchildren have done! Although I confess I had no hope of ever seeing either of you! It's enough to give me added years, I swear it is! Shea, break out the brandy! We must have a celebration drink!"

"On Sunday? In the morning?" Aunt Hesper asked.

"We're not going to get drunk, only celebrate a little! My grandchildren have come to brighten my old age!" He insisted on the brandy, which Shea silently poured into small glasses, even for Chris. I felt somewhat perturbed about that, for my father would surely never have permitted it, yet I was too insecure in my own position to protest in more than a murmur.

Chris handled it well, though I could see that his eyes watered a bit. I had had no more brandy than he, and I sipped at it cautiously, not particularly liking the taste but interested in the warmth that spread from the initial area of contact.

"Shea, I shall want to talk to Smithers at once," Grandfather said, upon draining his own glass, and again I sensed that there was meaning in the silence of the others.

"Who is Smithers, Grandfather?" Christopher asked, perhaps emboldened by the spirits.

"My lawyer. See to it, Shea."

"It's Sunday, Uncle Alex." Shea spoke evenly, without visible emotion. "Tomorrow will do, I take it?"

"I suppose, I suppose. But I'm an old man, and who knows what the night will bring? Twice I've nearly died from these terrible pains" —he tapped his chest—"and who knows when the next ones will take me? I must see my grandchildren provided for, just in case."

It was as if someone had turned on a powerful light over our heads. How could I have been so obtuse as not to see it at once? Of course. Grandfather was a very wealthy man, and these other people, these grandnephews and the widow of his nephew, had been counting on a pie to divide among the four of them.

No wonder they hadn't welcomed us here. No wonder, I thought in a state of numbness, they hadn't told the old man we were coming. Had he known, he might well have made provision even before our arrival. Had they hoped that we would be shipwrecked somewhere on the journey? Or that my grandfather would die before we could arrive?

The heat of the brandy still burned in my throat and stomach, but the rest of me was cold.

5

There was an accident that afternoon.

Christopher related the circumstances to me later, when he'd been taken to his room to rest after we'd dressed the wound on his head.

I was more shaken than he was. Although, of course, as he pointed out, there was little sense in being upset. He hadn't been killed, had he?

He had been out to the stables with Ned, looking at the horses, and then the two boys had come back to the rear of the house to sit in the sun and talk. For two boys whose backgrounds were so completely different, they took to one another surprisingly. Chris told Ned about life in China, and Ned contrasted this with tales about life in Eureka, and they were completely engrossed in their conversation.

It was only chance that Ned stood up when he did, having decided that it was worth trying to see if he could talk Cook out of some bread and jam. As he stood, he heard the slight sounds above and looked up to see rolling toward them, on the shed roof over the pantry area, a large stone urn, one of a pair that decorated a wide ledge across the back of the second story.

"He yelled and shoved me to one side, only not quite fast enough," Chris said, touching the bandage on his head. "Otherwise, it would have slid right onto me. As it was, it hit my chair and splintered it past anything. It just grazed me, or my head would've been as smashed as my foot was."

He sounded rather gratified about it, not that he was alive but that he'd had so narrow a miss. I felt a bit sick.

"But it's so heavy, so large . . . how could it possibly have fallen off?"

"I don't know. Ned says maybe it got jarred loose in the earthquake they had a few months ago. They have earthquakes every once in a while. I hope they have one while we're here, don't you, Sissy?"

I shuddered. "No. I don't. But there was no earthquake today, so why should it fall?"

"Who knows why things happen? Anyway, it doesn't matter, does it? Nobody got killed."

I said no more, but there was no denying that the episode was vastly disturbing to me. I was ashamed at the suspicion that entered my mind, yet not so ashamed that I neglected to look at the site of the suddenly mobile urn.

There was a single tall window at the end of the second-floor hall, which looked out on the stables and the shed roof. Anyone standing at the window could tell that the boys were below. He might also, when the window was open (as it had been, to admit fresh air during the warmest part of the day) have reached the decorative urns.

However, upon examining the remaining urn, I didn't see how anyone could have pushed one of them off. I shoved tentatively at the one still standing, carefully at first and then with more strength, and was unable to move it at all.

I leaned forward, out the open window, to examine more closely the spot where the missing urn had stood. This was clearly evident; the urn, apparently, had been a bit closer to the edge of the ledge than its mate. Still, it wasn't balancing on the edge, and there had been no tremor of the earth to unseat it.

A hand touched me from behind and I stifled a cry, sure that I was being sent after the urn, to break my neck far below.

"Here, what are you trying to do, commit suicide?"

I was pulled back into the house and set on my feet, inwardly a quivering mass, to see Shea frowning at me. "That's a bit dangerous, Cousin Jade. What were you doing?"

I told him about Christopher's accident.

The thick dark brows met over the hawklike nose. As incredulous as I, he, too, leaned out the window to examine the premises.

"Seems an unlikely thing to happen," he observed.

"So I thought. But it's so heavy . . ." I stopped, knowing I could not say, *no one could have pushed it.*

Apparently that idea didn't enter his mind. "Well, we'd better have someone check the rest of the ornaments on this place. God knows there are enough of them. I thought they were all secure, but we'll make certain of it. It won't do to have the damned things falling on people's heads."

It was accepted by the others as a shocking, but inexplicable, thing to happen. The old man, Ames, was dispatched with a tall ladder to make sure nothing else was loose that might fall.

Was I making a mountain out of a molehill, simply because I'd decided the family resented our turning up to share in the Robards fortune? I didn't know, and I wanted to warn Christopher, without knowing how to do it. When I said, "You must be careful," he'd given me an impatient look.

"Well, how can you be careful about something like that? If lightning strikes you or a tree falls on you, how can you be careful enough to keep from being hurt?"

"I'll keep an eye on him, miss," Ned said, and I nodded, unable to say more. I couldn't even ask Ned if he thought there had been anything peculiar about the accident. I could only pray Chris would be safe.

Grandfather felt so well that he insisted on joining the family for dinner, downstairs. The Sunday night meal was served cold, as it was prepared earlier before the servants took their afternoon off, but it was substantial and tasty. It was a fairly lively time, with Grandfather and Chris in especially high spirits, and for the first time we heard tales of how the Robards fortune was made in the woods.

I had thought surely the stories about the enormous trees, the giant sequoias, or "redwoods," were exaggerated, but it seemed that they were not. Some of the trees were as much as three or four hundred feet in height, and many reached twenty-five to thirty feet in diameter. Chris was wild to go out and see them; even if his chair hadn't been destroyed I thought this would be difficult to manage, but Shea assented casually.

"I'll take you out, first chance I get. Not tomorrow, I've too much else to see to. But soon. I'll get someone up here to measure you for crutches, and I think you may be able to learn to walk with them. Then you'll be able to get out into the woods with the rest of us."

My own reaction was one of increased apprehension. If this accident today had not been an accident, at all—if I were not giving in to a rampaging imagination—then how much easier would it be to arrange a second and fatal accident in the woods? Shea had been crippled there, his father killed there, and four of my mother's seven brothers had also died in logging accidents. Yet the family clung to their mill, their forests, their logging operations, and from what I could make out they were not content to hire help and give orders but worked with the saws and the teams themselves.

Yet if we were to live in this country, in this house, how could I stop them from taking Chris into the woods? Especially if they made him crutches so that he could walk.

He was ecstatic at the thought. We had both taken it for granted that he would be confined to a wheeled chair for the rest of his life; Shea took it for granted that he could walk if he wanted to, with the aid of the carved sticks.

By the end of the meal, which we finished up with an apple cobbler served with heavy cream, there was so much pleasurable anticipation in the air that my fears were lulled somewhat. Grandfather was delighted to have us with him; he made plans and gave orders so fast that I couldn't keep track of them.

My cousins, too, were relaxed and cordial; Aunt Hesper contributed little to the conversation but was at least not actively hostile. Indeed, when we were leaving the dining room she actually smiled at me and spoke in a pleasant manner.

"I understand that you play the organ, my dear. Perhaps you would play for us some evening."

I felt the warmth climb my neck and flood my face. "I'm not at all accomplished, I'm afraid."

Still she nodded and smiled. "Modesty is becoming in a young girl, I think. But of course you would want to try out the instrument in private before you played for the family."

Lawrie had agreed to entertain briefly, at Grandfather's request. We sat in the beautifully appointed music room, even Chris, although he was squirming before the music began. Lawrie played far better than my mother had, or perhaps it was only that his choice of musical selections was more sophisticated. He played no hymns at all, but the great music of the concert halls—Mozart, Beethoven, Bach.

It was still early when Grandfather rose, signaling that the evening was at an end. "Very nice, very nice indeed. What more could a man want than his family around him, in his own comfortable home? Lawrie, that was well done."

Lawrie smiled quietly. "Thank you, Uncle Alex."

Christopher, now confined to an ordinary chair unless carried by one of the men, scarcely waited until the old man had withdrawn before he turned an eager face to our oldest cousin. "When can I get the crutches, Cousin Shea? When will I be able to walk? Will I know how right away?"

"We can probably find a set of some sort here in town tomorrow.

I'll try. I don't know how long it will take you to learn to use them; I had a homemade one, and I fell flat a couple of times, but it didn't take long, as I recall. A lot depends on how determined you are."

Christopher inhaled deeply. "I want to walk more than anything. Really I do."

Shea nodded. "If that's so, you will."

I remembered, then, the gift I had brought for my grandfather, the jade figurine my mother had intended to bring herself.

"Grandfather!" I stepped to the hall and called after him; he paused on the landing, for his progress up the stairs had been slow, and leaned over to peer at me, one hand resting on the railing.

"Sissy, yes, what is it?"

"I brought you a present. From Mother. Are you too tired to look at it tonight, or could I bring it along?"

The smile spread across his strong features. "When I've had a sit-down for a few minutes to catch my breath, I'll be more than ready to see it. Come along in a few minutes, child."

I turned back to my brother, almost colliding with Aunt Hesper, expecting some sign of disapproval. There was none. She simply nodded in my direction. "I'm sure Edward would like an opportunity to become better acquainted with you, my dear. Lawrie will go on playing for hours; he always does, once he gets started." Indeed, he was playing again already, something I didn't recognize, poignant and plaintive and ineffably sad. "Edward, you said something about showing Cecilia around."

Edward sauntered toward us, completely sober, and far more attractive in dress clothes than he had been in the rough garments of Saturday night. "I would have, but I understand Shea beat me to it. Although he may have missed some details—he didn't have time to cover everything. How about it, Cousin? Would you enjoy seeing the pictures on the stereoscope?"

"I would, indeed. We had one at home. Only I have something to take up to Grandfather in a few minutes, and before that I'd better see my brother settled for the evening."

Edward surveyed me intently for a moment, as if judging whether I was making excuses not to spend time in his company. I wasn't sure, myself; our initial meeting had been unfortunate, but perhaps I shouldn't hold that against him. I knew that many men drank; indeed, in some circles it was considered only manly to do so. And he had been immediately apologetic when he realized who I was. Still, given my choice of the three cousins, Shea was the one I would have chosen, I knew.

I smiled in what I hoped was a convincingly pleasant manner, and he let me go, hands in his trouser pockets; I thought he was a bit disgruntled, as if he weren't used to being turned down for grandfathers and small brothers.

Chris was by no means ready to settle down for the night. The idea of being provided with devices that would enable him to walk was so exciting that I doubted he would sleep at all.

"Just think, Sissy! I can get up stairs, and hills, and all sorts of places I could never go with the chair!"

"I think stairs are rather difficult," I cautioned. "You won't learn that the first day."

"Ned says he knows a fellow who lost his whole leg, in a logging accident, and he has crutches and he goes everywhere. He works for the Robards mills, he helps tallying something or other, Ned says. He even has a girl friend."

I shot a look at him, trying to gauge how much thought he'd given to that aspect of his life. *I* had thought of it, heaven knows. That a man in a wheeled chair would have difficulty in earning a living, or in winning a wife. At his age, though, I hadn't expected Chris would be much concerned as yet.

"Ned has a girl," Chris went on. I glanced at the older boy, who sat on the edge of the cot that had been moved into the room for him. His ears were pink, and he shuffled his feet. "Oh, she's not my girl, really. She just—we just—" He broke off, embarrassed and confused.

I smiled at him. "I'm glad you're here to be a friend to Chris, Ned. Everyone needs friends, and since his accident it's been very hard for Chris to get out and meet anyone; there weren't many boys to meet in China, anyway, not American ones."

He shrugged, further embarrassed, and I decided it would be easier on him to turn my attention to Chris. "You're not to stay up late, now."

"I'm going to read to Ned. He doesn't read so well. And then maybe tomorrow I'll get my crutches and he can help me learn to use them. He has to work in the stable in the morning, but in the afternoon he'll have time."

"Don't expect the crutches too soon. They may not be available tomorrow." I hated to see him disappointed, but tonight he was uncrushable.

"They will be. Shea will see to it. Ned says when he sets out to do something, it gets done. Sissy, guess what? Ned says there are some real Indians that live outside of town. When I get my crutches maybe we can go out and see them."

"Christopher . . ."

"It's all right, they don't shoot anybody any more, hardly ever. Do they, Ned?"

Ned shook his head. "Hardly ever."

I had to laugh at their faces after the initial stir of alarm within myself. "And that's to be reassuring to me, is it? Well, we'll see what happens, and what Cousin Shea thinks of the idea. Good night, boys."

I heard them chattering before I had closed the door, and I was glad that Chris was not alone down here in the back of the big house.

Aunt Hesper was with Grandfather when I tapped on his door a short time later. She opened it to admit me, stepping back for me to enter, and I covered my disappointment, for I wanted this time alone with him.

"I'm getting Alex settled for the night," she told me. "Would you like me to give it to him?"

Involuntarily, my fingers tightened around the object in my hand. I hadn't brought it halfway around the world to do anything but place it in his hands myself!

"Hesper, I don't need you in the slightest. Go on, let the girl be with me for a few minutes, I'm sure she don't bite!" He grinned at me mischievously. "At least not hard enough so I'll object to it!"

He waited until she had reluctantly left us before he snorted, "That woman is enough to drive a man crazy. I can't think how my brother stood her all those years; it would have been kinder of him to have lived longer than me, so I didn't have to take her into my own house."

I wondered if, from the other side of the door, she had heard his words. I suspected Hesper was the sort of woman who would linger at a doorway to see what was said before or after she was in the room.

I advanced to the bed, where he was propped against a pair of fat pillows, extending the figurine. It was exquisitely fashioned from pale green jade. It was some eight inches tall, a benignly smiling old man in his Chinese robes; one could almost count the hairs in his beard, so delicately was it made.

He took it into his hands with a sigh of pleasure, bending nearer the lamp so that he could examine it more closely.

"Mother said you must be an old man by now"—would that be

offensive? I worried, too late—"and she wondered if you looked as lovely as this one."

His lips curved in an unconscious smile as he turned the figurine, running a gnarled old finger over the smooth flow of the robe. "Beautiful. Beautiful."

"It's a puzzle, really. Mother said you liked puzzles."

His eyes lit as he turned them toward me. "A puzzle? How's that?"

"He's hollow. Can't you tell by the weight? Although they were clever, it's weighted, to make it harder to tell. He comes apart."

He was as delighted as Chris would have been with a new toy. He tugged at the head, and nothing happened. "Where? How does it work? No, don't tell me! That would spoil the fun of it. A puzzle! How well Charlotte knew me, didn't she?"

"We none of us figured out how to open it," I confessed. "It was a gift, from someone for whom Mother did a great service—at least she said it was a great service, the old lady did. The figurine was a valuable possession, and she insisted that Mother take it. Poor Father, it bothered him when people gave us valuable things—but Mother really loved the jade, and she convinced him that it would be uncharitable not to accept a gift freely and lovingly given."

He laughed at that. "Aye, she could twist a man around her finger, that one could. How well I remember . . ." He was off on a reminiscence about my mother's childhood, and I listened, smiling with tears in my eyes.

We had been talking for some twenty minutes when there was a tap on the door. Grandfather's mouth twisted in annoyance. "Dratted woman . . . COME IN!"

It was not Hesper, however, but Shea who stood there.

"Oh, come in, come in! Look at this, Charlotte sent it to me!"

Shea took the figurine into his hands, turning it over and over. "It's a lovely thing," he agreed.

"Almost as lovely as the one who carried it to me, eh?" The old man's eyes were sly as he rolled them in my direction.

Shea's smile deepened. "I'll not argue with you there. In fact, I myself prefer the white jade to the green."

Grandfather hesitated, glancing from one to the other of us. "How's that?"

"He's teasing me," I said, despising the way I flushed so easily. "He doesn't like the name of Cecilia, he says he won't call me Sissy

. . . So he's learned my middle name from the flyleaf of my Bible, and he says he'll call me Jade."

"Oh, that's it!" He nodded approvingly. "Well, what are *you* wanting? Surely *you* don't feel called upon to check and see if I'm tucked in for the night?"

Shea laughed. "No. Nor any desire to make sure you've cleaned your teeth or washed your face. I wanted to tell you all the arrangements are complete; the Shaw Mill has officially been absorbed into the Robards Mills."

Not understanding the significance of this, I nevertheless realized that this was more than a casual statement of no importance. My grandfather fixed his eyes upon Shea's face with some intentness. "You're sure that's the way you want it?"

"I'm sure."

Grandfather nodded. "Very well, then. Very well. And now I'm tired. You two run along and look at the moon together or something."

This last suggestion was embarrassing to me, for I feared Shea might feel compelled to respond to it, whatever his own inclinations.

"I'm afraid this climate isn't conducive to evening walks, even in the summer. Not without a good warm coat, anyway," Shea observed.

"But it's good for growing redwood trees," Grandfather said. "And that's what we're here for, isn't it? To cut lumber. But don't forget to take time out for other things once in a while, boy."

"I will," Shea agreed, and let us out of the room. He looked down on me with a lingering smile. "You look tired, and I'll be in the woods at dawn, so I'll not ask you out for a stroll tonight. But one of these nights I'll do it, and not because the old man suggested it, either."

It was a warm thought to take with me to my own room, where I retired with my book of poetry. The book itself reminded me of the girl I had met on the stairs the previous night, and when, shortly after the stair clock had chimed out the hour of quarter-past eleven, I heard a door close softly, I listened. Ears straining, I tried to figure out which door, but it was impossible.

Later on, in my dreams, I heard the sound again, as if whoever had gone out had come in, or vice versa, whichever it had been, but I was too drowsy to note the time by the chiming clock.

Only next day did it take on any significance, and then again I could not be sure I wasn't coloring things with my own imagination.

For Chris greeted me at breakfast—we were usually to eat by ourselves, as the rest of the household ate very early, except for Lawrie, who never ate breakfast at all—with disconcerting news.

I knew at once that he was excited; he could scarcely wait until Annie had gone after leaving our dishes. He made a pretense of concentrating on putting brown sugar on his oatmeal, but the moment the girl was out of hearing he leaned toward me and said in a loud whisper:

"Sissy! Have you heard!"

"Heard what?" I asked in a normal tone of voice.

"Shhh! They all know about it, and they're upset for sure, they are! Didn't you notice Annie? She's white as a sheet! And she and Cook and Mrs. Dutton have been having a regular row ever since I came out, because Annie says she's got to leave before dark, and won't come until it's broad daylight, not ever again!"

I considered our fare and poured thick cream over my own cereal, deliberating between butter and honey for my bread. "You're being very dramatic, Christopher."

"It's not *me;* it's what happened! I'm not making up a thing, and I didn't just hear it from Ned, either! In fact, he didn't know it till he went out to the stables, but now they're all talking about it!"

"What is it that's happened?" I asked, and took a big bite of bread.

"There's a girl been murdered! Right off there in that thicket to the west of the house, practically on our property!"

For a moment I didn't credit what he'd said. I finished chewing and swallowed while he watched me with an avid expression.

"Who says so? Besides Ned?" To be truthful, I didn't think Ned had enough imagination to make up such a story, but it didn't sound at all likely.

"Everybody! Really, Sissy! She was stabbed! Over and over, Ned says, and she was covered with blood! Old Ames found her just on dawn this morning, and they've had the constable and all, and Ned says Cook was all for packing and leaving, herself, at first!"

I couldn't doubt that it was true. Suddenly breakfast didn't taste as good as it had.

"Who . . . who was she?"

"A girl by the name of Pearlie Grogan. She was seventeen, and she worked for some people name of Allrides, same as Annie does for us. Ned says they found out she hadn't been home to sleep, and because the blood was all dried and everything they think it must have happened last night. It was like she had an . . . an . . . assig . . . assig . . ."

"Assignation," I supplied, appetite completely gone now.

"Yes, like she went to the thicket to meet someone. Only they don't know who, but Ned says it was surely the murderer!" He took time to chew his mouthful of bread and honey, and washed it down with milk. "Ned says she sure was pretty, almost as pretty as you! She had black hair and big dark eyes with such thick lashes, he says, and a very tiny waist! And Sissy, you know a sad thing?"

He waited, as if for me to guess the impossible.

"Chris, stop it. Either tell it in a straightforward manner, or stop talking about it at all," I said with some sharpness.

"She was a Christian girl; she must have been, because she was wearing this little gold cross on a thin chain, and it was all tangled in her fingers, as if she held to it while she died! And it was all covered with blood!"

The room seemed to recede from me; the blue-and-white-papered walls blurred and for once in my life there was no unwanted color in my face. I must have gone chalky, for Christopher leaned toward me, touching my hand.

"It's awful, isn't it, Sissy? I'm glad we didn't know her, the way the others did, or it would be even worse."

I said nothing, but my thoughts were whirling. The girl I had met on the stairs, the one who had been visiting someone in this house the night before last, had been dark-haired, pretty, about seventeen. She had worn a small gold cross on a thin chain, and when I saw her, it had been caught in her fingers.

6

I don't remember how I got through breakfast, or even if I ate anything after those first few bites.

I did not think it was suitable that I should seek out the kitchen help and ask for more details of the tragedy, but I had to know. *Was the murdered girl the same one I had seen in this house?*

There could not be any connection, could there? Yet the memory continued to plague me: the girl on the stairs had been angry, upset, crying. Whoever she had been visiting had not bothered to show her out. Had she come back last night to see that person again, and had he then . . .

I stopped. I couldn't let my thoughts go any further.

Christopher, I know, ate a hearty meal, for I remember staring with astonishment at his empty dishes. "Ned says," he told me as he pushed back his chair and then remembered that he couldn't go anywhere without help, "that she wasn't keeping company with anybody. Any man who would have killed her in a jealous rage, or anything like that. Least not that anyone knows of."

I spoke with stiff lips. "I'm surprised that Ned doesn't say who did do it, then."

I had hurt his feelings. "You're being unkind, Sissy, and that's not like you. Naturally Ned tells me about things, because I'm a stranger here and I don't know. Wouldn't you like to know things?"

Wouldn't I, though. "Did . . . Ned wasn't there, when the girl was found. He didn't *see* her."

"No. He went over there, though, after he'd cleaned the stables, and he saw the blood. And Ames told him all about it, because *he* saw her, right up close. She was murdered, all right, no question about that."

I left the table, wandering about restlessly, unable to think clearly. How could I find out for sure if the girl was the same one I had seen? And what ought I to do about it if she *was?*

"I hope," Christopher said behind me, "that Cousin Shea will come soon with my crutches."

"He probably won't come before evening; he had to be in the woods at dawn, he said, and he has work to do all day."

"Call Ned, will you, Sissy? He can slide me on the chair back to my room, and I'll read or something until Cousin Shea comes."

Grandfather had his breakfast in his room; he had overdone last night, Aunt Hesper informed me, with a note of faint disapproval no doubt aimed at my part in his tiring, for had I not spent half an hour with him before allowing him to go to sleep?

So there was no going up to talk to him about it; I wasn't sure I would have, anyway. Annie might have been a source of information, but she was too busy to talk to me during the morning. Chris was right, though, she was terribly upset; she was pale, and she dropped things, and when Cook shouted at her she broke into easy tears. I did not think Annie was a girl who succumbed readily to tears.

At last I sought refuge in the music room, with the organ. I had often soothed a troubled spirit by a stint of hymn playing, and I sat down to familiarize myself with the instrument. It was a fine one, and when I had discovered, buried beneath all the other books, one of church music, I played.

The music was not enough, however, to erase the memory of that dark-haired girl, her face smeared with tears, and that tiny cross on its thin chain tangled in her fingers.

To my surprise, and Christopher's gratification, Shea returned to the house around noon with a pair of crutches. He instructed both Chris and Ned in their use, and stayed long enough to watch the initial efforts to utilize them. It might have been amusing, but no one was much of a mind to be amused.

Shea had eaten elsewhere; he didn't intend to stay for the noon meal. I walked with him to the front door, uninvited, because I had to speak to him.

"Is it true? About the girl found not far from the house?"

He nodded, his voice controlled. "Yes. A servant girl."

"Did you know her?"

"I know who she was. In a community the size of this one, everyone knows who everyone else is. I don't think I'd spoken to her more than once or twice."

"She wasn't a friend of the family, then?" He gave me an odd look, which took me a moment to interpret. "But no, she was a servant, wasn't she? I didn't think . . ."

He was still watching me in that intent way. "Why did you ask that?"

"I . . . I saw a girl who seemed to answer the general description we heard, and I wondered if it were the same one." I tried to remember what she had worn . . . a brown shawl over a dark cotton dress, wasn't that it? "Do you know what the murdered girl was wearing?"

"I have no idea. Where did you see this girl you're speaking of?"

There was a hint of sharpness in his words, and my courage failed me. I couldn't tell the truth.

"Why . . . on the street. I didn't speak to her." That, at least, was true. "It only seems so . . . so horrible . . . that someone one has even seen would be . . ."

"Yes, it's a dreadful thing. No doubt they'll turn up a spurned lover or some such thing, and he'll be made to confess." He turned away from me. "I'll see you at supper, Cousin Jade."

Grandfather didn't feel well enough to come down to the table at noon. When I looked in on him directly after our meal, he was rest-less and chafing because his lawyer, Mr. Smithers, hadn't come.

"I told Shea I wanted to see Smithers. Didn't he contact the man?"

I had to admit that I didn't know.

"Well, when he comes in, tell him I don't want to wait another day, do you understand, girl?"

I met his eyes and what I saw there chilled me. I had viewed death too many times not to know a man who looks with certainty upon his own.

"Ah, Sissy, let me hold your hand a little," he said, and drew me to him for a moment. "I'm an old man, and I've lived a good, full life. My wife and all my children have gone on before me, and that's not a good thing, girl. None of my sons even reached the age to marry and give me grandsons; sometimes I think I must have stolen my extra years from them, and I would never have wanted to do that. Your coming has made me feel better, for a bit, but there's no chang-ing the fact that I'm old and my heart is bad. But before I go I want to provide for you and the boy, and that's why I want Smithers. You're not to be sad that I've gone, either, because I'm ready for it. There will still be family left for you, and money aplenty to see that you want for nothing." He released me and gave me a push, with so little force that I realized his strength was, indeed, failing. "Run along, now, and if Smithers comes, you see that he's sent up here at once."

I left the room with tears in my eyes, although I knew that what he said was true. His life was nearly over, and he did not want me to grieve.

Mr. Smithers did not come, and when any two people met for a moment of conversation they invariably touched upon the subject of the murder. By midafternoon Christopher was already mastering the use of the crutches well enough so that he and Ned had crossed over the yard to view the site of the atrocity. I had no wish to hear how the blood had spattered the bushes and the grass and com-manded him to talk about something else or not speak at all.

I was called upon to watch his performance, and it did seem that he would be much more mobile on crutches than he had been in the chair. He was very awkward, and tried to go too fast, so that he often fell, and Ned would have to get him up. Yet he took it as if it were a game, a challenge, and the spills left him undaunted.

I was seated on the grass in the back yard . . . in such a place that it was unlikely anything could fall on me or approach unnoticed . . . when Annie came down the back steps, her eyes red and angry.

Mrs. Dutton called after her from the back door. "There's no way you can expect to keep your position if you won't show up for work on time, miss, and that's that!"

The older woman slammed the door behind her as she retreated into the house. Annie, her back straight and her jaw out, strode toward me, not replying.

I thought she was going to pass me without speaking, but the need to express herself was too great. She paused, looking down at me, her bosom heaving.

"That's all very well for *them* to say! They live right here in the house, and they don't have to walk through the woods to get here, and before it's full daylight!"

I didn't know what to say. I wouldn't relish walking through the woods alone, in the dark, either; not after what had happened last night. I knew I must say something.

"Was she a friend of yours, Annie? The girl who was killed?"

Her eyes flashed indignation. "A friend of mine? Pearlie Grogan? I'm not so hard up for friends I have to settle for the likes of her!"

"She was very pretty, they said."

"Oh yes, she was pretty enough, but no better than she should be! That I know for sure!"

I licked my lips, knowing my parents would be horrified at my probing into such a matter, and with a serving girl, at that. But I had to learn all I could.

"I heard she wasn't seeing any particular man."

Annie laughed, a scornful sound without humor. "She'd seen plenty of them, ever since she was fourteen, but none of them was especially *particular,* I reckon!"

I wanted to ask if any of the men in this house had ever shown any interest in Pearlie, but I couldn't; my tongue wouldn't form the words. I wanted to hold Annie here, somehow, and I searched for some means of doing it.

And then she dropped beside me, plucking at the grass with work-worn fingers; perhaps she simply needed someone to talk to.

"You don't know how lucky you are," she said, with only a trace of bitterness. "To have a position of favored grandchild in old Mr. Robards' home. To have clothes and pretty things and know you'll never have to work for a living."

I looked at her with compassion. "Yes. I am lucky. But luck's not something I've always known, you see. Both my parents have died, as well as two sisters and a little brother. We came halfway around the world without knowing what we would find here . . . we couldn't be sure that Grandfather was still alive, we didn't know he was wealthy, nor what our welcome would be. We had no idea there were cousins." I claimed no kinship with Aunt Hesper. "So I do know how it feels to be in your position, Annie. Except that I don't know enough to do much of anything to earn a living, and I worried all the way back to America about it . . . how I should take care of Christopher if we didn't find a grandfather ready to take us in."

She stared at me as if this were a revelation. "But you've always had nice things . . ."

"My father was a missionary in China. We had very little . . . far, far less than the Robards have here . . . this seems the ultimate in luxury and opulence to us. And as for clothes"—I smoothed a hand over my gray cotton skirt—"I have exactly six dresses, and all of them are two or more years old. All of them have been mended; one of them is patched."

"But you'll marry well. Someone will take care of you," she said; I thought some of the antagonism had gone from her tone.

"I hope so. I suppose every woman hopes so, doesn't she? My mother considered that she married well, for she loved my father very much, but they never had any money nor anything in the way of material possessions of any sort. Don't you have a young man, Annie?"

She flipped her red-brown hair and ran a hand through it. "Oh, there's Arnie, all right. But he's only a hand at the mill, and I don't suppose he'll ever be any more than that. It was one reason I came to this house to work . . ."

Puzzled, I asked slowly, "What was?"

"The three unmarried men here, of course! Four, counting the old man, but he's not interested in women! Any of the Robards men would be considered a catch, don't you know." She cast a sly look at me through lowered lashes. "Of course you've a much better chance than I have at them."

Once more I felt the telltale heat in my cheeks. "It's too early to say, as to that."

"Oh, they're looking at you. All of them. Don't you feel it? *She's* looking, too, but I doubt she thinks anyone good enough for her precious son. Besides, she hasn't a penny to her name, except what they give her . . . the old man lets her live here, but that's all. Don't you see how it galls her, to have to live on charity? And if Edward was to marry, how could she know his wife would want her to share their income? Once the old man's gone, they'll come into money, no doubt, all of them." And then, remembering that she was speaking so casually of my grandfather's death, she quickly changed tack. "Oh yes, the young ones are all looking at you, I see that. Not that I haven't had my share of looks, too, if it comes to that."

She brought her chin up. "From Edward, at least. I was encouraged, to begin with, until I found out that Edward likes to look and touch, but he don't marry. Not my kind, anyway. But I suppose you're different."

Was I? I had no idea.

Annie rose in a lithe, easy motion, brushing off her skirts. "Well, I've things to get from town, and be back in time to help with dinner. But I'm going to go home before it gets dark, and I won't be here before dawn any more, either."

She set off walking and I watched her go.

"Hello! Are you getting the sun?"

I turned to see Lawrie walking toward me across the grass, smiling. He never wore the rough work clothes of the other men; he was immaculate and elegant, though in an understated way. He put down a hand to me, which I accepted, to bring me to my feet.

"Yes. It's lovely here. It's such a strange climate," I commented, releasing my hand from his. "So cold at night, and the terrible fog that comes in, and then such warm and lovely days."

"But good for the growth of redwoods. That's Uncle Alex's attitude, and Shea's. Redwoods are money, and we're lucky that Uncle Alex got here early enough to get his share of them. More than his share, some people think."

I looked into his face, which was more nearly on a level with my own than either Shea's or Edward's. "But you're not interested in the lumber."

"Not to work in it, no. I'll admit I'm glad it pays well enough so that I don't have to go out and chop and saw and haul and split and all the rest of it. I wasn't cut out to be a lumberman."

"You're interested in . . . painting, and music . . ."

"Yes. I do work at that, you know. A little, at least. I give drawing lessons twice a week in the schools. Not that it pays me enough to live on, but that isn't necessary, anyway, because I have a share in the Robards Mills. Because of my father, of course. So that supports me." He was staring off toward a small stand of trees, and I wondered with a shudder if that was where Pearlie Grogan had been stabbed to death. "Well enough, in fact, so that I could take a wife and keep her in reasonable comfort."

Startled, and more than a little alarmed at this change of subject, I swallowed hard. Was this no more than a casual observation, or did it pertain to me in some way? Well, of course, there was only one way in which it *could* pertain to me, and instinct sent me shying away from such a consideration.

Lawrie touched my arm, ever so lightly, and I was forced to meet his gaze.

"I know you've only just arrived here, Sissy, and no doubt your life's been so tumultuous these past few months that you're in no position to make major decisions. But I want you to know that . . ."

What he wanted me to know I was not destined to hear, at least not at that moment. Christopher and Ned came around a corner of the stable, my brother lurching along in an ungainly but rapid fashion, only to sprawl full length when he got ahead of the crutches.

It was with relief that I saw an excuse to escape from Lawrie, and run to Chris. Of course he wasn't hurt and was already getting up by the time I reached him; he was annoyed at the fuss I made, a fuss I knew to be unwarranted. But I did not want Lawrie to finish what he was saying. All my life I'd thought it would be most romantic to be proposed to, no matter by whom, yet now that I was faced with the prospect (that was what my cousin was leading up to, wasn't it?), I wanted only to flee.

"Oh, Sissy, stop it!" Christopher said at last, when he'd been righted and regained his footing. "Guess where we've been!"

"I can't imagine." I didn't care, either, but Lawrie was still there, right behind me, and I didn't want to be left alone with him again immediately. "Where?"

"Down to where they took her . . . that girl, Pearlie Grogan."

I forgot Lawrie at once. "Chris! What on earth possessed you, you can't have wanted to *see* her . . . !"

"We never saw a murdered person before," Chris said, and Ned nodded. "It sort of made me feel sick to my stomach, a little bit."

"I should think it might. It makes me feel that way just thinking about it."

"The constable is asking questions of everybody who lives around
here. Asking if they saw her last night. Or if anybody saw her recently with a man. Or if anybody's found any bloody clothes. Whoever killed her, they said, had to have got blood all over themselves.
He'll be coming here . . . the constable, I mean . . . to ask everybody if they saw her."

Lawrie had forgotten his amorous impulse, if that was what it had
been. His mouth went flat. "There's no reason to ask questions of
any of us. We didn't know her."

I said without thinking, "Shea said in a town the size of this one
everyone knows everyone else."

"Well, by sight, of course. But the girl was not an acquaintance.
There's no need for any of us to answer questions about her. If the
man comes around, leave him to Edward, or to Shea. They'll dispense
with him in short order."

A fine tremor shook my legs. What would I say, if they asked me
about the girl? Admit that I had seen her in this house night before
last, the night before she was killed? But no, I did not know for sure
it was the same girl.

There was a way to find out, of course. If the boys . . . mere
children . . . had been allowed to see her, I would also be allowed
to view the body. Especially if I told them why.

I wouldn't go, of course. It was unthinkable. Yet the need to know
the truth was strong.

"I can't imagine what they were thinking of, to let a pair of boys
see the poor girl."

Chris was tiring, and he leaned heavily on the unaccustomed
crutches, shifting to avoid being cut under the arms. "Oh, they didn't
know. She's laid out, and this friend of Ned's let us sneak in for a
few minutes. She isn't bloody any more, they washed her up and her
mother brought a clean dress for her to be buried in. We saw the
clothes they took away, though."

This was said with an appalling degree of relish, by a boy who had
been raised in a God-fearing and protective family. I knew I ought
to put a stop to it, that it would give him nightmares and turn his
mind in an unwholesome direction. Still I had to know.

"What . . . was she wearing?" I asked in little more than a whisper.

"A blue dress . . . her best one, that she wore on Sundays, her
mother said. Her mother was crying."

"I don't mean to be buried in, I meant . . . the clothes they took away."

If either of them found this question to be odd, they didn't show it.

"A black dress, wasn't it, Ned? It was hard to tell, it was so caked with blood. And a brown shawl, that was all I saw. And the cross on the chain. It was real gold, her mother said, someone gave it to her, and they decided not to bury it with her because it's valuable."

A brown shawl. The same as the girl I'd met on the stairs. I felt numb. Surely there could not be two girls of such similar description and apparel. Pearlie Grogan had to be the girl I had encountered in this very house.

7

I made sure there was not another opportunity for Lawrie to approach me alone. Indeed, he didn't act as if he was trying to do so, but I was taking no chances. I spent the rest of the afternoon with the boys, telling myself that they needed a steadying hand and a change of subject matter; I read to them from a book on the history of Humboldt County, a large volume printed in 1882, and far more suitable for perusal than the matter of Pearlie Grogan.

Once more Grandfather did not come down to the table; he had a light supper in his room.

I conveyed his message to Shea. "He's upset that Mr. Smithers hasn't come by to see him; he wants to be sure you gave him the message."

"I tried, but he wasn't in his office," Shea said from across the long table. "I'll make another attempt tomorrow."

"Oh, he was here," Annie said, hovering with a heavy platter of roast beef. "The old gentleman saw him."

There had been a murmur of conversation around the table. It was not my imagination; it came to an abrupt halt, and all eyes fixed on Annie.

"Who was here?" Aunt Hesper demanded sharply.

"Mr. Smithers. Isn't that who you were talking about?"

Edward, too, sounded rather intense. "Are you sure?"

"Of course, how could I mistake something like that? He rang the bell and asked to see Mr. Robards, and I took him upstairs. He wasn't there for long, not over ten minutes. He came down and let himself out. I heard the carriage drawing away."

"What did they talk about?" Hesper asked. Her hands were quite still on the white tablecloth.

"Now, how would I be knowing that, ma'am? I didn't stay to listen outside the doors." Was there a touch of insolence in Annie's manner? I wondered if she'd caught Hesper doing just that. I expected a remonstrance, at least, but there was none. Hesper picked up her silver fork and attacked her meat with unusual vigor, saying no more, and gradually conversation resumed.

I had hopes that Shea would engage me in conversation after dinner, but he made pleasant excuses, saying that he had a brief engagement in town. "I hope to be back around nine. If you haven't retired, I'd like to talk to you, then," he said, and I felt my heart lurch.

I assured him that I would not retire so early, and then there was nothing else to do but accept Edward's proposal that we withdraw to the music room to look at the three-dimensional pictures of the stereopticon.

It was soon obvious, however, that looking at pictures was not exactly what Edward had in mind. Innocent that I was, it took me a short time to recognize that he was maneuvering the "accidental" brushing of hands in handling the slides, and that he was sitting much too close to me on the blue-velvet-covered sofa.

He was actually a more handsome man than his cousin Shea, and while he had not Lawrie's air of elegance he was certainly well turned out in dark broadcloth and spotless linen. Though his scent was a trifle heavy I had no doubt it was expensive and it was not unpleasant.

When he rested one large hand carelessly over mine in the seat between us I withdrew it almost too quickly. "My, what an enormous tree! Was this picture taken here in the redwoods?"

He didn't answer at once. Somewhat flustered, I turned inquiringly to him, only to find that he was smiling in a way that disturbed me. He took the instrument out of my hand and put it to one side.

"Cecilia, I'm sure many men have told you what a beautiful girl you are," he said.

He was too close to me, and I was much too warm. He reached again for my hand and I managed to elude him, but only by standing up.

"No, they haven't," I told him, and was horrified that I sounded as schoolgirlish as I was.

"Well, if they haven't, they will. The men in Eureka, certainly, once they see you, will do so. You haven't been here long enough to have come to any conclusions about us, I suppose, but you'll be giving some thought to your future." He gave a rather self-conscious laugh. "My mother thinks it's time I stopped playing the field and settled down, and while I know this is rather soon to broach the subject to you . . ."

I felt breathless and as if my waist was too tight. I backed away from him, spreading a hand between us to ward him off. "Please. It is much too soon for me to think of anything. It was so nice listening to Lawrie play last evening; I wonder if he might be persuaded . . ."

Something shifted in Edward's face, and I glimpsed annoyance, impatience. "To hell with Lawrie . . . if he wants to play we can hear him from here. Cecilia, you're a woman grown . . . almost twenty, aren't you? You must have given some thought to marriage. I'd see you were well provided for . . ."

"Grandfather said he would provide for me, so I don't think that's an immediate problem." I welcomed the small sound at the door, for it made it possible for me to move quickly away from him. Christopher and Ned were there, giggling together as if much younger than they were. "Did you want something, boys?"

"We've been reading in this, and Ned doesn't believe it says what it does." Chris indicated the book in the older boy's hands, and I saw that it was the one on family medicine.

I took it before Ned could protest; not that he would have, of course. "I told you before, I don't think it's suitable reading matter for a boy of your age. I'll put it back, and I don't want you to get it out again."

"Ned's fifteen. He's old enough."

"Well, you're not." I didn't really care all that much about the book, although it wasn't anything I'd have offered him to read, but I had to get away from Edward. The remembered touch of his hand was enough to send me rushing down the hall to the library, where the book was fitted into the empty space.

The boys, not disconcerted, were still giggling, or at least Chris was. "You see, she wouldn't take it away unless it was the way I said, would she?" Chris demanded. Ned shot a sidelong glance at me, uncertain of my reaction.

Edward had come to the door of the sitting room; that he was displeased by the interruption was clear from his stance, although he struggled to conceal it with his facial muscles.

"Cecilia . . . we were trying to have a serious conversation. I'd like to finish it."

So far as I was concerned, it was finished, yet I had been taught to be courteous. I pushed gently on my brother's shoulder. "Run along, Chris, and try to find something to do that won't bother anyone else. Why don't you teach Ned to play chess?"

Ned shook his head. "I tried, miss. It just don't make sense to me. There's such a lot to remember."

"Some other game, then. Something not noisy."

Edward was still waiting for me when the boys had vanished into the rear of the house. I didn't know how to handle him, and I looked around for some innocuous diversion.

"We didn't look at all the slides, did we?"

He blocked my way to them. He was heavier-set than either his brother or Shea, wide through the shoulders and a bit thick in the neck. I wasn't sure why that bothered me; perhaps it was only that he was so much larger and stronger than I that he seemed intimidating. Certainly there was nothing dangerous about a man about to propose marriage!

"Bother the slides. Let's go where we can talk in private, without a bunch of people running in and out."

Fresh alarm coursed through me. The last thing I wanted was to be anywhere in seclusion with Edward. I had dreamed of a proposal, like any other girl, but it had always been taken for granted the man would be someone I would want to say "yes" to. What did you do when you had trouble covering the fact that the idea repulsed you?

"There's a lock on the library door," Edward suggested, and put a hand on my arm, quite firmly. It was a large, heavy hand, and warm. My instinct was to jerk away, but it was impossible to do. "We can talk in there without being bothered."

"No," I said faintly. "I don't . . . there's nothing to talk about, Cousin Edward. This is not the time to . . ."

I wasn't sure how he had managed it, but I found myself compressed into the corner between sitting room and dining room doors, cut off from escape. The man was overpowering, up close this way, and as he bent toward me I caught a whiff of Grandfather's brandy.

"Now is exactly the right time, before there's a crisis that will take everybody's energies elsewhere," he said, and his breath was warm on my cheek.

"What . . . what do you mean, a crisis? Why should there be . . ." He was too close to me, actually pressing me into the corner, and I brought up both hands, palm out, to keep him from advancing any further.

"The old man's dying . . . we all know that. It may be days or weeks or a few months, but he can't last much longer. He's too sick. He'd be happy to see you settled before then, I know he would. Cecilia . . ."

He bent his head and captured my mouth with his, as if it were his right.

Indignation roared through me like a flame in a hayfield. I shoved as hard as I could, sending him slightly off balance for a matter of seconds. If there was no reasoning with the man, I would run from him; I had no wish to suffer his touch or his kiss . . . my mouth was burned and bruised.

Edward swore under his breath, taking a step after me that came to a halt when Lawrie appeared on the stairs. The younger brother surveyed us with comprehension, which wouldn't have been difficult because my hair was mussed, my face hot, and my breathing agitated.

Lawrie paused, then continued on down the stairs. "Uncle Alex is asking to see you, Sissy."

I fled past him, only too delighted to have an excuse for somewhere to go. I heard Lawrie's words behind me as I went.

"Edward, you great clod, couldn't you do it without scaring her to death?"

It was probably just as well that I couldn't understand what Edward said in return.

Grandfather was sitting in bed, but I saw at once that his color was poor and when I touched his extended hand it was cold.

"Ah, there you are, Sissy. I only wanted to say good night. Such a long time since I've had a young miss in the house to say good night to."

I bent to kiss his papery old cheek, knowing that what Edward said was true: he was old and sick and it could not be long before he would be gone.

The jade figurine stood beside the bed and he nodded at it. "I want you to have it back," he said. "I'll look at it a little longer, and think about Charlotte when I do, and then you take it back. It shouldn't go to any of the others."

And so, without saying it in so many words, I knew that he, too, was aware of impending death.

When I let myself out into the hallway again it was dark. I stood for a moment, reluctant to reopen the old man's door for illumination, for he was very tired. There was no furniture in the hall itself, nothing to run into, I reasoned. So I began to move slowly toward the front of the house, the fingers of one hand brushing along the wall in order to judge my whereabouts. Wondering if Edward lay in wait for me below, I was tempted to stop at my own room and barricade the door. But Shea had said he wanted to talk to me when he returned, and if I were not downstairs I doubted that he would seek me out. Not if he thought I had retired.

Admit it, Cecilia Jade Cummings. You didn't welcome Edward's advances, but you look forward with a quickened heartbeat to the attentions of Cousin Shea.

I paused halfway along the corridor, thinking about it. There was some logic in what Edward said, that a girl of nearly twenty should have a husband and protector. And it was not a rare thing that a girl should marry within the family, a cousin, particularly one who was not a first cousin, especially if there were family fortunes to be kept intact.

The thought of marriage with a man I could not love and respect was as repugnant to me as it would have been to any other female, although I knew there were many such marriages. Remembering what Edward's mouth had felt like, insistent and hard, covering mine, I shuddered. No, marrying Edward was no solution to anything. My problems didn't seem to me severe enough to warrant solving in such a way as that.

I began to move again, slowly, feeling that there was something strange about the darkness. It was so . . . so thick, almost tangible about me. What had happened to the gas lights ordinarily kept burning? Was it worth the effort to stop in my own room to light the kerosene lamp? But no, there would be lights downstairs, and there were no obstructions anyway; all I had to do was feel my way along.

Oddly enough, there didn't seem to be any illumination on the first floor either. Perhaps something had happened to the gas supply; I knew little about such things.

I had reached the corner; the wall ended, or rather turned, to make way for the stairs. I probed with a tentative foot for the top one. Another step, two . . . and again I halted, for I had the strong feeling that someone stood below me on the landing.

Why that should have frightened me I couldn't have said. Anyone else in the house, caught without lights, would be doing the same thing I was doing: feeling his way toward his destination, moving slowly and cautiously.

Yet my breathing was quick. I listened and heard nothing. My mouth opened to ask if anyone was there . . . but before I spoke I took another step down the long flight.

Something struck me across the shins and I plunged forward, losing my grip on the railing, a scream tearing my throat.

8

I might easily have broken my neck if I'd gone all the way down. But someone was there, coming up from the landing, groping in the dark the same as I. I struck a hard, unquestionably male body, causing him to emit a little grunt of surprise as his arms closed instinctively around me.

Fortunately he was only one step above the landing, so that when he pitched backward with my weight he landed against the wall, and we didn't fall any farther.

I caught the scent of him . . . soap and fresh air . . . and knew with relief that it wasn't Edward.

"Jade?" His hands verified my identity, for there was no other female in the house I could have been; Annie had left the house before dark. "Are you all right? What the hell's happened to the lights?"

I gasped a little in recovering my balance. "Cousin Shea! I thought I heard someone . . ."

"Are you hurt?"

"No. No, I don't know why I fell; it was as if something struck me across the . . . the legs, as I was starting down."

His hand closed around mine in a firm grip. "Let's go down and see if we can find out why the lights are all out. How's the old man? He's all right, isn't he?"

"He was, only a few minutes ago. He was ready to go to sleep."

We had reached the lower hall, now, and Shea grunted in satisfaction when we saw someone coming from the back of the house with a lamp. Mrs. Dutton, waddling along in a pair of carpet slippers, held the light aloft to reveal our faces.

"Ah, I've sent Ned out to see what's the matter. Seems the gas has been shut off or some such. I went to light a lamp, but the one here in the hall was empty. I told that Annie to fill all the lamps, but she's a lazy one, that girl, and all she's interested in now is getting home before dark! As if it isn't perfectly clear that Pearlie was murdered by one of them men she was always taking up with . . . no reason why he should want to do in any of the rest of us!"

Shea released me and made a sound of exasperation. "Well, let's get a few more lamps going and I'll go see what Ned's found. Maybe someone had better check on Uncle Alex, if he had a gas light going."

"No, he had a kerosene lamp when I was there," I told him. "And he said he was going to go to sleep."

"No need to bother him, then," Shea said. It was not until after he had gone that I stood looking up to the spot from which I had tripped; I had been walking slowly and carefully, so why had I fallen? I remembered being struck by something across the shins, but there was nothing visible to have caused a fall.

Lawrie appeared from the music room, and Edward, still disgruntled, from the dining room, where it was obvious he had made inroads into the brandy. There was a certain amount of milling around, and the two men went out to see if Ned and Shea needed a hand.

I was left alone for a few minutes, during which time I collected my thoughts and sorted my impressions. Shea had been there to catch me when I fell, and it was lucky I hadn't knocked him dangerously off balance along with myself, I thought. I relived those few moments when I had been in his arms . . . certainly not in an embrace, but in as intimate a contact as if that were the case. His hands had touched me . . . arms, shoulders, waist . . . and I had felt no aversion at all such as Edward had roused in me.

It was only a few minutes before they all trooped back inside. Shea explained succinctly that in some way the valve had been closed, shutting off the flow of gas. This had been remedied and they must all now go about making sure all fixtures that had been turned on were relit.

It was some time later when the company reassembled. Edward managed to locate me first, where I was sitting in the music room idly fingering the keys of the organ. I turned with some eagerness, expecting Shea, and it was with difficulty that I kept my face from showing disappointment.

Edward cleared his throat. "Cecilia . . . I . . . I'm afraid I was clumsy earlier this evening . . . Lawrie says I frightened you. I didn't mean to do that."

Transfixed, I clung to the edge of the stool, unable to make a reply.

He came closer, but this time at least he kept his hands in his trouser pockets. "Ought to have known better than to take a couple of drinks to get up my nerve. I never proposed to anybody before. I'm not sure I actually proposed this time, did I?" His smile was uncertain and made him look younger, more boyish. "Anyway, I was trying to, and I muffed it. I don't suppose it would be possible to forget it, and start over?"

I liked him better in this frame of mind, but not enough to sit through another attempted proposal. "Please. I'm not ready for anything like that. Can't we all just . . . have time to get acquainted, to make friends?"

For a moment there was a flash of something in his face—surprise that I should find it necessary to make friends?—and then he let his grin widen ruefully. "Well, if that's the way you want it."

"Am I interrupting something?" The voice was Shea's, and he didn't sound as if he really cared much, one way or the other, if he were intruding.

"Not at all," I said quickly, when Edward made no response.

Shea advanced into the room and leaned an elbow on the top of the organ, looking down on me. "Have you gotten brave enough to try it out?"

"A little. I found a book of hymns."

Humor gathered the skin around his eyes. "On the bottom of the stack, I'd be willing to bet. I don't remember ever hearing anyone play hymns in this house, do you, Edward?"

"No." The word was short, curt. Animosity radiated from the younger man to the older one, but Shea didn't seem to notice that he was on the receiving end of it.

"Cousin Jade, I told you I wanted to talk to you. I think . . ."

There was a sound of hurrying feet on the stairs, and Mrs. Dutton gasped out a strangled cry that brought us all to meet her in the lower hallway. She was carrying a kerosene lamp that dipped dangerously; Shea took it out of her hand and set it to one side, which enabled her to press both her hands to her heaving bosom.

"He's had a stroke, Mr. Shea! Oh, he looks awful bad; he's in terrible shape! I just looked in on him, to be sure he'd put out his light and there wasn't a gas jet turned on, and there he was, his face all pulled off to one side in such a pathetic way!"

Shea bounded past us and up the stairs; the rest of us followed, including the housekeeper, who continued to chatter even as she labored for breath for the climb.

"Poor old man, he didn't even speak to me when I called out his name, but he rolled his eyes! Ah, it's a shame, it is, poor man!"

I hurried along behind Shea and Edward. By the time we reached Grandfather's room it seemed the entire household had been aroused by Mrs. Dutton's cries, for everyone assembled there, even Ned and Christopher. I didn't ask how Chris had navigated the stairs; I was on my knees at the old man's bedside, tears filling my eyes as I saw that Mrs. Dutton had described his condition only too accurately.

One corner of his mouth was drawn down, and the eyelid on that side drooped as well. He knew me, though, and there was a faint answering pressure from his fingers when I touched them.

Shea turned from the bed and sought out Ned, the latest of the arrivals.

"Go for the doctor," he said. "And Reverend Whipple, but the doctor first."

In the big bed, where he suddenly seemed to have shrunk, Grandfather made a movement, working his lips in an effort that produced nothing I could understand.

"And Smithers," Edward said, too loudly. "Send Ames with the horses to bring back Smithers."

From the way my grandfather relaxed I thought that this was, indeed, what he had wanted.

I continued to kneel beside the bed, holding the big-boned but frail old hand. It was too much for him to maintain any pressure with it, but I hoped that it comforted him a little to know that I was there.

I wished they would all go away, the others, except for Shea, who stood at the foot of the bed, watchful, waiting. They were all waiting—in the dimly lit room I could imagine them as vultures hovering over some unfortunate creature, upon whose expiration they might feast—and I chided myself for such an uncharitable thought. They had known him all their lives; no doubt they loved him far more than I could, having come to him so late.

The doctor must have lived very close, for he came almost before I had time to become impatient. He was a tall, thin man with glasses, and he had obviously retired, for his clothes were hastily arranged and his hair uncombed.

He approached the opposite side of the bed from me; the others made way before him, but no one offered to leave the room until the doctor spoke. His voice was sharp, impatient.

"Get everybody out of here. There isn't enough air for a well man to breathe, let alone a sick one."

There was an uneasy shuffling of feet, and the servants retreated toward the doorway, but the others held their ground. Only I had made a halfhearted effort to rise as the old man's nightshirt was opened at the throat and an ear placed to his chest.

I heard no one breathing as they waited for the verdict. The doctor swiveled in exasperation. "Go on, the lot of you! He's had a stroke, and he doesn't need to be gaped at!"

He saw, as I felt, the slight tightening of the fingers around my own, and nodded at me. "You can stay, he wants you." He pushed with an outstretched palm toward the others, and reluctantly they began to edge away. Hesper and Lawrie went, their faces serious; Edward hesitated near the doorway, and none of them went any farther than just into the hallway.

Chris sat in a chair in a far corner, his eyes wide and solemn; I thought that he, as I, must be remembering the night our father had died. There was no sign of the new crutches; Ned must have hauled him bodily up the stairs without them, so as not to miss anything.

Shea had made no move to leave; instead, he shifted to my side of the bed and dropped a hand onto my shoulder. Like Edward's, it was large and warm, but there all similarity ended. It was a comfort to me, for I thought that he, too, loved the old man.

There was the sound of more footsteps, and the onlookers parted to allow this man through: a man almost as old as Grandfather, but sprier, rosier of cheek, and wearing a clerical collar.

He approached quickly and quietly, waiting until the doctor had completed his examination. Reverend Whipple, Shea had called him.

Shea's voice was low, scarcely carrying across the bed. "Is there anything you can do?"

For a moment the doctor looked at us, into the lamplight. Then, very slowly, he shook his head. *No.*

Shea's fingers bit into my flesh as he knelt, too, to put himself closer to the old man's face. "Uncle Alex? Do you hear me?"

There was the faintest of whispers. "Yes."

Shea had released me, but now he put a hand over mine as it lay atop the old man's. "Uncle Alex, I want your blessing on what I propose. This young girl will be alone and unprotected when you are gone. As the oldest of her remaining male relatives, I will make myself responsible for her and her brother, but I want to do more than that. I want to offer her the protection of my name, as well."

For a few seconds I didn't comprehend what he was saying; I was too much aware of the two hands in contact with mine: the old one, already cold, the young one, pulsing with warmth and life.

"Uncle Alex, I want to marry Cecilia Jade. Now. Tonight, while you are still able to know it." Shea spoke with a quiet intensity. As I realized what he was saying, paralysis rooted me to the spot; I sensed an uneasy movement among those waiting in the hall, but they were too far away to make out what was being said. "I didn't have time to talk to her about it myself, but I know that you would be happier seeing her safely married, to one of us. I think I am the logical one."

I must have gone as cold as Grandfather; only the heat from Shea's hand over mine kept my fingers from freezing solid. He leaned closer, his face only inches from the old man's.

"Do you agree, Uncle Alex? She should be married? For her own protection?"

It was with great difficulty that Grandfather moved his head in a nod of assent. His lips worked, and again we heard the whispered, "Yes."

Only then did Shea look at me. His face was so near that I could see the individual dark hairs in the thick brows that nearly met over his nose. His eyes were dark and almost hypnotic; I felt as if I were in some dreamworld, from which I would surely waken any moment.

"Jade?"

Marry Shea?

Such a short time ago . . . this afternoon? . . . Lawrie had hinted that he would find me acceptable as a wife. And even more recently Edward had pressed himself upon me . . . literally . . . in a similar advance. And now Shea . . . Shea, whose touch had not repelled me at all, and to whom I had been drawn at our first meeting.

The doctor's voice was low but rather harsh. "If you want him to witness it, you'd better get on with it."

Edward spoke sharply from the doorway. "What's going on? What are you talking about?"

No one answered him. Shea stood, drawing me with him as if I were mesmerized. My knees felt weak, but perhaps that was from kneeling for so long. Shea's words carried an urgency that was compelling as he addressed Reverend Whipple.

"If you please, sir. A very brief service, because Uncle Alex is tiring."

I had not given any response to the question implicit in that single word addressed directly to me, that saying of my name only. Yet here I was, at my grandfather's deathbed, my hand held by this man whom only a few days ago I had not known existed, listening to the beginning words of the wedding ceremony.

They were almost completed when the other members of the family grasped what was taking place. Edward swore in protest and moved toward us, but it was already too late.

"Ring—we have no ring," the minister said, and Shea pulled a heavy signet ring off his little finger and put it onto mine. It was too large and I had to hold it with my thumb to keep it from slipping off, which I did in a state of numbness approaching shock.

"I now pronounce you man and wife." The words should have been followed by "You may now kiss the bride," but the Reverend Mr. Whipple stopped uncertainly, perhaps thinking the final words inappropriate under these circumstances.

I had been aware of small scuffling sounds behind us, but was too bemused to try to sort them out. Someone else had come into the room—the lawyer, Smithers, I gathered from the greetings. Shea released my hand. I glanced down into my grandfather's face, and thought that he was trying to smile at me, although it was impossible to tell for sure.

The others had all moved back into the room with the lawyer, and Edward advanced angrily toward the bed. "What the hell are you pulling? What have you done?"

"I've married Cecilia Jade." Shea's voice was cool in contrast to his cousin's. "Don't make a fool of yourself, Edward; this isn't the time for it."

Fury mottled the younger man's face, but I thought that was all it was. Not regret at the loss of a chance to marry me himself so much as rage that someone else had accomplished it.

"He's trying to say something," Smithers said crisply. "Shut up, so we can make it out."

The room feel silent, so silent that I heard my own rasping breaths as the enormity of what had just happened began to shake me. Christopher's face was a white moon in a shadowy corner; I couldn't tell how he was taking it.

Grandfather's lips worked helplessly for a moment, and then he said a word that was intelligible to all of us.

"Will."

"He wants to make out his will," Hesper said, and her voice sounded like a file grating across rough metal.

"He's made a will," Smithers said, puzzled.

"A new one? Since Cecilia and the boy came?" Edward demanded.

"No. We talked about it, and I convinced him that what he had in mind was unwise." The lawyer looked into Edward's face and I thought some message passed between them, for all that they revealed nothing to the rest of us. "It's a large fortune to put into the hands of an inexperienced girl . . . or a child. It will take a man to run the Robards empire."

"And I'm running it." Shea spoke quietly but with great force; I felt the impact upon the others.

"That's not for you to say," Edward began in a fresh burst of anger but Shea faced him with composure.

"I'll be happy to show you the papers, any time you like. They've all been signed and witnessed, including the old man's agreement. My mills and interests were joined with those of the Robardses, and that gives me majority interest and control."

Edward and his mother were staring at the lawyer in disbelief, and Smithers spread his hands, shaking his head.

"I don't know what he's talking about. I swear."

"There are other lawyers in Eureka," Shea pointed out dryly. "Who haven't made alliances elsewhere. It's all down on paper, signed, sealed, and delivered into my hands."

"Will."

All eyes returned to the old man, who had used superhuman effort to speak this word again. Shea leaned forward to touch him gently on the arm. "What is it, Uncle Alex? Do you want, even now, to change your will?"

"No." A single word was a challenge to him, a mountain to climb, but it was important enough so that he tried with all his remaining strength to make us understand. "Have . . . made . . . new . . . will."

The effect on the assembled company was electrifying. In a room containing over a dozen people, there was not a sound of breathing for countable seconds. It was the lawyer, Smithers, who broke the silence. He bent over the foot of the bed, his knuckles gripping the massive footboard.

"You made a new will? Is that what you say?"

"Yes. New . . . will."

"Where is it?"

Afterward I was to wonder about the lawyer's intensity of feeling in a matter that ought to have been no more than routine business—unless, as Shea had suggested, he had some understanding with Edward or the others regarding Alex Robards' will.

We might all have been carved from granite . . . or struck by lightning . . . as we waited for his reply, but it was too much for him. Grandfather strained to speak, feebly gripped the hand I put out to him, and then fell back against the pillows.

We all knew before the doctor said the words.

"He's dead. He's gone."

A collective sigh ran around the room, and someone—I think it was Mrs. Dutton—burst into loud sobs.

My own sorrow welled up painfully through chest and throat and eventually reached my eyes in scalding but quiet tears. Gently, I laid the frail old hand at his side and turned blindly away.

Shea's arms came around me and he held me without speaking. I scarcely knew when one hand came up to cradle my head and press it into his shoulder.

Sisters, brother, mother, father—and now my grandfather. The tears that flowed so copiously were for all of them, all the loved ones I had lost. And I was held by the man who, though still nearly a stranger, was now my husband.

9

There was little time allowed for the luxury of tears. Mrs. Dutton's wailing was ended when Aunt Hesper administered a therapeutic slap on the cheek. Edward was clearly furious—and not entirely as a result of the brandy he had imbibed earlier—over the trick Shea had perpetrated upon the rest of them. He was in conference with the lawyer, Smithers, in one corner of the room; I think they had not noticed the small boy curled there behind them in an oversized chair with the shadows thick around him.

Shea held me very briefly, then set me firmly aside. There were things to be done. Arrangements to be made. He murmured something I didn't comprehend, and strode into the midst of the rest of them; I was somewhat reminded of David marching upon Goliath and the Philistines, for though he was not a small man he was outnumbered, and his angry cousin, Edward, was taller and heavier.

It was not to become physical combat, but the anger and resentment of the others was something they made no effort to conceal. Still numbed by the rapid-fire events of the past hour, I stood aside from the family while the hot words flashed back and forth. A sheet had been drawn up over my grandfather's face; I looked once in that direction and did not want to look again.

The doctor viewed us with visible distaste. "Perhaps you'd like to send for Mortimer?"

Mortimer was the mortician. There would be a funeral to get through . . . I'd had enough of funerals to last a lifetime. Was I doomed never to get out of my black bombazine?

"Yes," Shea said, his word incisive, leaving no doubt in anyone's mind that he had assumed head-of-the-family status. "Thank you, Doctor. And you, sir," to the cleric who was fumbling with the buttons on the coat he had not had time to remove.

Reverend Whipple paused beside me, looking unhappily into my tear-swollen face. "I am so sorry, my dear." His eyes shifted to Shea. "If there is anything further I can do to be of assistance, Mr. Robards . . ."

"Perhaps you can be of value to my wife. I won't be able to be with her immediately," Shea said.

His wife. It was not until then that the full implication of the words began to penetrate the cocoon of torpidity which encompassed me.

Shea's wife. I had stepped from girlhood to wifehood so swiftly, and I was not ready for the step. I began to tremble, and Whipple put a comforting hand on my arm.

"Perhaps if we could sit down somewhere . . . a cup of tea might be helpful. Or perhaps even something stronger, this once . . . this is very difficult for you, I'm sure."

I did not want to sit down with the minister for a cup of tea or anything else. I did not want to hear the words of solace I knew he would voice; I had already heard them, and they did not help—or at least not immediately, and not enough—and I was afraid that if he didn't go at once he might be here for hours—hours I couldn't bear to sit with him, listening to familiar biblical quotations and renewing all my old griefs as well as prolonging this fresh one.

Drawing myself together, I looked him in the face and spoke calmly. "Thank you, Mr. Whipple, but I'll be fine. I'm sure you have other things to do. Thank you for coming, but there is no need for you to stay."

I read the relief there, and the shame that he should feel relief, and I knew that he was a good and decent man. We shook hands, quickly, and he let himself out.

My grandfather lay dead, not yet buried, and the family were working up to a pitched battle, right here in his death room. I don't know where the resolution came from, but I knew this was not fitting, and I raised my voice to carry over the hubbub.

"Please. Can we not go downstairs to discuss what must be discussed? Mrs. Dutton, I think everyone could use something hot to drink—if you would serve it in the family sitting room, please?"

There was an astonished silence. Hesper's majestic bosom heaved convulsively, and she bit down on her lower lip, as if to keep from saying what had come to mind. The servants were staring, too, for I had not previously given any of them an order.

Shea gave me a glance of approval, his dark eyes touching me only briefly. "Jade is right. There are better places for discussing, and there will be things to do here. You heard Mrs. Robards, Mrs. Dutton—some tea, and put out the brandy bottle, as well."

I saw Cook form the words *Mrs. Robards* without sound. Only then was it borne upon them that I was, by virtue of my marriage to Shea a few minutes ago, the new mistress of this household.

Tomorrow, I thought, the idea will probably terrify me; now, I was glad that I had some authority to order them out of this room, the jackals away from the expected feast.

They began to move—sluggishly, to be sure, but at least I had broken up what threatened to become a shouting match if not a physical brawl. If it came to that, it was not going to be in my grandfather's bedroom.

I led the way, hoping the others would follow, and then I remembered Christopher. He was still curled in his chair, and I didn't see Ned. He must have gone for the mortician.

I turned back, pressing myself against the wall until they had passed me, and I didn't miss the malevolence in the air when Hesper stared into my face. Lawrie gave me a small, sad smile. Edward didn't look at me at all. Shea was the last, and he smiled, too.

"Good girl," he said, and went on with the others.

When I went back into the room, the doctor was still there beside the bed. He turned his head and nodded at the jade figurine which he held in his hands.

"Interesting piece, this. I don't remember seeing it before."

My lips felt stiff. "I brought it from China. It was a gift from my mother."

"Oh. Lovely thing, lovely. I'm sorry you've encountered so many problems, Mrs. Robards." It made me feel very strange to be so addressed, though I couldn't have said exactly how. "I suppose it's one more thing they'll fight over." And then, realizing that he had been critical of the family to which I belonged, he began to stammer an apology.

I cut through it quietly. "No. He wanted me to have it back. I'll take it now." I accepted it from him, the stone cool and smooth and beautiful. "Please join the others downstairs, if you like, Doctor, for something to drink."

He shook his head. "No, thanks just the same. I'll wait until Mortimer gets here, give him a bit of a hand."

I left him there, and stopped in my room to leave the figurine, then went on down the stairs. Although the lights were on again, indeed blazing from every available jet, as well as lamps lit in all the rooms where doors had been left open, I moved cautiously on the stairs. Right here was where I had fallen—why had it happened?

I even bent to look at the wall and the banister, but there was no mark, no irregularity, nothing to suggest what I had felt striking my lower limbs.

I continued on down to the hallway, where I met Mrs. Dutton. She breathed heavily as if she'd been hurrying, and spoke when she saw me.

"Oh, there you are, miss—Mrs. Robards—" Confusion turned her pink. "Cook is seeing to the tea, and I've put the brandy bottle and the glasses out. I thought you'd want the best glasses?"

I couldn't have cared less which glasses she put out, but I nodded approval.

She turned to go back toward the kitchen and paused, puzzlement screwing up her round face. "Now, what in heaven's name is *that* doing in here?"

That was a broom. A perfectly ordinary kitchen broom, with a handle about the height of my shoulders. She snatched it up, muttering, and made off with it.

I stood for a moment, feeling a chill as if a draft blew over me. And then, quite deliberately and ignoring the possibility of someone coming through the house and seeing me, I lifted my skirt and petticoat and tried to see my legs through my stockings.

I could not, of course, but a finger brushed across a shin found the tender spot, all right. Something had struck me right there, and caused me to pitch down the stairs. Something hard and unyielding. Something, I thought, that could have been a broom handle.

The idea was incredible. Surely none of the adults in this house would have resorted to such a cruel trick. And while Christopher was mischievous, he had never been cruel. Not that a crippled child could have managed it anyway . . .

I stared upward, knowing with a cold certainty that a broom could well have been the instrument used to trip me. But that implied deliberate, malicious, active malevolence—a far cry from a glare or a hateful word.

The constriction in my lungs was painful. I hesitated a moment longer, to see how it could have been done. It would have to have been held rather high up—too high for even the tallest of the men to have accomplished it while standing on the floor. But directly under the step where I had been there was a small table on which now burned a beautifully hand-painted lamp. The lamp had not been there during the minutes of darkness. Anyone stepping onto the table could have pushed the broom handle between the carved posts. It wouldn't have taken any particular amount of strength, either, because the rail itself would have held it well enough to do the job.

Behind me, the doorbell rang. It was loud, loud enough to penetrate to the back of the enormous house, and at close range it was earsplitting. I jumped, turned, and smoothed back my hair before opening it to admit Mr. Mortimer.

There wasn't time, then, to think about the broom that had been left in the front hall, nor to speculate as to why it had been there. I took the man upstairs, endured his condolences to my utmost limits, and fled once more.

I had reached the head of the stairs when I realized that I had completely forgotten my purpose in turning back the first time. Where was Christopher?

A surge of panic washed over me. He could have gone out a window, he was so small and so helpless . . .

"Hey, Sissy! This is some room you've got—I'll bet Queen Victoria doesn't have it much nicer than this!"

In the wake of fear, annoyance was a pleasurable experience. He was standing in the doorway to my room, a crutch under each arm, only a little unsteady on his good foot.

"Chris! You scared me half to death!"

"Why should I have done that? I haven't been doing anything."

"Where were you a few minutes ago? What have you been doing?"

"Looking around. Maybe I was in the bathroom." His face lit in a grin. "I *know* Queen Victoria hasn't got anything fancier than that! Little rosebuds painted on those handles you work to make the water come! There's a little water closet thing on the first floor, but nothing like this. Do you think I can ever move into a room up here where I can use this bathroom, Sissy?"

"I don't know, I'm sure. The stairs would be very difficult."

"I'll learn to do stairs. I can walk remarkably well already, Ned says, and it won't be any time and I'll learn to do stairs. I didn't know you were going to do that—marry Cousin Shea. Do I still have to call him Cousin, now that he's my brother-in-law?"

"I don't know." Suddenly, and quite positively, I didn't want to discuss my unexpected marriage, not even with Chris. "I thought you were stranded up here without the crutches, and I came looking for you."

"Ned brought 'em, when he came back with the doctor. It's too bad about Grandfather, isn't it? But everybody knew he was going to die, he'd been bad sick a lot lately. And he was awfully old. Boy, I thought they were going to start hitting each other right there in his room, didn't you? What are they all so mad about, Sissy? I didn't quite understand it all."

"I don't quite understand it all, either, but I'm sure Ned can explain it to you. He's better informed about the family business than the family is."

Chris nodded as if he found this reasonable. "It has something to do with control of the money and the mills and the lumber. I guess there's a lot. Are we rich now, too, Sissy? Like the rest of them?"

"I don't know that, either, but no doubt we'll find out when the time comes."

"Cousin Edward wanted to hit Shea. I heard him say so. He said, 'I'll beat his bloody face to a pulp,' and that other fellow, Smithers? he said, 'Don't be a fool.'"

Newly alert, I stared down into his innocent face. "What else did they say?"

"I don't know; I didn't understand all of it. But Edward was angry because of something to do with the will . . . he said, 'You swore he didn't change his will,' and Mr. Smithers said, 'Don't cry over your milk until it's been spilled. You didn't see any new will, did you?' and then Edward kept saying things about Shea, how he'd like to break him into bits, and Mr. Smithers told him not to be an ass. Why didn't you tell me you were going to marry Shea, Sissy?"

Why, indeed? I inhaled deeply. "There isn't time to talk about it now. Where is Ned? I hope he's going to help you back down to your room."

Chris leaned against the railing and shouted over it. "Hey, Ned! Are you down there?"

I clapped a hand over his mouth. "Christopher, for pity's sake, this is a house of mourning!"

"I forgot," he said, instantly contrite. "Sissy, Edward said something else, and he was talking about me. He called me a little bastard."

"He was using it as an expression of vulgarity, no doubt. He's very upset, perhaps he didn't think what he was saying. Ah, here's Ned. Ned, will you see that my brother gets back to his room, please?"

Poor Ned, who had been sent running all over the city tonight, looked a bit tired. But he cheerfully undertook to get Christopher back where he belonged. They managed it with awkwardness and some subdued hilarity—subdued only when I reminded them again that it was out of place at this time.

I was reluctant to descend myself. I had no wish to face them all, the vultures closing in around us. So Edward had referred to Chris as a little bastard, had he? Well, if I'd had to marry one of them I was glad it hadn't been Edward.

Which left me thinking about the one I had married.

I was Mrs. Shea Robards. And being a wife involved a great deal more than answering to a new name.

My parents had been very happy together, had loved each other very much. I had always envisioned a marriage such as theirs—not to a minister, although I, too, had loved my father—but to an ordinary sort of man with whom I would make a home and raise a family. I had imagined meeting him, and coming to know him, and being married in a small, simple church, like one of those we had passed on the way here from the wharf.

And now here I was, quite without preparation, totally unready to assume the role, married to a man who was little more than a stranger, for all that I had found him to be attractive and exciting.

"Mrs. Robards?"

I jumped, for I hadn't heard them coming; if the doctor hadn't caught at my shoulder I might have taken a second fall down the stairs.

"We're going to remove the body now. Perhaps you would rather not be here while we do it."

"I'll give you a hand," Shea called up from below, and I stepped to one side to allow him to pass. The other two men retreated to Grandfather's bedroom, but Shea lingered, looking down on me with compassion.

"You've had a long and dreadful day, haven't you, Jade? I suggest that you go to bed and get some rest."

My heart began to hammer in my chest until I was sure he could see it pulsing there. He touched my elbow, and guided me toward the open doorway to my room. "I'll help with Uncle Alex, and then I have some things to see to. I'll have to be out for a time—perhaps for several hours. There are many decisions to be made, many people to be contacted. I won't be able to spend much time with you tomorrow, either, probably." A smile came, faint, touching only his lips. "You'll manage. You stepped in very nicely tonight. That's the way to do it. Let them all know you're the boss, now."

My mouth was dry and my throat ached. I couldn't think of anything to say. He took my hand, the left one, where I was still keeping the signet ring on by holding it with my thumb, and slid the ring off. "Getting a cramp that way, aren't you? I'll get you something more suitable as soon as possible. Maybe you could put this one on a chain until then?" He dropped it into my palm and closed my fingers over it, where it felt hot from the warmth of my own pounding blood. "Good night, then."

He bent his head and kissed me . . . our first kiss. It was cool and chaste and while not at all repulsive it left me shivering uncontrollably when he had gone. I closed the door and leaned against it, wondering how I would ever find the strength to undress and get into bed.

For this one more night, then, I was to sleep alone, in this room. And tomorrow night? I thought. What then? Would I be expected to share the adjoining room with Shea?

The blood moved sluggishly in my ears so that they seemed to roar and I could hear nothing, not even my own breathing.

What about tomorrow night?

10

That I slept at all was the result of complete exhaustion. For a long time I lay awake, hearing them as they passed the door with my grandfather's body, hearing the others as they came up. It was late, very late; the clock on the landing counted out the hours—twelve full strokes, and half an hour more before Shea opened the door next to mine. For a time I was rigid, expecting that he might change his mind and come in through the connecting door that I knew was unlocked, but he did not. For a few minutes he moved around, and then all was quiet and the house slept. Even I, its new mistress, sank into a sleep as deep as if I were drugged.

In the morning the house was swathed in fog. It was so thick I could scarcely make out the trees only a few yards away.

I lay staring at the fronds of a displaced palm tree outside my window, wondering who had brought it here to this place, and why. It seemed an alien growth in this land of giant conifers, but there were quite a number of palms in this city.

And at last my thoughts had to move to something more important than palm trees.

I had thought, ever so briefly upon coming to this house, that my problems were solved. I would be safe and cared for under my grandfather's guardianship, and eventually there would be a marriage and a home of my own.

Now . . . now my grandfather was gone, and while it seemed I faced no immediate physical needs, I was plunged into a totally different world, simply because I had married my cousin Shea.

I didn't want to get up, didn't want to face the day or the life that loomed as insubstantially as the palm fronds in the fog out there. The clock on the landing counted out the hour . . . seven, eight, nine . . . and I knew I could delay no longer. Whatever was to be met would be no less difficult because I met it later in the day.

I sat up and swung my legs over the edge of the bed, then stared at the exposed flesh. As clearly as if marked in ink along the edge of a ruler, a blue bruise showed across each shin, just below the knees.

The room was suddenly even more chill than I had previously thought it. I hadn't dreamed the horror. Someone had deliberately attempted to harm me, had gone to some pains to do it. Perhaps, rather than just taking advantage of the moment when the gas lights went out, the one who wished me ill had contrived that part of the plot as well. The lights out, a broom at hand, and it was only a matter of waiting until I could be heard returning down the stairs. If anyone came along with a kerosene lamp, what harm would there be in being caught with a broom? And if the ploy didn't work, why, there was always another chance at me, wasn't there?

I dressed quickly, in the oldest of my black bombazines. It was almost too shabby to pass muster, but if I were going once more into deep mourning everything I owned would have to be put into service. My fingers shook over the buttons, and I wondered how I could face them and keep my suspicions from being written all over my countenance?

Who?

Who hated, resented, feared me enough to want me to break my neck?

Not Shea.

The protest had been there, I think, ever since the dreadful idea entered my mind. It could not have been Shea who stood on a table to wedge that broom handle across the stairs. For Shea had been on the landing, he had caught me when I fell and possibly saved me from serious injury.

I ought to have felt better with that rationalization, but my mind went right on, without my conscious control. No one would have had to hold the broom in place for it to do its work. Once wedged, it would have held firmly enough to trip me. It could have been placed there moments earlier and the perpetrator could have climbed the stairs to meet me . . .

"What sense does that make?" I asked aloud. "Why would he try to hurt me and then save me? It doesn't make any sense at all."

But, in a curious, distorted way, it might. What if Shea had wanted me to feel in his debt? What if he wanted me frightened, so that I would turn to him? What if he had even then been planning to thrust me into a hasty marriage, and thought that rescuing me might help him to do it?

My head ached and when I put a hand up to my forehead it was hot. I would not be sick, I could not be. There was too much to do, too many things to think about.

I drew a deep breath and opened my door.

The family was assembled in the dining room, except for Shea. My seeking eyes found everyone but my husband, and I didn't know whether I was disappointed or relieved.

From the look of them, none of them had slept well. Although it was not yet midmorning, Edward was already into the brandy and no one was even commenting upon it.

Annie was there, pale but composed, her freckles standing out against the milky whiteness of her skin. She was busily bringing in food; it wasn't attracting anyone but Christopher, who had cleaned up ham and eggs and was working on pancakes and syrup while the others sipped at coffee.

Annie shot me a vivid glance that acknowledged my new status; I couldn't tell whether she was admiring or envious or only surprised.

"Would you like coffee, miss . . . mum?"

I wasn't sure my vocal cords were still working, so it was amazing to hear myself sounding confident and assured. "Yes, please."

"Would you care for eggs?"

"One, please." I felt the eyes turning in my direction, as if I were committing some unpardonable breach of etiquette by being hungry the morning after my grandfather's death. "I've had enough of buryings to know they're easier to get through if one isn't faint from lack of food," I said, and drank the hot, sweet coffee.

It was understandable that they weren't talking much, not with the interlopers sitting among them. I wanted to know where Shea was but couldn't bring myself to ask.

Christopher, however, volunteered the information. "Shea's gone off to see about closing down the mill operations. They're going to bury Grandfather tomorrow morning."

Edward tossed off another glassful of the aged brandy. "I didn't think there was anything Shea thought important enough to shut down the mills for . . . but I guess when you've just taken them over, you have to show your weight in some way."

I hadn't known the spirit of anger was so strong in me until I heard my own words. "He is doing it as a mark of respect for my grandfather; it has nothing to do with who will run the mills from now on."

Edward's laugh was short and rather ugly. "Is that what you think? You don't know Shea very well, Cousin! Business is everything to him! Why do you think . . ."

"Edward!" Hesper spoke so sharply that her son broke off in the middle of a sentence. Her eyes were fixed upon him with some intense message I couldn't interpret. "I think you forget yourself."

"You're right." He sank into a chair, still nursing a glass of amber liquid. "I'm sorry, Cousin Cecilia. I apologize. I'm afraid I'm upset."

Hesper's tone took on a smoother quality. "We're all upset, and with good reason." She moved her lips in a grimace intended to be a smile, nodding in my direction. "We didn't want to wake you because we knew you'd had a difficult night, but you may be interested in knowing some of the family plans, my dear. As the little boy said"— I felt Christopher stiffen—"the funeral is set for tomorrow at ten. And in the afternoon Mr. Smithers will be here to read the will."

I looked from one of them to the other, unable to read any more than they wanted me to read in their faces. Lawrie was stirring his coffee and staring into it rather than looking at me.

"Have they found it, then? Grandfather's will?"

"It was never a matter of finding it," Edward said with more force than seemed called for. "There's a will on file with the lawyer, has been for some time."

"But he said . . ." I faltered, uncertain now. "I thought there was a *new* will?"

Hesper smiled with less warmth than anyone I had ever known. "It was very unclear to any of us that this was actually the case, dear Cecilia. Alex was very sick, and possibly confused as well, and he had trouble making himself understood. Quite likely he was only trying to refer to the fact that he had made a will . . . he wanted to reassure us that matters were well taken care of."

"But I distinctly heard him say—" I bit off the rest of it, knowing they had heard as well. Or at any rate Shea had, and the doctor and Mr. Whipple and Smithers himself who had been at the foot of the bed. And earlier, before he had been taken ill this last time, the old man had made it clear that he intended to revise his plans in order to provide more fully for Christopher and me.

Lawrie pushed back his chair; it made a screeching sound on the polished hardwood floor. "I think I'm going to take a walk."

"In the fog?" Hesper looked toward the windows, which gave the appearance of being packed full of cotton. "There are things we need to discuss, my dear."

"You and Edward discuss them and tell me what you decide." He smiled at me as he passed my chair. "Whatever the outcome of the discussions, you need have nothing to worry about, Sissy. Shea will see to it that you're taken care of."

"The way he took care of . . ."

"Edward!" Hesper's words were a razor-slash that penetrated the alcoholic haze in which he was wrapped. "There are some things that need to be done—I must visit a dressmaker, for one thing, and see about letting out my black crepe this afternoon so that it will be ready for the funeral. Cecilia, my dear, will you be needing her services, as well?"

"No, thank you," I said quietly. "I've had ample need for mourning clothes; they are in order."

I was glad when they had left us alone, Christopher and me, and I discovered that the atmosphere seemed considerably lighter. Enough so that I broke off a bit of bread and spooned honey onto it, nibbling with the beginning of an appetite.

Christopher had finished, and his crutches lay beside his chair, but he made no move to use them. He stared after our departing relatives, scarcely waiting until they were out of earshot to comment on them.

"Did you know she drinks, Sissy?"

"Aunt Hesper?" My disbelief must have been evident, for he leaned toward me across the corner of the table.

"It's true. Ned says he saw her once, she could hardly climb the stairs."

"It's quite possible Ned misinterpreted what he saw. Hesper's an older woman, and she may have infirmities we know nothing about."

"She drinks. I saw one of the bottles. I forget what Ned called it, but it doesn't have so much smell as the others, so nobody can tell she's been at it. Except that sometimes she can't walk straight."

"Where did you see the bottle?" I asked, torn between curiosity and the need to reprove.

"In her room. I looked in there when I was wandering around last night, waiting for someone to help me downstairs."

I felt the prickle of rising hair on the back of my neck. "Christopher, you didn't!" A quick glance confirmed my hope that no one was within hearing distance of us. "You know better than to snoop into people's rooms!"

"Oh, Sissy, don't be such a priss! I didn't go in and poke into their drawers or anything like that, I just looked in. Didn't you ever want to look into someone else's room?"

Since I was not entirely blameless in this area, I was ashamed to press that point. He soon saw that and continued with relish, "I saw the bottle, it wasn't even hidden, just sitting on the floor beside her bed. It was nearly empty. Ned says she takes the bottles out of the house late at night when she thinks nobody is watching."

I had a sudden thought. "You didn't see anybody walking around with a broom last night, did you? Just before the gas lights went out?"

"A broom?" His face was blank. "No. Ned and I were trying again to teach him chess. Lawrie got the idea right away, but it seems hard for Ned. I told him I'd learned when I was only four, but he says it's difficult to remember all that stuff."

The incident on the stairs could not have been accidental. Which made it likely that the heavy ornamental urn falling onto Chris had not been accidental, either. How could I warn him without frightening him half to death?

"What's the matter?" Some of my emotions must have played across my face, and my concern alarmed him. "Sissy, is something terrible going on? Something more than Grandfather dying?"

"I don't know," I said slowly. "I don't know . . . perhaps. Chris, be careful."

"About what?"

"About . . . everything. Oh, I don't know how to say it—or what to say. But possibly someone in this house wishes us less than well. It might be wise to be on guard against . . . accidents."

Far from sending him into a spasm of fear, this statement brought an eagerness to his eyes. "You mean we're rich enough so somebody might try to murder us for our money? Really, Sissy?"

"Keep your voice down! No, that isn't what I mean at all . . ."

"Then what?"

Yes, what? I knew nothing, absolutely nothing, and hadn't a clue as to who might be the enemy.

I sighed. "Couldn't you let it go at that, for now? That it would be wise not to let yourself get caught in a situation where you might be hurt?"

He gave a low whistle. "Boy, wait till I tell Ned . . ."

"No. Don't say anything to Ned. Not yet." As much as Ned talked to Christopher, I couldn't believe that he didn't talk to others as well. "It will be safer, I think, if this is a secret between just the two of us."

"But I don't know anything," he pointed out with some logic.

"And I don't know enough to be definite about anything; please, just use a little common sense and don't get yourself into potentially dangerous situations. I promise, when I know—*if* I learn something I'm sure of, I'll tell you more."

He was intrigued and wanted to know if something had happened to *me;* I declined to discuss that and repeated my promise. If I learned anything I could be sure of, I would tell him more, and he had to be satisfied with that.

The day was an uneasy one. Shea didn't come back, and I both longed for and dreaded his return. I didn't even know how to greet him, and had no idea at all what he expected of me.

By noon the fog had lifted, burned away by the sun, and the day was glorious. I wasn't sure it was suitable for me to go for a stroll on the day after my grandfather had died, but I had to get out of the oppressive atmosphere of the house. I got a warm shawl and wrapped it around me against the wind which blew in off the sea, slipping out the side door without telling anyone where I was going.

Eureka was a pretty town, very clean, with wide streets and attractive houses. There had never been a major fire here, Ned had informed us, mostly because, it was thought, the buildings were constructed of redwood, which is nearly impervious to fire. I walked for a long time, wondering about the people who lived in the houses nearest us, and wondering if they would ever be my friends.

Nearing home again, I met Chris and Ned. It was difficult to believe how well and how quickly my brother had mastered the use of the crutches; how much more easily he got around, although he tired quickly and had to rest often.

His face was pink with exertion and the dark curls blew into his eyes, but it was clear that he was enjoying his new freedom of movement and the companionship of another boy.

I stopped, holding the shawl about my throat, for it was growing cooler as the fog began once more to creep in across the bay and encroach upon the land. "Well, where have you been?"

"To the mortuary. Don't look like that, we just wanted to see Grandfather laid out. He looks very nice, peaceful, not sick at all. Doesn't he, Ned?"

Ned nodded, eying me warily, sensing my disapproval, although there was really no reason why they shouldn't have gone, I supposed. Other friends and relatives would be viewing him there up to the time of the funeral service tomorrow.

"That Mrs. Grogan was there. The mother of that girl that was murdered. She was all upset."

I had forgotten about Pearlie Grogan. "Do they know any more about how she died?"

Christopher shook his head. "No. Mrs. Grogan wanted to know what they'd done with Pearlie's brooch. Mr. Mortimer said he didn't see any brooch, but Pearlie's mother insisted she'd had one on, and it was her grandmother's, and she didn't want to lose it. She said it was a white cameo on a dark red ground, with lace filigree around it, and it was valuable. But Mr. Mortimer said he didn't know anything about it, and they were still arguing about it when we left. Sissy, are we to go to the funeral tomorrow, too?"

"I suppose everyone will go." I hoped fervently that I wouldn't have to attend another funeral for twenty years. "You'd better check to see if your good clothes are fit to wear; maybe Annie would press them for you if they need it."

We walked on toward home together, enjoying the fresh air in spite of the nip to it. Only when I reached the house did I admit to myself how little I wanted to re-enter it.

"Ned has to go round and water the horses, and I'm going with him," Chris told me. "I'll see you at dinner, Sissy."

I let myself in the front door with its colored glass panes and was unwinding the shawl, when Shea spoke sharply behind me so that I spun, startled and off balance.

"Jade, where have you been? I've been looking all over for you!"

His thick brows met over the bridge of his nose; for a moment he resembled an angry hawk, poised over its prey, and the ferocity of his voice caused mine to waver.

"I—I was taking a walk."

"For the past two hours? Never mind. Here, let me take that." He removed the shawl from my unresisting fingers. "Come upstairs. I want to talk to you."

11

When the door closed behind us, the two of us together in my large and lavishly appointed room, I sought to keep my nervousness from showing. Perhaps my hands trembled slightly, though, for he took them in both of his, chafing at them gently.

"Are you cold? Devilish climate, sometimes . . . you go out when it's warm and freeze before you can get home again. Would you like to sit down?"

I would have known better what to answer if I'd been able to determine his frame of mind. Was I in for a dressing-down because of some unknown transgression, or even for the walk itself?

"No, I'll stand." I didn't feel so inferior, standing. "I'm sorry if I wasn't supposed to go for a walk . . ."

Some of the blackness went out of his face. "Oh, it wasn't that. I was concerned because I couldn't find you, afraid something might have happened . . . Jade, it's time I talked to you, past time, in fact."

He had released my hands and I clasped them together at my waist, seeing myself reflected in the oversize mirror across the room. My shabby dress, the careless dressing of my hair . . . I looked out of place here, in this elegant bedchamber.

"I know I took you off balance last night; I hadn't intended to do it that way, but with Uncle Alex dying . . . I felt it had to be done at once. I took advantage of your own shock, and perhaps I ought to apologize for that . . . but it was for your own good."

"My . . . own good." I felt stupid, thickheaded.

He stood facing me, only inches away, and he was enough taller so that I had to lift my face to look into his. "Jade, do you realize the situation you've walked into here?"

I was aware of my tongue moving over my lips and I forced myself to stop doing that. "I'm not sure what you mean."

"The Robards fortune is very large. Until there's an accounting there is no way of giving you a definite figure, but it runs into hundreds of thousands of dollars. There are timberlands, and two mills, this house, and various other properties. Most of it Uncle Alex acquired on his own. My father, and Edward's, were his brothers. They came in rather late and they worked for him, but they had no share in the actual ownership."

He was speaking with great seriousness, and I tried to concentrate on what he was saying, but he was so near and I was so conscious of him as a man—no, not just a man, but my husband—that it was an effort to follow him. I was distracted by the way his dark hair grew around his ears, and the slight unevenness of his teeth, and the shape of his mouth.

"Since both of his brothers were killed in logging accidents, and we were minor children, he took us all in. I think he looked upon us as his children. We were all the family he had left. Except for Charlotte and her family, of course, and you were all on the far side of the world. He had no assurance that he would ever see any of you before he died. Lawrie was never interested in the lumber business, but Edward and I have worked in the woods since we were young boys. We replaced his own sons, in a sense."

In the pause he seemed to be awaiting some reaction from me. I swallowed and nodded, trying to look intelligent. I wished I had accepted his suggestion that we sit down.

"He made his will long ago, after his first heart attack, and I think he's revised it several times since then. There was a nominal bequest to you and Christopher, but he didn't anticipate being fully responsible for you, not while your father remained alive. Only of course when you came here, when he saw you—that you were the image of Charlotte, and that you would need help with the boy—he knew that he had to do something more."

I was listening now. They had known I was coming, all the rest of them, and they hadn't wanted Grandfather to know it, for he might have changed his will at once in our favor. Whereas if we'd been sunk or shipwrecked or died of scurvy on the way over, there would have been no necessity for the rest of the family to give up any of their own portions for us.

Shea must have guessed something of my suppositions, for he nodded. "Yes. Several people would have been happier if you hadn't come. Even I felt that way, before I met you." My mind clung to that last phrase so that I missed a little of what followed it. "We had been told that we would inherit—Edward and Lawrie and I. Probably there is some sort of legacy for Aunt Hesper, too, I don't know. But since Uncle Alex's initial attack, I have been running the entire family business. You may have gathered that Edward doesn't agree with me on how to do it. He had hoped that after the old man died Lawrie would throw in with him to control the company. I've successfully blocked that, by joining the interest I had in another mill to the Robards industry, giving me a majority vote. Regardless of what is left to you, I will retain control."

I drew a long breath. "They told me—Edward and Aunt Hesper— that there is a will on file, an old will, and that there is no reason to assume he actually made another one since we've been here. They said Grandfather was old and sick and possibly imagined he had made another one . . ."

Shea laughed, a short, quick bark of sound. "Oh, they'd like to think he was out of his head there at the end! No one's even begun to look, yet, for the other will. If he says he made one, then I believe he did. That's nothing for you to worry about, anyway. Leave that to me. Business is what I'm good at, and I'll handle it. No, what I want to talk about is you yourself."

The room was not warm, and my hands were still cold, but there was a film of perspiration over my body, an oozing of nervousness that I could not control.

His eyes were suddenly more perceptive, as if he could tell what I was thinking and feeling.

"You're a young woman, with no business knowledge or experience, and the lumber industry is no place for a woman. But if he's left you a sizable portion of the estate—which I know he intended to do —then he's put you in a vulnerable position. That was obvious even before he did it."

I wished I had a drink of water—or maybe some of Edward's brandy would be more to the point, if it would put a little starch in my legs, and ease the terrible dryness of my mouth and throat.

His voice changed, and his eyes seemed to go right into me. "Jade, do you know what happened last night? There on the stairs, in the dark, when you fell?"

I felt almost as numb as I had been when Grandfather died. Yes, I knew what had happened—or thought I did—but I was unprepared to put it into words for anybody. To do so would make it only too real, too horrifying.

His fingers closed around my upper arms; I think he was unconscious of taking hold of me, but his hands bit into my flesh almost painfully.

"I don't want to frighten you unnecessarily, Jade, but I think you have to consider the possibilities for your own safety. I think someone tried to harm you last night. That's why I wanted to marry you at once, to put an end to whatever hellish idea they've hatched up."

My words came out in a jerky, unnatural fashion. "Someone . . . wanted me to fall . . . perhaps to . . . break my neck . . . so that I couldn't . . . inherit . . . no matter what . . . Grandfather did."

He seemed relieved that I grasped that, that I did not have to be further convinced, and his grip relaxed slightly.

"You should be perfectly safe now. There's no reason to think otherwise. Still, I was disturbed when I couldn't find you this afternoon, and for a time I think it would be better if you didn't wander around alone, or without letting anyone know where you're going."

I had missed something somewhere, I thought. "I don't understand. Why . . . why should I be safe because I'm . . . because we . . ."

"Because if Uncle Alex did leave you a major share of his fortune, getting rid of you would no longer let it slip into anyone else's hands. Legally, it would come to me." Again he gave that short laugh, without humor. "Of course, if they manage to get rid of me it would be a different story, but I think they'd find it a harder job to do it."

I stood there, as frozen as if encompassed in ice, and indeed I wouldn't have felt much colder if that had been the case. What he had said was true. They might have wanted to "be rid of" me because of the money, but the others couldn't hope to gain by my death now.

Except for Shea himself.

His wide mouth softened into a near-smile. "And now I've frightened you, and I don't want you to be frightened, Jade. I didn't want to do any of this the way I had to do it. If Uncle Alex had remained in reasonably good health . . . if there hadn't been any 'accidents' "— and I knew he referred to Christopher's as well as mine—"we might have had a time to grow to know one another, to develop a natural fondness, to fall in love."

I was glad now that his hands held me, for I might have fallen; at the least I would have been swaying, for my limbs felt as if they had liquefied.

His smile broadened, a gentle smile that lit his eyes as well as his mouth. "We still need that period of adjustment, don't we, Jade? We aren't quite ready to jump into being husband and wife, especially when you're grieving for your grandfather. So far as the family—and the countryside at large—is concerned, we are married. We are one. But what we do behind closed doors is our own business."

Heaven knows what he saw in my face. I scarcely knew what I felt inside, let alone what came through to the surface. He was very close to me now, although I hadn't been aware of him moving; only a few inches farther, and his lips brushed mine. Lightly, coolly, as he had kissed me before.

And then he set me apart, and his smile was full of the satisfaction he felt at this one-sided talk we had had. "The next few days will no doubt be difficult to get through. And I'll be busy, so I won't be spending as much time with you as I'd like. But I'll feel better with this left open . . ." he pushed the connecting door between our rooms into position against the wall, wide open, "and I hope you'll feel better knowing I'm near at hand." The faintest of shadows rested ever so briefly upon him. "If anything happens that seems—well, at all unusual, or out of the way—tell me. That's probably an unnecessary precaution, because you should be perfectly safe now. Do you want to rest before dinner? The shades can be drawn to make it dark enough to sleep. Oh, I forgot to ask, do you need anything? Clothes, anything like that, for the funeral?"

It was a wonder he could understand me, so wooden were my lips. "I have . . . plenty of black."

"Oh, God. Of course you have. I didn't think. Oh, here, I picked this up today. I think it will be a better fit . . . if not, we'll have it altered."

"It" was a ring. A beautiful, narrow gold band. He held it so that I could see it closely, and then slipped it onto my finger. "A little loose, but not much. Get some rest, now, you're looking as if you'd been sandbagged."

A final smile, and he was gone, leaving me with scarcely enough strength to make it to the bed.

I didn't bother with shades. It didn't matter to me whether they were up or down, the room dark or light. Outside the palm tree was again dissolving into the mist, and that didn't matter, either.

What mattered was that I was here in this house, married to Shea Robards, and that . . . someone . . . might want me dead because of a will my grandfather had made.

I slept, and woke to a tapping on the door. I was groggy and my head ached. The tapping came again, so that I called out in reply to it.

Annie was there, in her plain dark cotton with an apron over it, her hair looking as if she'd been out in the wind. It wasn't dark, yet, not quite, but I thought walking home through that fog would be every bit as unnerving as being out after dark.

"Mr. Shea sent me up to call you. To see if you'd like some tea."

"Tea. Yes, that does sound good. Thank you, Annie."

"He said to find out if you needed any clothes readied for tomorrow."

"No. Maybe the tea will help my headache."

She was curiously impassive. "Sometimes it does. Would you like me to bring you some hot water?"

"Yes, please." I pulled myself upright, with every muscle resisting. I wanted to sleep for a week—or at least until after the funeral was over, the will read—but they didn't have the latest will, did they?

When she had brought hot water I bathed my face and felt somewhat better. It was a temptation to plead illness, which indeed I was not far from experiencing, and simply take to my bed. Only the memory of what my mother would have said kept me going; Mama was a great one for duty as opposed to self-indulgence.

The family were assembled in the back sitting room. Shea was leaning against the mantle, more elegantly dressed than I had yet seen him in a dark broadcloth suit and white linen, with highly polished boots. He moved toward me with a smile, holding out a hand.

"Jade, come sit down, and have some tea." He bent his head to give me a perfunctory kiss, no more than a brushing of his lips across my forehead. Solicitous, husbandly . . . and chaste.

Why did I think that? Didn't I want him to be kind and considerate?

I accepted a seat on a small sofa and Shea sat beside me, pouring from the silver pot on a low table. It was a pleasant, peaceful scene: a few lamps lit against the encroaching dusk, a lovely room soft with chintz and polished woods, an assemblage of well-groomed, attractive people.

Yet I sensed an underlying current that was cold and dark. Was it directed at me? Had one of these people tried to maim or kill me? The tea was hot and sweet, the way I liked it. I was conscious of Shea's arm along the back of the sofa, touching me across the shoulders until I leaned forward, away from him. For a moment I had an impulse to lean into his arm, to feel it tighten around me . . . and then the moment passed. It was only a room, full of strangers, including the man beside me.

Annie stood in the doorway. It seemed to me that she was thinner than she had been only yesterday, which must be my imagination. "If there's nothing else, mum, I'd like to be leaving now. Before it gets clear dark."

I didn't realize she was addressing me until Shea touched me lightly on the shoulder. "We won't need Annie any longer, will we, Jade?"

"No. No, of course not. Go ahead, Annie."

She bobbed her head, but there was nothing subservient in her manner. Was Annie hostile to me, too? I didn't know any reason why she should be.

They were making polite conversation, and after a time I didn't try to follow it. It was a façade, all on the surface, masking what they really thought and felt. After a time someone—Hesper?—suggested that a poetry reading might be appropriate. Lawrie was dispatched to bring back a slim volume, and for a time we listened to his quiet, soothing voice—I, at least, without comprehension, busy with my own thoughts.

It was with a sense of release that I went up to freshen my person before supper. Again I was tempted to plead a headache and ask for a tray in my room; again I was shamed out of it. Annie was gone, the only servants left in the house were Mrs. Dutton and Cook, both of them far older than I, both fat and with bad feet.

Someone was in the bathroom, so I bathed in cold water in my room, much aware of the open door between Shea and me. I caught a glimpse of him seated at a desk, bent over a paper covered with sketching and figures, but he didn't look in my direction.

It was necessary once more to make the trip down the long corridor to the bathroom, which this time was free. I paused, however, because since I'd been here a short time earlier someone had closed the door opposite, to my grandfather's room.

Only curious at first, I stepped to it and tried the knob. To my astonishment, it was locked. While I stood, puzzled, I heard from within the sound of rustling papers, or perhaps skirts, I couldn't be sure.

I spoke without thought. "Is someone in there?"

The sounds ceased. This time, frowning a little, I rapped and called out more loudly. There was no reply, and the door resisted my efforts to open it.

I turned away, walking briskly back to my room and striding to the connecting door. Shea still sat at the desk, his back to me, working over his figures. I cleared my throat and he turned.

"Jade? You want something?"

"There seems to be someone in Grandfather's room. They've locked the door, and it sounds as if they might be . . . sorting through papers, or something like that. They didn't answer when I knocked."

I was coming to know the way his thick brows met over his nose when he was disturbed or angry. He shoved back his chair and came out of it in a fluid motion, for all that he retained that slight limp.

He led the way back down the hall, but when he grasped the knob it gave beneath the pressure and swung inward—on an empty room.

However, the unlocked door didn't give the lie to my story, for it was obvious that someone had been there. Drawers were incompletely closed, bedding had been stripped and dropped onto the floor, and a few cushions tossed out of their chairs.

Shea observed it with a grim face. "Someone wants to find that will before the rest of us do, it seems."

"But they told me there *was* a will, and that it was the one that would be accepted . . ."

He laughed. "Let us turn up the latest one and see how far they get trying to foist the earlier one on us. Well. I wonder if they found what they were after?"

"I interrupted whoever it was. They must have had to leave very quickly, before we came back."

"So there's a good chance they didn't find it, eh?" He turned to the door and removed the key from it. "Let's just lock it from the other side, and after supper we'll have another pass at finding the document. I should have done it sooner, I suppose." He locked the room, from the outside, and pocketed the key. "You didn't get any clue as to who it was, did you?"

I remembered the soft sounds—which might have been either

rustling paper or rustling taffeta. "No. Just small sounds of movement."

He stood for a moment, looking down on me. "I think I did the
right thing, for all that it swept you along on a tide too strong for you
to handle. I'm sure it was what Uncle Alex wanted . . . to see you
safely married to me. I hope it will be what you want, too."

I had no ready answer to that, and luckily he seemed to expect
none. "Come along," he said briskly, "let's go down and eat."

The meal was a dull one, up to the point where Shea announced
that immediately following it he intended to open up Grandfather's
room and search it. "Anyone else who wants to join in is welcome.
After all, we all want the same thing, don't we? The final will to be
admitted as the legal document to decide all Uncle Alex's affairs?"

No one responded to the hint of sarcasm in his voice. But no one
wanted to be left out of the search.

Even Christopher asked if he could come along and watch. Shea,
with a bit of humor, included him in the party. "Certainly. You can
keep an eye on everyone, see that they don't slip anything into their
pockets unbeknownst to the rest of us."

It was anything but a jolly party that made the search, however.
Search we did, into, under, behind, beneath everything. There were
plenty of papers, including what appeared to be an incomplete rough
draft of the document we sought, which had been crumpled and
dropped into a wastebasket. It was Shea who found it, displaying it
before us all as evidence that the old man had actually written a final will since my brother and I had come here.

"It proves nothing," Hesper said fiercely. "Nothing! There is so
little there, and he entertained himself these last few months, writing
wills! They were all destroyed, as he intended them to be! This is no
more than a beginning of a will, a few meaningless lines."

Shea smoothed the paper and folded it. "Nevertheless, I think I'll
just hang onto it. In my opinion it shows intent to write a new document, naming his grandchildren as principal heirs. Certainly *Cecilia
Jade Cummings* is spelled out clearly enough."

Edward snorted in derision. "Intent be damned! What will count,
in court, is what turns up in a genuine legal will, and Smithers has
the only one there is!"

Shea refused to rise to matching anger. "Then why are you wast-
ing your time helping to hunt for one Uncle Alex only imagined he
wrote?"

"I'm here," Edward stated flatly, "to see that you don't pull any shenanigans in concocting your own 'will,' Cousin."

Shea's smile was thin. "I don't have to do any such thing as that, Edward. Regardless of which will you turn up, I'll still control Robards Industries—the mill and the woods."

The dislike—no, the hatred—between them was palpable. I wondered why they continued to live here in the same household, and knew the answer before I had completely formed the question. They had all wanted to be near Uncle Alex—to influence him, to protect him from one another—and they had to be on the scene to do it.

Hesper's bosom rose and fell like a majestic ship at sea. "You're finished searching, are you? We've found nothing. No will, no proof that he ever made another one. Where else is there to look? We've torn the place apart, unless you want to peel back the wallpaper! If he wrote it, and told no one until he was dying, then he hid it somewhere in this room. He was too ill to go anywhere else with it. He didn't even cross the hall to the bathroom the last two days of his life; he was too weak to walk that far. And except for his body, nothing has been removed since he died. Nothing. We have found no will because he didn't make one! There is nothing here to find!"

A muscle twitched at the corner of Shea's mouth; no more. He turned and walked away.

I began to pick up the pillows and replace them, to straighten the things we had disarranged. Was she right? Or was Shea?

And whichever way was the right of it, how much difference would it make to me?

Shea had gone out, Mrs. Dutton informed me, when I had finished putting Grandfather's room to rights. No, he hadn't said where.

We had worked hard for several hours, searching. I was tired and dirty, and I took my first bath in the gigantic enameled tub. It was an oddly luxurious experience, for hot water came out of the little tap with its rose-painted handles, and there was something in a tall blue bottle to scent the water (Hesper's? I wondered guiltily, but it didn't seem like Hesper, to me) and I soaked in it for quite a long time. While lying there my eyes roved about the room, which was quite large but so sparsely furnished that it offered little in the way of hiding places. If Grandfather had left his room during those crucial last days, this was the only other place he'd have come, and there was no place here to put a valuable document.

I dried myself on a big towel and dressed in an old flannel gown, the only one I owned. My clothes were so few, and so worn . . . I would need new ones before long. Was I to come to my bridal bed in a rag such as this?

Even the thought was enough to generate heat in the chilly room. Shea had offered me a "period of adjustment" of undetermined length. But he had intimated that eventually we would assume the natural marital relationship.

No one had ever spelled out that relationship to me, although along with the other girls in the school in Peking I had speculated and giggled under the covers at night. I knew more than some of the others, for I had assisted in the birth of a baby when I was fourteen.

My little brother Rodney was born then, a month early, and when my father was away. Mama's pains had taken her unaware, and my oldest sister, Rachel, was sick in bed with a fever and a sore throat. Hannah, a year older than I, was dispatched for the midwife half a mile away. But there wasn't time to wait for the midwife: being early, and very small, the baby was born quickly and easily, and there was no one there but me to do for him.

Up to this time I'd heard only vague tales about how babies were born. Mama was concerned that I should be there, so young and so innocent, to witness the birth, but she was too weak to care for the baby entirely by herself and I had to be allowed to help. For myself, I was so entranced by the tiny creature that I gave little thought to the rest of it, at the time.

Later, of course, I thought about what a curious way God had chosen to bring children into the world; and having seen the baby emerge from my mother's body I drew my own conclusions as to how he had gotten there in the first place.

My friend Grace was a fund of information, too. She read all sorts of racy novels that would have been immediately confiscated had the Reverend Mr. Wingate learned of them. In actuality, they were couched in such roundabout terms that they could scarcely have corrupted anyone. Without Grace's interpretations, we would have remained unenlightened regarding the facts of life.

At any rate, I was certainly no more ignorant than most girls of my generation and upbringing. And where the thought of entering into a marriage with Edward, for instance, was totally repugnant, it made a good deal of difference to put Shea into the title role in my imaginings.

I pulled a robe, equally worn, over the nightgown, and made my way back to my own room.

The door stood open to the connecting room, which was dark. I could see enough to tell that the bed was flat, unoccupied.

My emotions were in a state of turbulence. I stood before my mirror, examining the figure I saw there. Excluding the shabby robe, I was attractive enough, I thought. My hair had a tendency to curl and my lashes were thick and dark. Green eyes—Father used to laugh and say Mama had known best about calling me "Jade," after all—a small, straight nose, and a reasonably pretty mouth.

I understood Shea's explanation for the "period of adjustment." It was true we'd scarcely had time to get acquainted, let alone to fall in love.

Still, it was my understanding of the nature of men that they didn't need all that much time to desire a woman. Naturally he had had the sensitivity to withhold himself from me on the night of my grandfather's death. But tonight? Mightn't I have expected he would seek me out tonight?

Business, everything was business with Shea, they said. At all hours of the day or night. Still, a man was a man, wasn't he?

I blew out my light and got into bed, but not to sleep. Tonight the chiming clock on the landing was an irritant . . . every fifteen minutes, that little four-note melody, adding four more notes on the half, four more on the three quarters of an hour, until on the hour there was the entire tune and then the striking of the hours . . . ten, eleven, twelve.

My stomach muscles tightened in apprehension when I heard his footsteps at last on the stairs. He let himself into the adjoining room, and I listened to him moving about, undressing without lighting a lamp. Since there was no door closed between us, I heard the faint protest of springs as he got into bed.

My stomach muscles remained in a knot.

There was no holding back the idea, once it came, and I knew it had been there, off on the periphery of my mind, for some time.

Had Shea married me, not to protect me or because he was attracted to me, but in order to retain or expand his control of Grandfather's business?

Was I no more to him than another bit of Robards business?

12

The day dawned looking as if it had been created solely for a funeral. The mist was so heavy that it dripped from the eaves; by the time we were ready to leave the house it had strengthened into a thin rain.

A total of three carriages had been brought around, all drawn by horses with black plumes already sodden. Christopher, Ned, Shea, and I went into the first carriage, and even the umbrella held over me on the dash for the vehicle didn't keep me from being damp by the time I was seated; and as the sides were open and the rain swept in on a slant there was insufficient protection in the greatcoat Shea put around me. Hesper and her sons went into the second carriage, and the servants into the last one. We started with a lurch, mud spurting from under the wheels, and I prayed that it would soon be over.

The church was filled. There were far more men than women; employees of the Robards Mills and the lumbermen who felled the trees, Christopher whispered to me. Because Chris needed help, Ned was allowed to sit with the family, where he was obviously awed and uncomfortable in his Sunday best.

I didn't listen to the minister's words. I sat with my hands clasped in my lap, not even my black gloves capable of warming them, my head bowed. I knew there were curious glances in my direction, and I was glad my hat had a veil so they could not clearly discern my face. They would all know, I guessed, that Alex Robards' granddaughter had come from China, and that she'd married Shea at the old man's deathbed. No doubt they also knew far more than I about the kind of man my husband was, and what my portion of the estate would be.

It was raining harder when we left the church. The coffin, of magnificent and glossy construction, was mercifully hidden in the hearse that moved just ahead of us. I had passed by the coffin, as had the others in the church, guided by Shea's hand on my elbow, but I had closed my eyes rather than look into the dead face. I had no wish to remember him that way.

By the time we reached the graveyard the rain was coming down with such force that it ran in rivulets into the open grave. Shea spent only a moment assessing the situation, and decided that we would stay in the carriage; behind us, the others had mostly decided the same thing, although there were some who came on foot and stood

around without even the protection of umbrellas against the outpour-
ings of the dreary sky.

Somewhere off to one side I heard a woman sobbing. I didn't look
around to see who it was. For myself, I had already shed my tears.
I might do well, I thought in an uncharacteristic burst of pessimism,
to save any more for my own plight.

And then the casket was lowered into the ground, the brief words
spoken . . . "ashes to ashes, dust to dust" . . . and the first shovelful
of earth thrown atop the polished box. Shea gathered up the reins,
deciding we'd had enough; we were all shivering and wet.

Even Christopher was subdued and silent, and Ned was never
talkative in the presence of any adult. The horses, eager to get back
to their stables, needed no urging to canter.

When Shea lifted me down I was stiff with discomfort. The carriage with the servants was right behind us, and Shea spoke over my
head.

"Annie, will you help Mrs. Robards out of her wet clothes, please,
and see that she's made comfortable?"

Before I could protest that I needed no such help, he was gone;
the boys had ridden on around to the back with him.

We walked into the house together, Annie and I, and although
she was polite enough, I sensed once more that something was amiss
between us.

"See to yourself—you're as wet as I am," I told her, and was re-
warded with a rather sullen assent.

My dress buttoned down the back, dozens of tiny covered buttons
which were difficult to grasp with numbed fingers, and I was still
struggling with them when Annie tapped on my door and entered.
She was into one of her usual dark cottons, with an enveloping apron.

"Here, let me do that," she said, and I stood while she performed
the task.

She caught the dress when I stepped out of it, lifting it clear. "I'll
see that it's dried and pressed, mum," she said.

I spoke on impulse. "Do what you like with it, throw it out, for all
I care. I don't intend to wear it to another funeral, ever."

She stared at me in astonishment. "But it's beautiful goods—silk,
isn't it? Real silk?"

"Yes. Take it, if you want it. We're nearly of a size. You could
probably alter it to fit; there's a generous hem."

Her eyes continued to widen. "You mean it? I can have it?"

"Yes, certainly I mean it. I don't care if I never see it again."

Annie ran her tongue over her lips. "If you're sure . . ."

"I'm sure."

A smile tugged at her full mouth. "Thank you, then. What will you be wanting to put on? The bombazine?"

How I longed for something beautiful, not black nor gray nor practical, but something soft and shimmering and beautiful! I stared into the opened wardrobe, hating everything in it.

"The gray, I think. There's a black armband somewhere in that top drawer. I don't think Grandfather would mind if I don't wear all black in his memory."

She put the wet dress aside and helped me into the dry one; I had to change petticoats, too, because I was damp to the skin.

"There's all sorts of things to eat. The neighbors brought in the funeral meats, the way they always do."

"I'll be down directly. Has"—his name stuck in my throat, and I couldn't say it—"Mr. Robards come in, yet?"

"I couldn't say, mum." She had dropped back into the reserved manner.

"Annie." I stopped her before she could leave the room with the wet dress over her arm. "Have I done something to offend you?"

For a moment she hesitated, and I thought she would not answer. "I suppose it's not your fault," she said at last. "That he stopped looking at *me,* when you came."

Before I could voice the demand to know whom she was talking about, she was gone.

Shea? Was she referring to Shea? Had she thought him interested in her before I arrived? I was already feeling bruised and shaken. Her flat statement did nothing to make me feel any better.

I met Shea on the stairs, and he greeted me with a smile. "I'll change my coat and be down directly. They've set out a meal for us," he said kindly.

I finished my descent with wooden-feeling legs. Kindly. That was the word that fit Shea's treatment of me. He had been kind.

But that wasn't what I wanted in a husband, I thought, and felt the hot surge of blood through me. I knew, from Grace's stories and the books we had giggled over, that there was something to be valued more highly, and that was passion. If he really cared for me, as a woman rather than a financial asset, wouldn't he reveal some passion?

A veritable feast awaited us, and by now everyone was hungry enough to indulge in it. At least eating took up some of the hours— the hours that stretched endlessly before me. What was I to do to occupy myself in this house? There was a cook, a housekeeper, and a hired girl to do the work. What was left for a mere mistress, ignorant and ill-trained as she was?

I put the question to Shea when we had eaten our fill and various members of the household went about their own business until the lawyer should come at two. He smiled a little at my earnestness.

"So you need something to do? There are books to read . . . the organ to play . . ."

"One can't read and play the organ for twelve hours a day."

"It's your house now. Do as you like with it. The servants are at your disposal."

"But don't you see, that's just it? The servants do everything that's necessary, and it's a beautiful house, completely decorated, everything finished—what is there left for me to do?"

"Would that be to your liking? To decorate a house?"

"There's nothing left to decorate! Even my own room is complete to the last curtain and picture on the walls! I'm not used to being an ornament, I'm used to working—cooking, cleaning, the things an ordinary woman does. There's none of that to do here."

He came to a decision; I saw it in his face. "Come along, I'll show you something."

He had been working at the desk in the library; when he first spread out the papers for me to see they were incomprehensible. Sketches, figures . . . I raised puzzled eyes.

"I know it's rough, and I'm no artist, but it can't be that bad. Here, view it from this angle."

"A—a floor plan?"

"A floor plan. I'm making the preliminary drawings for a house. Our house."

"Our . . . house." I wasn't sure what emotion this roused in me.

"This house belonged to Uncle Alex, and while I was single it was the logical place to live, so that I could discuss the business with him. Now he's gone, but the others will continue to live here. I don't intend to live with them. There's an architect coming from San Francisco next week; I'll show him these and ask him to design us a house. As grand as this one. I already have the lot for it—approximately half an acre, out on Hillsdale Street. There are some fine homes going in there, the equal of any in the state, including those in San Francisco. Of course, it will be some time before they get into actual construction, but I'll ask him to hurry along the plans, and our own men will build it. Would that please you, to have a house to furnish and decorate?"

"A house . . . as grand as this?" Already I was warming to the idea; just getting away from Aunt Hesper would be a step in the right direction.

"Grander, if you like. A home to raise a family in. The plan I had in mind," he bent over the plans, so that he didn't see the color in my cheeks, "has seven bedrooms. One downstairs, and six up. Will that be enough, do you think?"

"Seven . . . seems rather a lot," I said faintly, wondering what Mama would think if she knew of it, after the tiny cramped quarters she had lived in all her life.

There was a spark of amusement in his eyes when he looked at me. "Too many?"

"What . . . ever you say, of course."

"I've used basically the same floor plan as this place, with only a few changes. A bathroom downstairs as well as up, for instance, would be convenient, don't you think?"

He talked on about it at some length, and it was the first time I'd seen him enthusiastic about anything that wasn't strictly business. Although perhaps it was, in a way. As new head of the Robards Mills, he needed a home befitting his position.

"You won't have to wait until it's built to pick out your wallpapers and draperies and carpets—that sort of thing. Do you sew?"

He asked the question abruptly, straightening so that he was once more looking down from his superior height.

"Yes, of course."

"You'll be needing clothes. You won't be wearing mourning forever; in fact, I'm in favor of a gradual change to colors very quickly; you're too young and pretty to dress like an old woman. Mead's Department Store has a new device they call a sewing machine; you might go in and take a look at it, see if you think it would be worthwhile."

"A machine that sews? I've heard of them, but I've never seen one. Yes, I would like to sew . . . some clothes." The idea was exciting.

"At Mead's. Your credit there is unlimited; I've already discussed it with the owner. Just tell them who you are. Now." He grinned at me. "Will that satisfy your need to have something constructive to do?"

The strident ring of the bell at the front door kept me from having to make a verbal response, but perhaps it was all there in my face. I'd never had even limited credit anywhere, let alone *carte blanche* to buy anything in the store. I wondered how soon I could decently investigate Mead's Department Store.

"Is it time for Smithers already?" Shea drew himself up to his full height, and his limp was scarcely perceptible when he went to open the door.

The lawyer was there, shaking off a dripping umbrella. He came into the hallway, with a smile that held no warmth at all, although he greeted me politely enough.

"The front parlor, I think, is where we're going to meet," Shea said, and touched my elbow to guide me there.

I would have liked to go off by myself and contemplate the prospect of a grand house of my own and unlimited credit at Mead's Department Store, but I was quickly brought down to earth when the family assembled. Shea chose one of the yellow brocade sofas for us to sit on; it was strategically situated in that from it we could see the faces of all the others, which was certainly what Shea intended.

There was no doubt that it was serious business. Even Lawrie, though he gave me his usual friendly smile, was tense.

The servants were called in, as well, for they were all mentioned in the will. They filed in, uncomfortable but eager, too. Smithers stood before us, his back to the sliding paneled doors that divided this room from the next one, and adjusted his spectacles. He cleared his throat and the small scuffling sounds ceased at once.

"As you know, we are gathered to read the last will and testament of Alexander Joseph Robards, dated July nineteenth, 1884," he began. His eyes flickered toward us, but Shea was impassive, lounging on the sofa as if this were a social afternoon of no importance. Only his eyes, hard and dark, gave him away.

"I will not bore you with the legal jargon, which would no doubt be incomprehensible to you," Smithers said in a condescending manner. "Instead, I will summarize, as clearly as possible, so that there will be no misunderstanding. The first bequests are those to the servants. Mr. Robards was most generous, as you will see. To those in his employ for more than six years, he left the sum of five hundred dollars each." He beamed at Cook and Mrs. Dutton, who were appropriately overwhelmed. "To those of no less than two years employment, the sum is two hundred and fifty dollars."

This, I judged from their reactions, included Ames and Annie. Ned stood in a corner, for all the seats were occupied, trying to think what to do with his hands and his feet. He brought them all to a standstill, however, at the next bequest, which was obviously directed at him.

"For those with a year or more employment, the sum is one hundred and twenty-five dollars."

Ned's face flamed, then went white as the enormity of the sum was impressed upon him. Hesper shifted restlessly in her chair; she had come in too late to appropriate one of the upholstered seats, and this one creaked under her weight. I half expected her to urge the lawyer to forget the domestic bequests and get on to the important ones.

There followed a list of similar sums to people whose names I didn't know; perhaps they were workers at the mills. I let a glance slide toward the man beside me, who looked perfectly relaxed, but when he shifted position to put his arm along the back of the sofa I felt that it was rigid.

"To the surviving children of my beloved daughter Charlotte," here he read from the paper in his hand, "I leave the sum of one thousand dollars each." The lawyer smiled in my direction, his eyes flinty, as if this was more than I had any right to expect. Hesper was breathing heavily and trying to do it quietly. Beside her, Edward was silent and stolid, no doubt fortified for this ordeal by another nip from the brandy bottle. Lawrie's smile was apologetic, I thought, when his eyes met mine.

"To my sister-in-law, Hesper Jessica Robards, I leave only the lifelong privilege of remaining in the family home. I do this in the belief that her sons, who upon my death will be independently wealthy, can well afford to care for their mother."

Hesper's raspy breathing stopped altogether. I saw incredulity flash across her broad face, to be followed by rage so great that it set her to trembling. I think everyone there could have read her mind. *"And after all I did for him!"*

Unaware, Smithers was continuing. "And to my nephews, Shea Alexander Robards, Edward William Robards, and Lawrie Stenton Robards, I leave the business interest incorporated under the name of Robards Mills . . . there follows a legal description of said property . . . to be divided equally between them, with the stipulation that Shea and Edward will draw the same salaries as they now draw before the profits shall be divided, since they are the ones who have chosen to actively work in the business."

I shot a glance at Lawrie and saw that he had relaxed, was half smiling. So this was as much as he had hoped for; he was content to draw enough to enable him to devote his time to painting and music.

Edward half turned in his seat, seeking out Shea. "To be shared equally between us! That doesn't sound as if you're going to play God Almighty forever more!"

Shea was unperturbed. "One third of the original business, to each of us. That doesn't take into account that just before he died Uncle Alex signed the papers incorporating my personal business interests into the Robards Mills. That gives me an additional percentage of the whole, which means I will permanently outvote you"—his eyes touched on Lawrie and returned—"since only you and I control voting stock. Even if this will stands. Which it won't."

There was an immediate hubbub, from the servants, on a subdued level, as well as from Hesper and Edward.

"This is Uncle Alex's last will and testament. There is no reason why it shouldn't stand!" Edward said, his tone ugly.

"Mr. Robards," Smithers addressed Shea formally, "are you able to produce a more recent will than the one I have just read?"

"No. But a dozen people heard him say he'd made one. I do have a rough draft of one he began and discarded, which would seem to prove intent."

"Intent, in this instance, has no legality whatever," Smithers told us. "Unless the will you mention is produced, the one I have just read will stand."

"I have a lawyer who thinks differently. He thinks there is sufficient evidence to take into a courtroom, even if the will doesn't turn up. There are witnesses to the fact that he stated he intended to provide more fully for his grandchildren, and the paper I have here, in his own handwriting, states fairly fully what he intended that provision to be."

"Is the document signed?" Perspiration stood out upon the lawyer's brow, although the room was not overheated.

"No, although the handwriting can be verified, as there are plenty of other samples of it. There is some possibility that the latest will has been found by those to whom it is a disadvantage—and destroyed by them." Shea had to raise his voice to finish his statement over the outcry *that* brought forth. "My lawyer is preparing a case to take to court; it is there that the matter will be settled, Mr. Smithers—not here, not by you."

Edward came out of his chair, his face suffused with blood; he reached for Shea, pulling him off the sofa with a handful of shirt front. I had not even time to become alarmed, for Shea broke the hold by sinking a fist into the other's midsection. He followed it by another blow to the jaw that sent his cousin reeling across the room, knocking over two chairs.

"And that's what you'll bloody well get any time you put a hand on me," Shea said. I saw that his knuckles were bleeding where they had connected with jaw—or had it been teeth?—but he was unaware of it.

"Mr. Shea, sir . . ." That was Mrs. Dutton, fluttering anxiously in the background. Edward was getting to his feet, but Shea turned his back on him to face the housekeeper. "Mr. Shea . . . if there's going to be a court battle over the estate . . . does that mean, sir, it may be months or maybe years before we get our money? Before we even know if we ever will get it?"

"No, not at all. The provisions for all of you would have been the same, no matter how many wills were drawn. I'll see to it that you have your money immediately, from my own personal funds, if necessary. You have nothing to worry about."

There was a collective sigh of relief; I could see them all spending it in their minds. Perhaps they, too, would for a short time have "unlimited credit" at the department store.

"It can't be right," Edward said, pressing a handkerchief to a bleeding lower lip, "that he can bring in the Shaw Mills and take control. How can that be right?"

Smithers was tight-lipped. "I haven't seen the documents he refers to. We will, of course, be privileged to examine them."

"In my lawyer's office, at your convenience," Shea agreed.

"The Shaw Mills!" I could see that Edward was consumed with jealous anger. "Mills he got by murdering his wife . . . ! And now he's using them against the rest of . . ."

He didn't get to finish his statement. Shea hit him again, and this time there was a spurt of blood from Edward's nose; but Shea didn't get off scot-free, either, because a reciprocal blow alongside his head sent him reeling.

Hesper moved into the momentary lull as both men were recovering themselves. "Stop it. This is accomplishing nothing except to wreck the room. Shea is right about one thing. This will be settled in court, not here by a bloody fist fight. And we'll see how the court decides when there is a legal will in evidence on our side, and none on his." She swept from the room as if she were, indeed, Victoria; all she needed was a crown.

The servants melted away; Edward and Smithers withdrew for a further conference elsewhere, with Edward sopping at the flow of blood from his nose. Lawrie gave me a regretful smile as he left; a moment later I heard him playing the organ, the volume up enough to cover any number of private conferences.

Shea put up a hand to one ear, as if it were tender. "I'm sorry. This was a nasty affair for you to witness."

Used as I was to a happy, close-knit family situation, this afternoon had indeed left me somewhat shaken. I stared at the oozing blood on his knuckles.

"That ought to be bandaged."

Shea glanced at it, dismissed it. "It's nothing. It'll heal." The dark eyes swung to meet my own. "I owe you an explanation of that remark of Edward's. About . . . murdering my wife."

Across the hall the organ soared in the glorious notes of Beethoven's Ninth Symphony. The constriction in my chest was so painful that I couldn't speak at all.

"I was married to Anthea Shaw for two years. She was drowned last summer . . . I found her on the beach, drowned." Although he put no particular emphasis on the word *I,* nor any emotion into his voice, I felt something twist inside me. If he had loved her . . . and found her, dead, lying on the sand . . . "It wasn't possible to tell exactly what had happened. There was a thorough investigation, however, and a note came to light. In Anthea's handwriting." He was still trying to maintain a flat, even monotone, but he couldn't quite manage it; he spoke dryly, looking past me at the fog-shrouded windows. "She had fallen in love with another man . . . and since she could never have him, she had decided to end her own life." He turned back to me, that muscle jumping at the corner of his mouth. "The letter was turned over to the constabulary. The official investigation was at an end. We saw no reason to brand her a suicide; there were too many people to hurt that way. It was easier to let it be thought her death was accidental."

My words were little more than a whisper. "But Edward said— murder." Ned had reported it that way, too, I recalled. *People said it was murder.*

Shea spoke even more dryly. "It would have pleased Edward if I'd been suspected—and convicted—of a crime. After all, with me out of the way, he'd have a clear field with the Robards Mills. That wasn't the way of it, however, and the official verdict was accidental drowning."

I couldn't make my voice any stronger. "So much hatred between you—how have you stood living here in the same house with—the others?"

"I lived here because Uncle Alex was here. I was needed." I knew the subject was dismissed. "There are people I must see. I'll do it this afternoon; tomorrow I'll be back in the woods, which means you'll be more or less on your own. Remember, the house is yours; Hesper is only a guest in it. Do as you please, only don't go out without letting one of the servants know where you are."

When he had gone I had no wish to subject myself to any more of the company of my relatives. I withdrew to my room with a book I did not read; lying on the bed, thinking, I could hear the organ from below, for it carried with far more power than mere voices, and Lawrie's mood was reflected in his music. I thought he was genuinely sorry for me, but there was elation on his own behalf. His future had been assured; there would be funds to support him while he did the things that were important to him.

I could only wish my own future happiness was secure.

13

The third night of my marriage was spent as the first two had been: alone. I wondered that Shea had the energies to run the business, for he seemed never to sleep. Never in bed before midnight or one o'clock; up and gone by dawn.

Rumor had it that Shea had murdered his young wife—a wife who had obviously brought to the marriage some financial rewards in the form of another mill. Shea said she had left a suicide note, but it had not been revealed to anyone but the legal authorities. I didn't doubt that it was possible for a man of influence to persuade them to keep it quiet, if they were convinced that it was genuine. However, I had only his own word for the existence of the note. And I knew that I would never go to the constable and ask for proof.

Did I need proof? I wondered. The evidence of Edward's efforts, through the lawyer, to keep Grandfather from making a new will, his crass behavior, were a far cry from what I had observed of Shea.

Edward had come close to suggesting that Shea had married Anthea Shaw in the expectation of gaining control of her business properties, and had as good as said outright that he'd killed her for them. Did he also insinuate that the same held true in my case?

How could I know? Gradually the music wove its thread through the fabric of my emotions, calming, strengthening. I knew what I *wanted* to think. I wanted to believe Shea, wanted to believe that his restraint was self-imposed out of consideration for my innocence, inexperience, and grief.

I'd had enough of grief. I was ready to start living. It would be so much easier, out of this house. For all its luxuries, it was not a homey house. Not with Edward and Hesper in it. A home of my own would be a different matter.

I daydreamed a little, about a house and a family that would expand to fill seven bedrooms. I even thought for a time that while ready for bed I would not go to sleep; I would keep a light on, so that Shea would at least look in to say good night.

As the clock relentlessly chimed out the hours, however, I had to give up on that. The room grew cold, and at last I put out the light and burrowed under the covers to say my prayers.

It was after two when I finally heard Shea's footsteps on the stairs. He was making a concentrated effort to be quiet; I heard him stumble into something in the darkness of his own room, heard a muffled oath, and wondered if he, too, had sought solace of a sort in the brandy bottle.

If I cried a little then, in my own private darkness, it was no longer on behalf of the dead but for myself.

Had there been any way to avoid the rest of the family while managing to stay fed, I would have taken it. As it was, I was forced to descend to the room where Hesper was having her breakfast. To my surprise, she greeted me cordially enough, and raised her voice to summon Annie with my food.

I slipped into my chair, wondering where Christopher was. Had he eaten already? I asked Annie.

Annie nodded. "Oh, he was up with the birds this morning. He and Ned went with Mr. Shea to the woods."

Alarm coursed through me. "To the woods! But he doesn't get around well enough yet for that!"

"He'll be riding most of the time, more than likely. Anyways, he was up and he begged to go, so Mr. Shea said all right. The boy was dying to see the big trees, and learn how they're cut down and sawed up into lumber."

Her choice of words struck me as ominous. *Dying to see.* I hadn't wanted Chris out of my sight. He'd had one accident, he might easily have another; even if there were no foul play the woods were highly dangerous, as proved by the mishaps to men of normal agility.

I was unable to control my uneasiness, apparently, for Hesper gave me what I thought was intended to be a reassuring smile.

"No doubt the men will watch the boys." She stirred sugar into her coffee; the aroma of it wafted across the table to me, increasing my appetite. "I thought the funeral went very well yesterday, didn't you?"

The stiffness extended to my entire body. The last thing I wanted to talk—or think—about, was funerals. The woman seemed not to notice the aversion that must have shown on my face.

"Alex looked so natural. So peaceful. I don't think he suffered much there at the end, do you? He'd had several painful heart attacks, and he *did* suffer terribly. I'm glad it wasn't another of those, with everyone there to see it."

I stared down into the oatmeal Annie had set before me. A moment ago I'd been ravenous. I tried to swallow the lump in my throat.

"Of course I went over to the mortuary beforehand to see that he was properly done up. Mortimer is the only mortician we have, although I understand there's another one coming in soon. At any rate, he didn't do a very good job on a friend of mine—Frances Vernelly. Of course she did die in a good deal of pain, so perhaps that makes it harder . . ."

Her voice went on, and I was aware of the sound yet understood nothing of the words. It was impossible not to visualize my grandfather as he must have been, laid out on some cold table while men did strange things to his body in an attempt to make him look "natural."

"Cream?" The word cut through the blanket of insulation I had built around myself, as Hesper thrust the pitcher toward me. "It's very good and thick this morning. Do you prefer brown sugar, or white?"

"Brown, please." I prepared the oatmeal, wondering if I could eat it.

Hesper went on with the monologue from which I was mercifully missing some bits. "I think that woman is going right out of her head, I really do. Of course, grief does strange things to people."

I blinked, wondering who she was talking about.

"Making such a fuss over a missing brooch! As if the mortician or his helper would be likely to steal it! Why would they? They'd never be able to give it to anyone who could wear it, apparently it was such a distinctive thing it would be immediately recognized. Mrs. Grogan said it was valuable, but I doubt that, very seriously. The Grogans never had anything else that was valuable. They came out of Georgia after the war . . . poor white trash, I think they called them, back there."

She didn't seem at all discouraged by my lack of comment, nor did she notice that I was eating slowly and with an effort.

"She was carrying on in a hysterical fashion—I could hear her all the way out in the street, before I went in, if you can imagine! I felt sorry for poor little Foster—that's the assistant—she had him backed against a wall and was saying, 'It was a white head upon a garnet red ground, and there was gold lace filigree all around it! She had it on when she was killed, so where is it now?' As if the poor man could tell her that! He suggested it might have come unclasped and fallen off at the scene of the crime, and she said she'd looked, and it hadn't been there, and there was nothing wrong with the clasp, no reason why it should have fallen off. I felt sorry for her, of course—can you imagine what it must have been like, poking around looking for a cameo where the grass was all beaten down and covered with your daughter's blood?—thinking what had taken place there—but the woman was totally unreasonable—is something wrong?"

I had risen quickly, fighting the nausea that rose in my throat. Murmuring an incomprehensible excuse, I hurried away, glad I hadn't eaten more than a few spoonfuls of the cereal, so that there was nothing of it to come up.

I stood in the front hallway, sucking in deep breaths. I had to get out of this house, I thought. I couldn't spend the day here listening to Hesper relive every moment of the day of the funeral. I had a fleeting moment of pity for my grandfather, who had endured her presence in his house for years.

The day itself, beyond the windows, was inviting. The sky was clear and brilliantly blue, with only a few fluffy clouds that moved inland as the wind blew off the ocean. Grandfather had told me not to grieve, and while it was impossible to feel no sorrow at his death I certainly did not intend to spend much of my time thinking about the deaths in my recent past. Life is for the living, my father had often said, and my own future stretched ahead of me, unknown but potentially exciting.

Would I be thought shameless if I went shopping the day after Grandfather had been buried?

Quite possibly, but I was determined to go anyway. I hurried upstairs for the shawl that would be necessary until midafternoon. I was on my way out the front door when I remembered Shea's admonition: I was not to leave the house without telling anyone where I had gone.

Hesper was still in the dining room, and in only a few minutes away from her I'd regained my appetite, but I didn't want to lose it again by making another attempt to eat with her. Mrs. Dutton had come to pick up my dishes, which she was viewing with concern.

"Was there something wrong with the oatmeal, missus?" she demanded.

"Not at all. I'm simply not hungry yet. Mrs. Dutton, my—Mr. Robards asked me not to leave without telling someone where I was going. I'm going to walk into town and do some essential shopping."

She nodded, relieved that I wasn't being critical of the food. "Very good, missus. Will you be back for a meal at noon, then?"

And give Aunt Hesper another chance at me? Not bloody likely, I thought, and was astonished that one of Grace's old phrases had come so readily and so wickedly to mind. "No . . . it will probably be . . . oh, perhaps late afternoon, before I come home," I said recklessly. I didn't know what there was to do, if shopping should fail to fill the essential time. But I was determined not to spend any more of today alone with Hesper, and the men would be present at suppertime.

"Very good. If Mr. Shea comes in afore you do, I'll tell him. Not likely that he will, though . . . he said they'd all be eating at the cook-house today, so the boys could see how the lumberjacks eat."

Once free of the house, I felt as if a great weight had been lifted from me, or the door of my prison opened to set me loose. It was cool enough so that the shawl was welcome, and vigorous exercise was exactly what I needed. There was no need to hurry—I had the entire, glorious day—so I took a roundabout way, looking at the houses with their neat lawns, bright flowers, and picket or wrought-iron fences. Some of the houses, three full stories high as our own, had flat center roofs that were also encircled with the wrought-iron railings, and I wondered if they actually served as captain's walks where families could look to sea for their returning sailors.

There were several large ships in the harbor, some of them an-chored on the far side of the bay, which was quite narrow at this point, where they were apparently being loaded with lumber. There were also a few smaller vessels at the dock where Christopher and I had landed; I knew that most of the supplies for the city came in by ship because it was a long, arduous trip from San Francisco by land —nearly three hundred miles, and all of it uphill, as one dry-voiced traveler had put it as we had disembarked from the city.

It wasn't the harbor I was interested in, however; I was eager to find Mead's Department Store, where I had unlimited credit. The entire concept was slightly unreal. While we had never gone either hungry or unclothed, there had seldom been any money for extras, and patched underwear and discreetly mended frocks were taken for granted.

It took me a little time to find the store I sought, for I did not ask questions but wandered along looking into windows and reading signs. Mead's, when I found it, was gratifyingly large, modern, and well equipped.

A middle-aged man, thin and neat, came directly toward me almost as soon as I had entered the establishment. He smiled, bowing slightly, and to my astonishment spoke my new name.

"Good morning, Mrs. Robards. Mr. Shea said you might be com-ing in. I'm Adolphus Mead. Is there something in particular I can show you?"

But of course, he must have attended Grandfather's funeral, and made his conclusions as to my identity since I sat beside Shea.

"I'd like to spend some time just looking around, if I may. I'll want to buy some dress goods, I think."

"We have some lovely things, just got in a shipment two days ago. Your husband said you would be needing a good many things, and of course we will deliver anything you wish."

It was like drifting into a dreamworld. I forgot funerals, and Aunt Hesper, and the unfortunate girl who had been stabbed in the thicket near our house. And although this excursion was made possible by my new husband, I very nearly forgot about him, too.

Most of my dresses had been hand-me-downs from my older sisters, and occasionally, when Mama was unable to mend one of her own gowns, it was cut down for me. New dresses had been a rare thing in my lifetime, and the prospect of being able to select freely of these marvelous fabrics was a heady sensation indeed.

The shop owner hovered at my side, never aggressive, but pointing out the features of various selections.

"You'll be wanting something like this, perhaps . . . it's an all-wool silk Henrietta, imported from Germany. Very practical to use, as it's eight inches wider than most of our fabrics, forty-four inches. It's one of the finest dress materials we have in stock."

I fingered the material, eye lighting on one labeled *cardinal,* which I knew was an out-of-the-question shade for me, at least for a long time. It was indeed elegant and luxurious. "How much is it?"

"Eighty-seven cents a yard. It's comparable to what my competitors sell for a dollar and a quarter."

Eighty-seven cents a yard! I swallowed and dropped the fabric, turning to the bolts across the aisle. "This is a Henrietta, too, isn't it?"

A pained expression crossed his face. "That is a domestic cotton, Mrs. Robards. Fifteen cents a yard. Really, Mrs. Robards"—he paused, obviously caught up in a dilemma, then plunged on—"I'm sure your husband would be very angry with me if I allowed you to go home with anything of that quality. I am going to be very presumptuous, simply to spare myself a tongue-lashing." He smiled, to show that though he meant it, he didn't want to be thought an overeager merchant. "Mr. Shea buys nothing but the best for his own dress clothes, and I know that is what he intends for you. He stated clearly to me that you were to have whatever you wanted, and that price was no object."

My voice was rather faint, echoing in the large room. "I'm afraid I'm not used to shopping without regard to price."

"Of course. I perfectly understand. However, we both want to please your husband, don't we? May I make a suggestion? Why don't you sit down over here, and I'll ask my clerk to bring us some tea, and then I'll bring some materials for you to study at your leisure, and we won't discuss prices at all? We'll simply let you choose what you like from the bolts that I know are suitable. How would that be?"

The idea was outrageous; my mother would have gone into an apoplectic seizure at the very notion of shopping without asking prices.

It was also tremendously exciting.

"I could use some tea," I hedged, knowing full well that he would take it for consent to the entire proposal.

He was delighted. I was given time to consume not only tea but several slices of bread and butter, with jam, and a dish of wild strawberries. These latter, I suspected, had been intended for his own luncheon. As I was by this time in the late stages of starvation, I ate them shamelessly. My mother had talked about strawberries, but I had never had any before.

The next few hours passed in a haze of delight. If occasionally guilt reared its ugly head (a dollar and twenty-two cents a yard for silk taffeta!—but it was such a lovely shade of old rose, and I'd never had anything that color in my life), Mr. Mead managed to help me suppress it.

After I'd selected enough materials to keep me busy sewing for the next two years, Mr. Mead was only too happy to show me his household furnishings, including catalogues of things that could be ordered from as far away as Kansas City and Chicago.

Other customers came and went, all attended to by one of the other clerks; Mr. Mead devoted himself to me exclusively, and insisted upon taking me out to a restaurant for a noon meal, which he paid for.

No wonder it was a heady day for me, and that I let it run on far too long. When I finally left the store, allowing the proprietor to think that I had a carriage waiting for me, the afternoon fog was moving with incredible swiftness across the waters of the bay, enveloping everything like some monstrous carnivore.

With the fog came chill. I was glad of the heavy shawl, and thought that next time I came I would buy yarn, as well, for knitting more of them. This black one was the only shawl I had, and it had already done service for years.

I walked briskly, but the fog moved faster, rolling ahead of me in what seemed like balls, and then swallowing me up as if I were Jonah in the whale. I had often contemplated that poor man's fate, and thought how terrifying it would be to exist in total darkness—but this was almost as bad, for now the mists were no longer swirling, they were simply so dense that I could not see the houses on my own side of the street if they were more than a few yards back.

Beginning to be alarmed, I paused to look up at a street sign on a post. I had reached the intersection of Fourth and E Streets, which could be no more than four blocks from home. Surely, with this system of numbered and lettered streets, I couldn't get lost, even if I couldn't see.

Somewhat reassured, I moved on. Twice wagons or carriages passed me in the street; I heard the creak of wheels and the clop of hoofs, but neither time could I make out the nature of the conveyance.

I knew that if I were to call out and identify myself there was a good possibility the unknown driver would see me safely home, but I couldn't bring myself to do that. I plodded on, beginning to feel damp now as the mist became more dense. What a peculiar climate it was, to be sure!

I had reached another street corner, but this one had no sign. I hesitated, wondering if it were worth the effort to cross the street and see if there were one on the other side. I actually took a few steps in that direction before pausing, irresolute.

The approaching horse could be heard for some distance, but I was confused by the fog; I couldn't tell where it was, and it came at such a speed that it was upon me before I knew it. Indeed, it was only by the grace of God that I wasn't killed, for the animal and heedless rider bounded into my line of vision, brushed against me, and were gone without slowing.

I was thrown backward, and down; I sprawled gracelessly in the street, scraping a hand on the stones so that it bled. Drawing a ragged breath, I struggled to my knees, and then to my feet, searching for a handkerchief to press against the stinging palm.

In falling, I had lost my sense of direction. I stood in the street, hearing nothing but the blood in my own ears, trying to get my bearings. There was a fence there, an ornate wrought-iron one. Wasn't it vaguely familiar? Wasn't it like the one around the house two blocks away from the Robards mansion?

After a moment of contemplation, I began to move again, hoping I was going in the right direction. Surely at the next intersection there would be a guidepost to set me straight.

However, I went on for some time without coming to an intersection. For some reason the block was an extra long one, and all the fences (which were the only things I could see) were too similar to be of much value in orienting myself.

It was therefore with a vast sense of relief that I finally spotted a building I was sure was familiar . . . was it our own stables? I had somehow gotten into the alley; I had walked on a block too far instead of turning into our street, but I was safe, now, for if this was our stable I had only to turn in through the back gate and make my way across the yard to the back door.

A peek into the half-open door confirmed my supposition; I recognized the wagon parked within. I wondered what time it was, and hoped that I'd have time to get in and put myself to rights before Shea came home; I had a notion he'd be considerably displeased to see me, dirty and bleeding, coming in the back way.

In the open space between stables and house I might have been suspended in a cloud for all that I could see. In my hurry I'd stepped off the path; I had a moment of further near-panic until I remembered that the grounds were enclosed; I wasn't likely to wander out through an open gateway without knowing it.

And then I saw her.

I didn't know, at first, that it was a person, of course. It was simply a dark mass on the ground, a tumbled heap as if someone had dropped a carriage robe there.

Black . . . a mound of black . . .

Horror rose in a paralyzing wave as I saw that protruding from beneath the folds of black silk was a woman's foot.

Black silk—surely *my own* black silk, for where it was turned back I saw the place it had been mended with the wrong color thread while I was on board ship—and a black shawl had slipped down from the girl's head, revealing a mass of red-brown curls.

"Annie?" It was no more than a whisper, going nowhere, held to me by the wall of fog. "Annie?"

I bent closer, heart pounding, to reach for the thin wrist outflung at an unnatural angle and to stop without touching it. I heard my own rasping breath—only my own—and stared with stunned disbelief at the knife handle that protruded from Annie's back, between her shoulder blades. Even as I watched the blood spread, soaking the black silk in the dark, irregularly shaped blot, and I knew that she was dead.

14

I don't know how long I stood there, voice gone, limbs trembling, hearing only my own harsh breathing and feeling the heavy mist on my face.

I wanted to scream for help, but I hadn't the wind for it, or, it seemed, the strength to run away.

"Annie . . ." my voice came from far off, a ghostly echo, and I strengthened it by sheer willpower. "Oh, dear God . . ."

The man's voice came out of the thick fog, disembodied yet familiar. "Who's there?"

Shea. Shea was there, coming toward me, his tall figure resolving as if out of nothing into solidity, and something liquefied throughout my system. I didn't have to scream, or move, and I managed to reply.

"Here. It's me, Sissy . . . and Annie. She's . . . dead."

"Dead?" He repeated the word angrily, covering the distance between us in two long strides. He, too, started to reach for the pale, freckled wrist that protruded from beneath the fringe of the shawl, and then stopped when he saw the girl's back. His oath caught in his throat.

He turned then to me, eyes searching my face for seconds before he wrapped me in a rough embrace, pressing his cheek to my hair. "Oh, God, Jade—are you all right?"

"Yes." I was, now. I could feel the strength returning to my knees, and the trembling was coming under control. I spoke his name for the first time, without thinking. "Shea, she's been murdered. Just like . . . that other girl."

For only a few precious seconds our embrace endured, and then I was set firmly aside. This time he dropped to his knees and folded fingers around Annie's wrist, his lips thinning.

"It can't have happened very long ago. She's still warm. Did you see anything? Hear anything?"

"No. Nothing . . . until you spoke . . ."

"What were you doing out here?"

"I lost my way coming from downtown, came a block too far and got into the alley by mistake. And . . . found her, like this."

"Why were you walking from town? Ames is at your disposal with a carriage." He sounded angry, but he wasn't looking at me; he still knelt beside Annie's body, which seemed so much more frail in death than it had in life.

"I wanted to walk, and I didn't realize the fog would come in so quickly—and be so dense I couldn't see."

"Go into the house and get some help—send anybody you find, and Ned for the constable."

When I hesitated, he lifted his face to look at me. "It's only a few yards—nothing can happen to you, I'll be able to hear you."

I turned, then, in the direction from which he had come, unable to see the house. But of course it was there, for the stable was back *that* way . . . my steps faltered, I felt as if I were Columbus, about to step off the edge of the world, for all I could see . . .

I looked back and saw Shea pick up something and drop it into his pocket.

I don't know why that should have lent wings to my feet, but it did. I ran, regardless of the fact that I couldn't see where I was going until I was there; I actually collided with a corner of the house, knocking the wind out of myself. And then I had jerked open the door and was in the back passageway, where the aroma of roasting meat and spices enveloped me.

"Who's making all the racket—oh, it's you, missus." Mrs. Dutton took one look at my face as I burst into the kitchen, her own eyes widening as her mouth went slack. "What is it? What's happened?"

"It's Annie. She's been stabbed. Shea says to send for the constable . . ." My eyes roved over those gathered there—Ned, and Ames, and Cook—fixing on the boy. "Ned, the constable at once."

Ned had gone white. "Stabbed? Annie's been stabbed?"

In the silence I heard the sputter of the meat and the bubbling of the water for tea. It was Cook who worked her lips into the crucial question.

"Is she dead?"

"Yes. I think so. Hurry, Ned." I knew he didn't want to go alone, but who was there to send with him? Ames would be wanted out back. Their shocked faces worked to calm me in some backward sort of fashion. "Mr. Shea would like you to go out, Ames, please."

The old man looked older as he shrugged into his jacket. He took

a last gulp of his tea, looking as if he wished it were fortified with
something else, and slipped past me.

"And I made a fuss about her leaving so early," Mrs. Dutton said.
Her skin had a greenish tinge, and there were beads of moisture on
her forehead. "She said she wouldn't walk home in the dark, no more,
and I said it was hours, still, until dark, and work waiting to be done
—and I was that angry when she talked to me, saucy-like, and stalked
out."

Cook glanced out the windows. "Blinding as if it was dark, that
blasted fog. Can't see your hand in front of your face."

"How long ago did Annie leave?" I asked. I poured myself some
of the tea, for I needed it.

"Oh, must be on ten minutes ago, wasn't it?" Cook turned to Mrs.
Dutton for confirmation of that.

"Something like. We hadn't none of us had our tea, yet. We'd all
had time to drink a cup. We didn't hear nothing. She didn't scream.
Was it . . . like the other one? Stabbed over and over, in the
chest . . ."

"No. So far as I could see she was . . . was struck only once. Mr.
Shea didn't go out right after Annie did, then . . . ?" I heard my
own voice, the question I was amazed to be able to ask, and my cup
shook so that I had to put it down.

"I wouldn't be knowing about that. I didn't see Mr. Shea after he
took care of the boy, and that's been some time back. He must have
gone out the front door, for he didn't come through here, at all."

"The boy?" Alarm flared afresh, and I realized that although Ned
had been here with the others, Christopher was not. "Chris? Has
something happened to my brother?"

"An accident, like," Mrs. Dutton said, and my knuckles turned
white as they curled over the back of the chair. She saw my face, then,
and reassured me. "Oh, he's not hurt so bad, Mr. Shea said, just
shook up a bit. It's the way of boys."

"Where is he? How badly is he hurt?" My forebodings about a trip
to the woods had been justified; I shouldn't have let him out of my
sight, I thought unrealistically.

"He's in the parlor with a rag on his head. He said he didn't need
to be put to bed."

There was more, but I didn't wait to hear it. I wouldn't believe he
was safe until I actually saw him.

Christopher lay comfortably on a sofa, peering out from under a wet cloth. He raised a hand in greeting. "Hi, Sissy. Don't go into fits; I'm all right."

"What happened?" I stood over him, although it was obvious his injuries were superficial.

"I got too close to a tree they were felling." He lifted the rag so that I could view the purple welt and accompanying lacerations. "The tree didn't fall on me, but some of the branches broke off and were flying around and I got hit by one of those. Shea gave Ned and me the very devil and brought us home."

"I should think he might have."

"You ought to have been there, Sissy. It was great! You wouldn't believe the size of those trees! Next time you come along and see how they do it!"

I shuddered. "No, thank you. And Chris, I don't want you to go again without my knowing it."

"Why not? Shea said I could go. What's going on in the kitchen? Is something wrong?"

I hesitated, but there was no way of keeping it from him.

"I'm afraid so. There's been . . . an accident . . ." But it wasn't an accident; someone had been waiting for Annie, or had followed her, with a knife in hand, for the express purpose of killing her.

Some of what I was experiencing must have shown in my face, for Chris lost some of his enthusiasm. "Is somebody dead?"

"Annie," I admitted. "Ned's gone for the constable."

He pushed the rag back so that he could see me better. "Sissy! Was she stabbed, like the other one?"

I nodded, feeling suddenly so weary that I could scarcely stand. "Oh, Chrissy," I said, using the name I hadn't spoken in years, "something's terribly wrong . . ." I stopped, unable to put my nebulous fears into words.

He stared at me gravely. "Sissy, do you think . . . it's somebody from this house? That did it, I mean?"

"No. No, of course not. I'm only very upset . . . I can't think straight . . ."

I left him, then, because there would be things to do, and because I couldn't talk to him any longer or he would pry the truth out of me. For I did think it was quite likely that someone in this house was involved, not only in Annie's death, but in the other one as well. And I was afraid to think who it might be.

Poor Annie was taken away, and the constable came into the house to have a cup of hot tea and to ask questions. I could see that Shea would have preferred that I be left alone and let him face the brunt of the questioning, but the constable was firm.

"If Mrs. Robards is the one who found the girl, then I'll have to talk to her," he insisted.

It took only a few minutes, for there was little to tell, really. I had seen no one, heard nothing.

"We've examined the ground about the body quite thoroughly," the constable said. "There's nothing to show who might have done it."

I remembered then, and knew I had consciously put it to the back of my mind, that Shea had picked up something. I thought it had been caught in the folds of Annie's skirt.

"I don't suppose you saw anything at all that might give us a clue, Mrs. Robards?"

I glanced at Shea, who was standing with his back to the open fire, watching me. Did he know I had looked back, for just a moment, and seen his action?

I swallowed, shaking my head negatively. "No. I didn't see anything at all."

The constable sighed. "Well, the knife may give us a clue. I didn't want to take it out until we'd done a closer examination. I'll bring it by tomorrow to see if anyone can identify it." In the electrified silence he looked to Cook. "I don't suppose you're missing any knives?"

Cook and Mrs. Dutton exchanged glances. "We've many knives here. It would be hard to say if anything was missing, not right off-hand, like."

He nodded and stood up. "Well, thanks for the tea. Raw day, a man appreciates a hot drink. I'll be talking to you tomorrow, no doubt. Good night, then." He nodded in my direction, and I sat rigidly in my chair until Shea had gone to walk him to the door.

For some minutes I had been aware of Shea's coat, the one he wore in the woods, which he had tossed carelessly over the back of a chair when he entered the warm kitchen. I rose now, picked it up, and moved toward the pegs in the rear hallway where such things were hung. The pulses were audible in my ears as I placed it upon an empty peg . . . and then slipped my hand into the right hand pocket.

It contained only one object, something small, hard, and cold. I curled my fingers around it, and shielding it with my body from view of the others in the kitchen I opened my palm.

It was a button. A perfectly ordinary white button, the kind that is commonly used on men's shirts.

It meant nothing. It could have come from anyone's shirt . . . perhaps it had fallen off Shea's shirt only moments before, as he was bending over her . . .

Feeling sick, I replaced it in the pocket and turned back to the kitchen.

Mrs. Dutton stood before the stove, salting something in a big kettle. She was talking to Cook, unaware of my presence.

"Another funeral. That's two—are we going to have a third, now, as well?"

"Annie makes three, if you count the Grogan girl," Cook observed. She was peeling potatoes, which were enormous, the sort they raised in this countryside. "Three—that's it, that's the end of them."

"The Grogan girl had nothing to do with us. But I hope you're right, that this will be the last." She turned and saw me. "She was right grateful for the dress, she was, missus. Said she'd wear it home to show her Ma. Gave me a start, for a minute, she did, when I came upon her in it; thought it was you, for she had her hair covered. She thought it was funny, I'd mistaken her for you. She laughed." Her own face pulled into doleful planes. "The last thing she ever laughed at, poor thing."

I couldn't reply. I suppose I'd been thinking it right along, from the moment I found Annie, but now I had to let it surface, I couldn't suppress it any longer.

I walked through the kitchen and the dining room and stood in the hall, which was beginning to grow dark, although the glass in the doors still glowed with subdued pinks, blues, golds, and greens.

Annie had been wearing my dress. Probably no one but Mrs. Dutton and Cook had known I'd given it to her. Her red hair had been hidden by a black shawl much like the one I wore to town earlier in the day.

Anyone in the household could easily have determined that I had gone to town and guessed that I would return as I had gone, walking, through the fog.

Unlike Pearlie Grogan, who had faced her attacker, Annie had been struck from behind. Not until she had fallen and the shawl pulled from her head would it have been obvious who she was.

Chilled, shaking, sick at heart, the question throbbed through my mind: had Annie been killed because someone thought she was me?

15

"Jade? What are you doing here in the dark?"

I turned so quickly I nearly lost my balance, and he put out a hand to steady me.

"Just . . . standing . . ." My voice was full of tears, and Shea was immediately solicitous.

"What a day you've been through, haven't you? Why don't you lie down, rest a bit until suppertime?"

"I don't think I'll want anything to eat . . ."

"Well, we'll see about that later. Maybe a bowl of hot soup . . . I think they're brewing up something like that. Here, it's time we had a light on . . ."

The chandelier, with the gas lit, was impressive and dispelled all the shadows, except the ones over my heart. My pulses quickened at this man's touch, at his voice, yet I could think such dreadful things. He had said I would be safe when married to him, for now the others had no reason to want to harm me. They could have nothing to gain by my death, now.

Yet the same was not true of Shea himself. His first wife had died under mysterious circumstances, leaving him a wealthy man in his own right, even before he inherited from Grandfather.

But the will . . . the only will that had been found . . . left me no more than a thousand dollars, I reminded myself. A man who has just taken over a business worth many thousands of dollars doesn't kill for so small a sum.

"You look very pale. Come upstairs and lie down," Shea insisted, and I moved with him, toward the stairs.

I couldn't help it. When we parted at my doorway, I looked at the buttons of his shirt, as unobtrusively as I could. They were all there.

I went inside, feeling relieved until it occurred to me that he could well have lost the button at the time Annie was struck down, then come inside and changed his shirt, before returning to "discover" Annie and me.

My father had taught me to pray, in times of trouble, and often I had found genuine solace this way. Today it didn't help. Nothing helped. I lay on the bed and wished for a cold cloth, like Christopher, but I didn't want to go after one. I needed a cold cloth on my very soul, I thought, for I felt bruised and aching all over, deep inside.

I heard Shea moving around in his room for a short time, and then he went out. The stairs creaked slightly under his weight as he descended.

This time I had no compunction about getting up and entering his room. I could love this man. For the first time I said it to myself, straight out. Perhaps I already did, or at least had begun to. But I had to know the truth about him. I could not live with a murderer.

He had, indeed, changed his clothes since coming home from the woods. It was his habit to wash and change before supper. His discarded garments lay across a chair.

My fingers were unsteady as I lifted the shirt, turning it to examine its front.

The next-to-the-top button was gone. I stared at the remaining threads with a sinking sensation that verged on physical illness. So lost in thought was I that I didn't hear him returning; when the door opened I made a quick and guilty turning, to face Shea across the expanse of white bedspread.

For an instant he was startled, perhaps angry, although if that was the case he quickly controlled any visible sign of it.

His voice was normal, friendly—or at least courteous. "Were you looking for something?"

The shirt slid from nerveless fingers onto the bed. "There—there's a button missing."

"Yes. Were you going to replace it?"

Our eyes locked across the room; his face was partly in shadow, and he was well schooled in concealing his emotions, but there was something in his eyes he could not hide, something that caused a pain in my throat, and stinging tears.

I had to know. I wanted to love this man, and I could not endure the sort of thoughts I had been entertaining over the past hour.

"There was a button like it in the pocket of your coat," I said, and the pain showed in my voice. "I saw you pick it up—out there."

For a few seconds I thought he would not reply, or that if he did it would be with fury, perhaps even with physical violence. For there was violence in him; he couldn't stop it pulsing at the base of his throat.

It wouldn't have surprised me if he'd struck me; I shrank inwardly, as he came toward me. He withdrew something from his trouser pocket, and thrust it out for me to see.

For a moment the object itself didn't register; I was looking at the hand, palm up, calluses showing. A man's hand, the hand of one who has worked at hard physical labor. Shea Robards might control an industry worth hundreds of thousands of dollars, but he hadn't gained that control without plenty of legitimate effort on his own part. He'd spent his life in the woods, along with the other men who made up the company, and he loved it—not just the money, but the business itself.

My eyes had blurred and I had to blink to see what he held for my inspection. It meant nothing to me—a bit of gold chain, only three lengths of it.

"What . . . is it?"

"This is what I picked up out there—it was caught in the fringe of Annie's shawl. Not the button—the button came off earlier, and I dropped it into my pocket then." His tone grew harsh, although I thought he tried to keep it level. "So whatever you were thinking about the button, you can now transfer your conclusions to this— it's part of a watch chain."

The lump in my throat was agonizing, almost preventing speech. "I don't understand."

"Part of my watch chain—it broke a day or two ago. The rest of it's there, on the dresser. I haven't had time to have it repaired or replaced."

He waited, as if for my judgment; I was too confused and upset to be able to make any.

"Don't you want to know why a few links of my watch chain should be caught in the shawl of a murdered girl?"

Was he being deliberately cruel? Baiting me? Or was he hurting as badly as I was?

"What do you want me to say?"

As my words became softer, his became louder. "What do you want to say? Do you think I killed Annie? Stabbed her in the back, and then returned when I realized I was missing part of a chain?"

I felt the tears begin to slip down my cheeks and was powerless over them. "But you said the chain broke—a day or two ago. You weren't wearing it—today."

"No. I wasn't. But I can't prove that. Is that what you want? Proof? Proof, one way or the other? I have nothing to offer you, Cecilia Jade. No proof."

"How . . . ?"

"How did it get there? On Annie's shawl? I'd like the answer to that myself." His mouth was a flat line, ugly with suppressed emotion. "What would you have done, if you'd discovered a clue that implicated yourself? Left it there for them to find? When you knew you were innocent?" He flung the bit of chain down on the dresser beside the rest of it. "There it is—take it and give it to the constable, if you like. Tell him where it was."

My mind was finally beginning to work again, and when it did, the moisture stopped forming in my eyes so that I could see him clearly.

"If it broke several days ago—and the piece was lying here—then it couldn't have caught on Annie's shawl when she was near the . . . the person who killed her."

Shea inclined his head slightly. "But I didn't mention to anyone that the chain was broken. I can't prove that I wasn't wearing it, and it's unlikely anyone would have noticed it was missing."

I wasn't talking to him so much as reasoning it out aloud, to clarify things for myself. "Annie was wearing my dress . . . and a shawl covered her head. From the back . . ."

"From the back she might easily have been taken for you," Shea said, and there was a different note now; the hostility had faded. "Do you think I would have tried to stab you in the back, Cecilia Jade? Do you?"

For timeless seconds I scrutinized the hawklike face. Then I slowly shook my head. "No. No, I don't think that."

Some of the rigidity went out of him, the ugliness out of his mouth. "Thank you for that," he said, and brought up both hands to cup my face.

What began as another of the chaste, gentle kisses ignited something far greater; I may have swayed against him, or perhaps it was he who pressed closer to me. At any rate, his arms caught me in an urgent embrace, his lips were hungry, and my own responded with a passion that surpassed my innocent imaginings.

I wasn't ready to be released when he drew back, smiling a little, seating me in a chair while he sank onto the edge of the bed next to it.

"Listen to me, Jade. There is someone in this house who wants the Robards fortune enough to kill for it. I'm sure of that now. I thought you would be safe enough, married to me, because getting rid of you would accomplish nothing but to let your share of the estate come to me. Obviously, my reasoning was too elementary."

I had felt so warm in his arms; I was once more cold. "Then you think . . . Annie was killed in place of me . . ." The idea was so sickening that I gripped the arms of the chair, fighting nausea.

"I don't know that for sure, but with that bit of chain caught on her shawl, what else is there to think? Someone wanted me connected with a murder. Maybe they knew it was Annie; maybe they thought it was you. A mistake would have been easy enough, when they caught her from behind that way. But the chain is proof they intended suspicion to point at me, because they had to have deliberately come into this room and picked up something to implicate me."

I tried to follow through on this, to comprehend the logic involved. "Because if you were implicated . . . in my death . . . you couldn't have inherited from Grandfather, no matter which will is produced as the legal one."

He seemed gratified that I had grasped this myself. "Precisely. If they couldn't get rid of you without losing the money, this was the only way to do it. To be rid of both of us—what a master stroke! Everything they want, free and clear. What difference would it make if I were hanged or spent the rest of my life in prison?"

"Then we're both still in danger," I said, and realized I was shivering.

"But now we're warned." The grimness returned to his face. "They couldn't have expected I'd be the one to find the body, that I'd retrieve the bits of watch chain. They may not have figured out what we know—or suspect—either. They can't be sure the chain wasn't simply lost or overlooked." He leaned toward me, reaching for my hands. "Jade, I don't think you're in danger so long as you avoid being alone with any of them—stay with the boys as much as you can, or with the servants. There's no reason to think *they* wish you any harm. If you have to be upstairs alone, lock yourself into your room. I'll get you the keys. I don't think a killer will want to take any chances that might get him caught and punished, but there's no sense in taking any chances. And don't leave the house at all, under any circumstances, unless I can be with you."

The idea of walking again through such a fog as today's, with a murderer stalking me . . . the tremor that shook me caused him to tighten his clasp on my hands.

"I'll see what arrangement I can make to get us out of here. Until then, there's only Edward and Lawrie and Hesper who have anything to gain. Whatever the danger is, it has to come from one of them."

Contemplating them one by one, it was difficult to conceive of any of them as a murderer. Even Edward, for all his rages and his too-frequent inroads into the brandy, was an ordinary person, not one I could visualize as a killer. Jealousy, envy, covetousness, hatred between brothers (or cousins) . . . these were common enough conditions among human beings everywhere, or admonitions against them wouldn't have been so specifically spelled out in the Ten Commandments.

Yet it was even less possible to look at the man beside me, to feel the pressure of his hands on mine, and think that *he* could be the one who had wielded the knife.

"You will be careful," Shea said. I nodded without further words, content for the moment to see the half smile on his face as he leaned to brush my lips with his. And while it was once more a gentle kiss, it was no longer so chaste; there was a hint of passion that lingered in my stirring blood after he had gone.

My newfound certainty of Shea's innocence of the wickedness around me was not as long-lived as I could have wished, however.

I returned to my own room, seeking out the Bible as I had so often done before in time of trouble. It was a chilling thought that someone wanted me dead, even though I could not be absolutely certain that Annie had been mistaken for me. I sat for some time, first in reading, then in thought.

What about the other girl, Pearlie Grogan? Certainly she had not been killed because she was thought to be me. For all their protestations that none of them knew her except by sight, she had been in this house shortly before her death. One of the people who had a room on this floor had let her in, spent some time with her, and then sent her fleeing in tears.

Whom had she been visiting?

Again there were three possibilities. Not Grandfather, and not

Aunt Hesper. Which left Edward, Lawrie, and Shea. She looked Edward's type, a rather full-blown beauty, but of course that didn't prove anything. Many men chose that sort of woman for secret liaisons, though they would not marry her.

Was that what the girl had been so upset about? Had she expected marriage, perhaps been promised it? And then, when I had come, had she been rejected? Each of the three men had made overtures to me, with varying degrees of sincerity. Edward had referred to the fact that his mother thought it was time he settled down—hardly, I saw now, an indication that he himself was stricken with love for me —and I thought Lawrie might have been inspired to propose from the same source—and been somewhat relieved when I brushed him aside.

Annie, too, had said she'd come to this house because of the attraction of three unmarried and potentially wealthy young men; at least one of them had paid attention to her before my coming, enough so that she'd resented it when the interest turned in my direction. Would it help to know which of the cousins had encouraged Annie? Or was that immaterial?

I could not but believe the two murders were tied together, committed by the same person. If it hadn't been for the links from Shea's watch chain I might have allowed myself to hope that the killer had no connection with this household and had simply happened to attack two young girls in the same vicinity.

There was no way an outsider could have gotten hold of the chain links. One of the Robardses had to have done that.

It was nearing suppertime. I roused from the chair, putting the Bible aside. Often it had offered me comfort; today the familiar words seemed to have nothing to do with my present circumstances.

I walked to the bathroom and washed my face and hands, marveling how even in moments of appalling disruption and disorder we continued to do such mundane things as wash our faces.

There was a murmur of voices in Aunt Hesper's room, and I stopped, curious. Any compunction I might have had about eavesdropping was overcome by the belief that someone in this house wished me evil. The old rules didn't apply any more.

The voices were Aunt Hesper's and a man's—Edward, I thought— but the words were too low for me to make them out. As if they were intentionally keeping them low enough so as not to be overheard.

A quick glance down the corridor showed it to be empty. Lawrie was playing the organ; its notes wafted up the open stairway. Neither of the fat old women was likely to come upstairs—and I'd hear them, if they did; I wasn't worried about being caught in the act by Shea, who might well have listened himself.

I pressed an ear to the door, holding my breath.

The words were quite audible; I had come in on the end of a profane diatribe against some unknown "he" whom I had no difficulty in identifying. I thought Edward paused only because he had run out of breath.

"Don't make the mistake of underestimating him," Hesper said sharply. "That could be dangerous. Shea is no fool; he didn't gain control of the Robards Mills right from under your nose by being a fool. He's clever, and he thinks on his feet; he's quick to seize any opportunity, and he'll stop at nothing to get what he wants. Witness his marriage to the little cousin. He's never at a loss for words, or explanations, and if he has to make them up, why, so much the better."

"I'd like to break his neck," Edward growled; he sounded closer to the door.

"And be hanged for it," his mother asked dryly. "Even the mills are hardly worth that. Don't be a fool, Edward. Don't let Shea provoke you into some reckless action. If you'd used a little finesse it might have been you who won over the girl, instead of Shea."

"And then I'd have been saddled with her for life," Edward said, confirming my guess that his mother had put him up to addressing me. "She's pretty enough, but she's got no fire to her. I'm just as pleased that didn't work out, if you really want to know. Lawrie tried finesse, and he didn't get any farther than I did. It wasn't our fault; if we'd had a bit more time . . ."

"Or thought faster. Shea didn't hesitate; the minute he knew Alex was dying he took the right step. You'll have to admit it was a brilliant bit of strategy, marrying the girl."

"It's not fair that she should have so much," Edward said, a sullen child in a man's body. "She never worked for it, she didn't even know the mills existed! Twice, it's worked for him! Twice he's married a fortune! And I don't care a damn what the official verdict was, I still think he killed Anthea!"

Hesper must have moved away, or turned her back to the door; I couldn't make out her reply, and then I heard Edward's heavy footsteps and knew I had to get out of sight.

Shea's door was nearer than my own; I closed it behind me only seconds before Edward emerged from his mother's room and went on to his own, which was to the front of the house from mine.

I leaned for a moment against the door, trying to sort out and evaluate what I had overheard.

So quickly my newfound confidence in Shea began to crumble. Surely they hadn't known I was listening, they hadn't been speaking for my ears. They believed Shea had killed his first wife for her money. And they thought Shea had been quick and clever to take advantage of my grandfather's death, to sweep me into marriage.

The phrases Hesper had used ran through my mind like a torrent, sweeping away everything else, all the pleasure I had felt, all the hope. *No fool . . . clever . . . thinks on his feet . . . quick to seize any opportunity . . . will stop at nothing to get what he wants . . . never at a loss for words or explanations . . . if he has to make them up, so much the better . . .*

He had come up with an explanation at once, when I charged him with picking up a button at the site of the murder. *The truth, or a rapid improvisation?*

I hadn't seen what he picked up. It would have been either a button or a few links of gold chain. He hadn't been defensive about it; instead he'd taken the offensive, telling me to go ahead and show the chain to the authorities, if I liked.

He had agreed at once that Annie might have been killed because she'd been mistaken for me. *Quick to seize any opportunity . . .* Quick to make an explanation and kiss a girl in such a way as to make her believe he cared about her? Had it been *Shea* Pearlie Grogan had visited? Shea who met her in the thicket to silence her once and for all because she was a threat to what he had decided he wanted—me and my share of the Robards Mills?

My head was aching fiercely and I fought the urge to cry. So easy, with Shea's mouth covering mine and his arms hard around me, to believe what I wanted to believe. And so impossible not to see some truth in what Edward and Hesper said about him. Dear God, *what was the truth?*

He would see it in my eyes, that again I doubted, I thought. How could I face him? How could I devise a convincing mask?

Most important of all, how could I determine the truth?

16

After my worry about getting through a meal under suspicious and discerning eyes, it wasn't necessary to face them, after all. Ned came up to say that since no one seemed in the mood for a large meal, and Shea had gone out on some sort of business, Cook wanted to know if we'd each take a light tray in our rooms? With Annie gone, there was no one to wait table, but Ned with his young legs could deliver trays.

I was only too glad to acquiesce. Christopher was feeling fine, not much the worse for wear except for a lump and the scratches on his forehead; he and Ned would eat together in the kitchen.

I kept Ned a moment longer, to ask the particulars about the afternoon's mishap in the woods. He shuffled his feet uneasily, but met my eyes straightforwardly enough.

"We stood where we thought we were supposed to stand, but afterward Mr. Shea was angry, he said he'd told us farther back. It might have been a lot worse; I saw it coming and shoved Chris, but I couldn't knock him quite far enough out of the way."

I held my face in its mold of calm despite the inward churnings. "But you thought Mr. Shea had told you to stand where you did?"

"Well, I didn't hear him, myself; he said it to Chris. And Chris was so excited he might not have listened. Even getting hit that way, he said it was the grandest day of his life."

"I see. Well, tell Cook a tray up here will be fine. Thank you, Ned."

Another inconclusive bit of evidence. Could Shea have seized upon *that* opportunity as well, telling the boys to stand in a dangerous place and then scolding them afterward and pretending they'd misunderstood his orders? Or had Chris and Ned, in the way of boys, simply pressed closer in order to see better?

For a time I paced my room, torturing myself with speculations. How could I possibly determine the truth? And how could I live with Shea as a husband until I did?

I ate with a better appetite than I ought to have had, under the circumstances. I justified this to my somewhat guilty conscience by the rationalization that if I didn't eat whenever someone around me died I'd have wasted away to nothing, long since.

The house grew dark and the lights were lit, but they couldn't quite dispel the atmosphere of menace. Two young girls had died, and their deaths were somehow connected with this house. Lawrie was again at the organ, and the music he chose tonight was haunting, sad, in keeping with my mood.

Shea didn't come back, and I wondered about the affairs that kept him away so much of the time. Was it special business, necessitated by Grandfather's death and Shea's own new position of authority? Or did he always keep this sort of hours, day and night alike?

There were moments when I relived that kiss, the first real kiss of my life. Moments when I allowed myself to believe that Shea was coming to care for me, and that it was safe to allow myself to care for him. And then the dark suspicions followed, suspicions that must be put down if I were ever to know any happiness or security.

I stood in the doorway of Shea's room, looking at his belongings. There were not so many. He didn't spend much time in this room. His life was in the woods, in the mills.

But there must be clues here to his past life. With scarcely a thought for what Mama would have said, I lifted my lamp and carried it into the adjoining room.

A girl named Anthea had lived here in these two rooms with Shea. She had died, drowned in the bay. Had she loved him? Had she, at the very end, come to fear him?

I moved quietly, alert to the sound of footsteps on the stairs, but methodically, too. Shea was neat; either that, or whoever put his clothes away was careful to fold everything and place it precisely in the drawers. I went through everything and learned nothing. He kept no papers in his room, except the sketches he had made of the proposed new house. I didn't want to dwell on those. Not until I knew.

There was a tall wardrobe, hung with clothes such as I had yet to see Shea wear. Beautifully cut trousers and jackets, elegant shirts, highly polished shoes. There had been a time when he had gone to parties, perhaps hosted them. A man who worked only in the woods and had no time for anything that was not business wouldn't need clothes like these.

And then, in a packet at the back of the top shelf of the wardrobe, I found it. A picture of Anthea, and some letters.

There was nothing to *say* it was Anthea, but I knew. The green room had been decorated and furnished for her, perhaps by her. She was a lovely girl; even the unnatural pose she'd had to maintain for the photographer couldn't hide that. She had long, silky fair hair, and a sweet, curving mouth. She had looked directly at the camera, so that her eyes seemed to meet those of the viewer.

I looked at it for long minutes, uncertain of what I felt about her. So young, so beautiful—and rich, as well. Had she been unhappy with Shea? Had she, as he said, come to love someone else and been driven to what she felt was the only way out, to take her own life? Or had she been unsuspecting, trusting—only to die for it?

I put aside the picture and looked at the letters. There were only a few, obviously written before she had married Shea. They were girl-ish, innocent almost to the point of being childish. The picture of Anthea emerged, and I felt that I had known her. Rich, pampered but not to the point of being selfishly spoiled . . . she had been her father's darling, and she obviously looked forward to having Shea take her father's place.

Nothing there to indicate whether she would have killed herself because she'd come to love another man. But these had been written a long time before her death, when her father was still alive, when she was looking forward to her wedding and her life with Shea.

I replaced them in the closet, wiping the dust off my hands. It had been a long time since Shea had looked at them, I thought.

There was nothing here for me, nothing to show, one way or the other, what manner of man Shea Robards was. If he'd had any per-sonal life since his wife's death, he kept no reminders of it about him.

Grandfather had loved him and trusted him. Grandfather had wanted me to marry him; he thought I'd be safe with Shea.

Safe. Would I ever feel safe again?

I left my door open, with light streaming into the hallway from the overhead gas fixture, and took my lamp to the other end of the house. To Grandfather's room.

Granted, we had looked everywhere for the will he said he'd writ-ten, and not found it. But if he'd done it—and I was sure he had, for his mind had certainly been clear right up to the last—then it had to be somewhere in this room.

I spent another hour there, an hour as fruitless as the previous one. It was time to go down and say good night to Christopher, I decided. Lawrie had been at the organ for hours; I wondered that his hands were not aching from the strain of it. The music was appropriate to the atmosphere of the house, but I was beginning to wish he'd stop.

I could feel it shaping my thoughts, my fears for the future I would have here.

I saw no one in my passage through the lower floor. Cook and Mrs. Dutton had gone to bed; the climb to their third floor quarters was strenuous enough so that they only made the journey twice a day; when they wanted to rest in between, they used the "cubby" which had previously been Ned's room, but it was empty now, and dark.

The boys were in the big room, playing something on the floor with small cubes that I didn't recognize until they looked up and saw me, when Christopher swept them up and out of my sight.

"What are you doing?"

"Playing a game," Chris said offhandedly. "It isn't time to go to bed already, is it?"

"Considering how early you started off today, I'd think you would be ready for it." Suspicion seemed to be my new way of life. "What's that you're hiding? Christopher, those aren't *dice?* Are you *gambling?*"

I crouched to pry them loose from his fingers, and it was a normal, healthy anger that shook me, the first ordinary emotion I'd felt in some time. "Shame on you! What would Father think!"

"It's only a game. We aren't gambling, Sissy. We haven't either of us any money," Chris pointed out. "Ned says everybody knows how to roll the dice in America."

"I don't think Ned knows that much about everybody in America." I dropped the confiscated cubes into the front of my dress. "I'm disappointed in you, to say the least."

"Oh, Sissy! I have to live in this place, I want to be like everyone else!"

"To the extent of forgetting everything Father taught us?" I demanded.

"I'm a Robards now." His face set in stubborn lines. "Shea says when I get old enough I'll be able to work for the mills. Maybe not in the woods, but he says if I'll learn bookkeeping it will prepare me for the day when I'll have an important position in the mills. I already have a good hand, he says, and that's important when you're keeping records."

"Having personal integrity and retaining your Christian values is important, too. I don't think rolling dice is a suitable pastime for a young boy, at any rate. And it's time you were getting to bed; you've had a difficult day."

"It was a grand day, Sissy. I wish you could have seen it, those trees coming down with such a crashing and the earth shook so you could feel it through the soles of your feet!"

Considering how close one of those trees had come to putting an end to him, I didn't want to think about it. I began to turn down his bed and laid out his nightshirt.

He made no move to reach for his crutches. "Is Shea back yet?"

"No. Did he tell you where he was going?"

"I heard him talking this afternoon. He made an appointment to go see that other lawyer, what's his name, Ned?"

"Priddy. Augustus Priddy," Ned supplied.

"To see if we have a case. Won't we get any money, Sissy, if the other will doesn't turn up? Won't we be rich, after all?"

"I'm sure I don't know anything about it. At any rate, we won't go hungry."

"I wasn't worried about going hungry. I want to be rich," Christopher said earnestly. "It has ever so many advantages, Ned says."

Such as making one a target for murder, I thought, chilled.

My rejoinder, however, was commonplace enough, a biblical quotation. *"It is easier for a camel to go through the eye of a needle, than for a rich man to enter into the kingdom of God."*

Christopher burst into laughter, which annoyed me until I saw the reason for it. Ned was staring at me with an incredulous expression on his face; obviously he had not been reared on biblical quotations.

"That's not saying it's impossible, is it?" Chris wanted to know, beginning to unbutton his shirt. "Personally, I'm willing to take a chance. On being rich and getting into heaven anyway, I mean."

Any other time I'd have carried the conversation further, but I was tired and had an idea that my little brother was baiting me.

"Put out the lights and go to sleep at once," I said, and listened to them giggling behind me as I closed the door. How marvelous, I thought, to be young and carefree and unworried.

But that wouldn't keep anyone from being dead.

I passed through the kitchen where the fires were banked for the night in the wood range. The gas one gleamed with polished blue steel. The bread pans were set out, the dough giving off a yeasty odor as it rose in order to be baked in time for breakfast. My lamp could not dispel the shadows in all the corners; my own distorted outline moved ahead of me across the scrubbed floor.

Lawrie was still at the organ. I didn't recognize the piece he was

playing, but it sounded to me of women sobbing. I passed the open
door and on up the stairs, wishing Shea would come home, and uncertain of what I would do when he did.

He had kissed me, this afternoon, as if he had some feeling for
me. I had returned it in a way that might easily have led him to believe I was ready to assume the role of wife. In truth, I didn't know
whether I was or not. In a way, I wished I hadn't overheard that
conversation between Edward and his mother. Until then I had had,
for a few brief minutes, a taste of happiness and hope.

I got ready for bed, conscious of the darkened, empty room
through the open doorway. Perhaps, I thought, slipping between the
sheets, Shea had feigned that, too: the affection, the passion I had
believed was there. Perhaps it was only to quiet me, to pacify me,
until he could do what he wanted to do.

But he didn't need to get rid of me to have control of the mills
and the money. He already had that. Surely a proportionately larger
share, if the second will should be found and I declared to be a primary heir, would not entice him to murder.

I reached out to turn off the lamp on the bedside table. My
thoughts were tumultuous, my uncertainties many. It was difficult to
block them out long enough to say my prayers. I listened to the chiming of the stair clock with the macabre reflection that it might be
counting out the remaining minutes of my life. It was enough to keep
one awake forever.

Strangely enough, or perhaps not so strangely considering what
an exhausting day I had had, I slept. Deeply and soundly.

Wakefulness came slowly and with reluctance. I struggled up
through layers of gauze, as thick as the fog that had hidden a killer.
I was tired; I didn't want to wake up, didn't want to open my eyes.
But there was a noise, I had to determine the source of the noise—a
crackling sound, and then a light beyond my closed eyelids.

Fire.

I sat up, eyes wide now as I felt the heat on my face.

Fire. Great orange tongues of it, consuming the curtains beside
me, licking at the spread across my bed.

It seemed, in those first terrifying moments, that the entire room
was engulfed in flames.

17

I wasn't aware of screaming.

I scrambled out the other side of the bed, even as the flames pursued me across the spread. A few more seconds of sleep and I would have been afire myself; the inferno roared up the wall, and a panel of drapery fell smoldering onto the carpet.

There was a pitcher of water beside my washbowl, but its contents made no impression on the fire. The entire house would go; I must rouse the other occupants before it was too late.

I ran through Shea's room and jerked open the door into the hall, scarcely knowing what I yelled. Whatever it was, it was effective, for heads began to pop out of doors all along the corridors. I couldn't have been asleep long, for all the others were still fully dressed, including Mrs. Dutton, who came out of the bathroom.

"Mother of God! The house is on fire!" she bellowed.

Edward stood in the doorway of the room beyond mine, seeming dazed for a moment. From the opposite end of the hall Hesper urged him to action.

"Get a hose! Get buckets! How bad is it? What's burning?"

Everyone was there except Shea; even old Ames came down from the third floor in his nightshirt, scurrying for buckets. A hose was brought into play; it seemed a pathetic effort, for there was not much pressure, but surprisingly, within a matter of minutes the fire had been reduced to a few smoking wisps of fabric and the ruined carpet and bedding.

"Was you burned, missus?" the housekeeper wanted to know.

"No." Now that it was over, I was icy . . . a cold film of perspiration drenched my gown. "No . . . I'm . . . all right."

We stood staring at one another and the mess. I became aware of my disheveled state and the lack of a robe; it had been lying where it caught fire, and was no longer recognizable.

Hesper brought me some sort of wrapper and helped me into it; it was much too large but at least it covered me. "How did it happen?"

"The lamp must have overturned," Lawrie said. "See, there . . . and the oil ran out and ignited the curtains. It's a good thing you woke up before it got any farther."

"But the lamp was out—I remember turning it out." My lips moved stiffly in protest.

"It's easy to fall asleep without realizing you've left your light on," Hesper said with more kindness than she had yet evidenced. "But very dangerous. The entire house might have gone."

"Takes a lot to fire redwood," Edward grunted. He had a smear of soot across his face, and his hands were dirty. "I'd just as soon not find out how much, though. Well, the room's a mess. You can't sleep in it."

In the ensuing silence we heard the front door open downstairs. A moment later Shea bounded up the stairs, breathing hard, his eyes wide and alarmed.

"What's going on? What's burning?"

"It's out now," Ames assured him. "The missus must have knocked over her lamp, somehow, but she wasn't hurt. It'll take some fixing, though. I think maybe we ought to haul that mattress outside, just to be sure it ain't got a spark left there."

Shea's gaze sought me, saw the truth of my condition, then swung toward my room. He stood for a moment in the doorway, surveying the destruction.

"Yes. Take it out, well away from the house." He kicked at a charred remnant of fabric. "Take it all out, to be on the safe side."

He came back to me. "You weren't burned?"

I shook my head, not trusting myself to speak.

"She can't sleep in that room no more, not tonight," Mrs. Dutton observed. "Do you want I should make up the bed in the old man's room, sir?"

"No." His tone was curt. "She'll sleep in here." He opened his own door, standing aside for me to precede him into it. "Just get everything out that might still be hot . . . leave the rest of the cleanup until morning."

He didn't speak to me until the door had closed on the others. He shut the door into my room, too, making a face. "God, what a smell! Maybe an open window will help." He threw up the sash and let the cold night air in, then turned back to me. "What happened? Really?"

"I don't know. I turned out the light—I *know* I put the lamp out, really I did—and when I woke up the curtains were on fire and the bedding was beginning to go."

I couldn't tell what he was thinking. His face was a mask, the mouth a flat line. He flipped back the spread on the big bed.

"You'd better try to get some rest. Do you want something to take? I think Hesper has some sort of powder that might help."

"No." I didn't want to take anything to make me sleep. I had the horrible thought that I might never wake up.

He moved toward me, then, and slipped the wrapper off my shoulders. "Go on, get into bed. It's safe to sleep. I'll sit right here in the chair beside you and see that it is. We can leave the light lit, if you like."

There was an uncomfortable pressure in my chest, as if something had grown too big for my rib cage to contain it. "You can't sit up all night."

"Certainly I can. I don't need much sleep, actually, and there are plenty of things to think about. That will, for one thing. I think we've got to intensify our efforts to find it, and settle this thing once and for all. And there's the matter of your safety—if you can't be safe here, we'll have to make other arrangements. You're shaking; get into bed. You'll be safe for tonight, I promise you that."

I did as he said, and Shea stretched out on the chaise longue, although it wasn't long enough for his legs. He turned the lamp down low, but not so low that I couldn't see him quite clearly.

I had never been less in the mood for sleep in my life. Tired though I was, sleep eluded me for some time as I lived and relived those moments of waking to flames and smoke. The acrid odor was heavy in spite of the closed door between this room and my own.

Whether or not Annie had been killed because someone mistook her for me, the attempt on my life tonight had been no case of mistaken identity. For all that redwood was supposed to be very resistant to fire, that had been a real inferno for a short time. Paint and fabric burn, as does bedding; had I slept only a little longer I might well have been fatally burned.

Had the fire endangered the rest of the house and its occupants? I didn't know. Perhaps it would have been worth burning the house to have me dead. Or, more likely, the perpetrator would have roused the household before it came to that, if I hadn't done so. I noticed that both buckets and hose had come readily to hand in the emergency.

It had taken a bit of daring to enter my room, relight the lamp, and turn it on its side so that the fuel would run out and ignite bedding and curtains. What if I'd wakened while it was being done, and recognized the arsonist? Would I have been silenced by some more direct method?

I tried to picture them, one by one, creeping through the darkened room and setting off the conflagration that was intended to kill me. It seemed as preposterous with one as with the other. But they had all been alone in their rooms when I dashed into the hall, except for Shea, who had apparently been outside the house. None of them could alibi the others.

I stared through half-closed lashes at the man across the room, his hawkish face both highlighted and shadowed from this angle. Shea could not be ruled out any more than any of the others, I thought. Could he have done it? Could he pretend to my face that he cared for me, that he was planning a life for us together, while at the same time plotting my death?

I didn't think so. Only was there logic in my belief, or no more than wishful thinking?

There had to be some way of finding out. I racked my brain to think what that way might be. The only idea that occurred to me was so frightening that it was a long time before I grew warm enough to sleep.

Even then, sleep was fitful. Several times I woke, fighting terror, as if the flames were once more licking at my bedclothes. The smell of scorched paint was strong, for all the open window.

The first time I surfaced with a choked cry, coming upright to find Shea beside me, his hands capturing my flailing fists.

"It's all right. The fire's out, you're safe, Jade."

I fell back, gasping, onto the pillow.

The second time I made no sound, and once I'd come awake I saw that Shea had fallen asleep, a robe tucked around him against the chill. Still, he was there, and if he'd wanted to smother me himself he'd have done it by this time. On that note of dubious comfort, I went back to sleep.

When I woke again it was morning. Shea was gone, the window had been closed, and there was a carefully penned note beside me on the nightstand.

"Jade:

I've asked Ames to sit outside your door until you're awake, to see that no one disturbs you. I will make arrangements for us to

*move to a hotel as soon as possible, until our own house can
be built, to make sure nothing like this happens again.*"

It was signed simply with the letter *S*.

I read it with mixed feelings. It was only natural that I should want
to get away from a house where someone wanted to harm me. But
how could I know for sure that my potential enemy didn't go with
me? How could I protect myself, if that were the case?

It was not until I had dressed and relieved Ames of duty that I
remembered the idea I had had last night. In the cool gray light of
dawn it seemed absurd, too bizarre to consider seriously.

Yet it continued to work within me, like yeast, bubbling up, ex-
panding, impossible to suppress.

Could I set a trap for a killer?

I knew nothing of killers, and even less of traps. Yet it seemed
to me that it ought to be possible to induce my enemy to reveal himself, if I could devise a sufficiently clever trap.

The bait, of course, would have to be myself.

That was what alternately tantalized and paralyzed me.

To have any chance of success, I would have to make it appear
that I was completely vulnerable and that I could be eliminated at
little or no risk to the perpetrator.

That was relatively easy. The hard part was to make sure that my
enemy was not successful.

My imagination ran riot with the idea all the while I was having
breakfast; it was a waste of food, for I might as well have been eating
potato parings for all I tasted.

By the time Christopher showed up I had come to a reluctant
decision. To attempt any sort of trap by myself was out of the question, suicidal. I had to have a conspirator.

While Christopher ate and chattered, I thought over and around
my idea. The only safe conspirator was one I could be certain was
trustworthy, someone who couldn't possibly himself bear me any
malice. That left such a narrow range of choice that when Chris had
finished off a meal substantial enough for a lumberjack I took the
only preliminary step I considered feasible.

"Come with me for a few minutes, Chris. I want to talk to you
in private."

His eyes were wary. "What about?"

"In private," I emphasized. "It's getting nice outside. Maybe we
could sit on one of the benches in the garden."

He caught the significance of that at once. "So nobody can hear us? Can I bring Ned, Sissy?"

"No. Just you and me."

"You can trust Ned, Sissy. I tell him everything."

I looked at my younger brother. He was filling out from Cook's good food, and since he'd been graduated to crutches I imagined that his muscles were developing; certainly he looked healthy and vigorous. But the fact remained that he was crippled; he couldn't move quickly and would be no physical match for any adult.

Probably Ned wouldn't be a match for a man, either, but at least he had two good legs and he could run if he had to.

I lowered my voice so that it wouldn't carry beyond the two of us, looking into his eyes so that he would be impressed by the seriousness of the situation.

"It's a matter of life and death, Chris. If Ned can't be trusted it could get me killed—and maybe you, as well."

Excitement sparked in his green eyes, and he shoved back one unruly curl. "I'd trust Ned with my life, Sissy. In fact, I already have. I might have been killed by that falling tree, if it hadn't been for Ned."

"All right. Bring Ned," I decided, hoping to God I was right to include him.

The day was sunny and warm in the sheltered places. We went to one of the ornate benches that dotted the gardens, far enough from buildings or shrubs to be sure that we could speak unheard; there was no way for anyone to approach within hearing distance without our knowledge.

I expected them to be shocked by my revelations. The shock was my own, to some extent, for they accepted what I said at face value, without asking for proof.

"Someone is trying to kill me," I said, watching their faces as they sat before me on the ground.

Ned's eyes grew a bit larger, but Chris only leaned toward me with an air of excitement.

"I knew you weren't stupid enough to go to sleep after you'd knocked over a lamp. Who is it, Sissy?"

"I don't know. That's what I have to find out. And I have to do it quickly, because Shea is planning to remove us to a hotel, to a safer place." I didn't mention that Shea was included in the list of possible suspects. "I don't want to leave this house without being sure of who it is."

"How are you going to find out?"

"I can't, without your help. Not without taking a chance on getting killed." I wished the entire prospect of action were as stimulating to me as it obviously was to my brother; instead of excitement I felt only a churning dread that caused occasional waves of nausea.

"We'll help, won't we, Ned? What do you want us to do?"

"I have to know, first of all, that you will help. And then I have to plot something—make them all think I'm helpless, so that they'll . . . try something—only you'll have to keep them from succeeding."

"Like staking yourself out, and letting them come after you," Chris agreed, as if this were the most ordinary thing in the world. "Let's think what would be best to do."

He had ideas aplenty—all of them outrageous and potentially fatal. I saw Ames walk across the yard toward the stables and knew I had to keep this session as short as possible, to make plans before we were interrupted or noticed by anyone who might figure out what we were doing.

"Or I could be lost," Chris was saying, "and you'd come looking for me, all of you, in the dark. You could go over near the thicket"—it was mercifully out of sight, but he gestured toward the place where Pearlie Grogan had died—"and the killer, whoever he is, would be able to follow you and finish you off before anyone else got near."

"The idea is to keep him from finishing me off," I reminded. "We only want to know for sure who he is."

Ned who hadn't said a word but sat wide-eyed through Chris's inventive monologue, spoke for the first time.

"You might tempt them with the will, miss. They're all very anxious to get their hands on that will. I've heard them talking."

"But I don't have the will . . ."

"Some of them think maybe you do," Ned said.

"How could they? Why would I be hiding it, if I had it? It's no good to anyone unless it's produced and turned over to the proper authorities."

Ned shrugged his ignorance of wills and legal matters, or of grown-ups. "I don't know. But I heard Mr. Lawrie saying that if they could be sure the will didn't turn up there was nothing to worry about, was there? and Mrs. Hesper said that was the trouble, they couldn't be sure of anything."

"You could say you'd found the will, Sissy. Even if you hadn't. That would bring them, all right."

"It would help," I agreed. "But unless I can produce a genuine will for them to destroy, I don't think they're going to be satisfied until we've been eliminated, you and I. There's a great deal of money and property, and they don't want to share it with us. All I really need to bait the trap, I think, is to pretend that I'm easy to get to —give them a chance to think they can catch me in another planned accident."

Christopher had some more ideas about this, all of them terrible. I had to point out, again, that I didn't really want to be killed; I only wanted someone to think it would be easy to reach me.

"I've thought of one thing. I nearly fell on the stairs the other night," I didn't mention how unaccidental that had been, "and I could stage another fall, perhaps spraining my ankle so that I couldn't walk. Shea mentioned that Aunt Hesper has some sort of sleeping power; I could pretend to take that, and they'd think I was helplessly sedated."

Chris frowned, pointing out what I ought to have thought of myself. "But Shea stayed with you last night, didn't he? That's what Ames said. If he stands guard over you, how are you going to tempt anyone to come after you again?"

"Perhaps I can wait until Shea has left the house—he's almost always gone during the evening—and then fake the sprained ankle," I said, but I wasn't sure how that would work. If Shea were genuinely protecting me, as I wanted to believe he was, he could ruin any scheme we came up with. If he knew about it.

"He's going to be gone again tonight, I think," Ned said. He was very shy of me, and he always blushed when he spoke in my presence. "I know he made an appointment for this evening with his lawyer. He's very worried, because Mr. Priddy doesn't think he has much chance in court of getting most of the estate in your name unless the new will turns up."

I didn't like the implications of that—when Shea already had a controlling interest it didn't seem necessary to me that he acquire even more of it through me—but it might help get him out of the way for the experiment with the others.

"If they know you're drugged to stop the pain," Christopher observed with altogether too much relish, "and they think you have the will in your room, someone will come in and try to smother you. And then we'll stop them."

This was the part I'd been dreading; getting someone to come and make another attempt on my life wasn't going to be particularly difficult, but surviving that attempt might be.

"That's what I haven't figured out," I confessed. "How you're going to do that."

"We'll shoot them," Christopher said.

I stared at him. He'd never touched a gun in his life. And we both knew our father's philosophy regarding killing. Still, in the Bible a man was entitled to defend himself against his enemies, and probably the only reason David and Gideon and all the others hadn't used guns was that there were none available in biblical times. I hoped it wouldn't be necessary to actually shoot anyone; the idea was simply to prevent them from killing *me*. Still, the idea of guns was unnerving.

"There's a pair of pistols in the drawing room," Ned offered. "In that glass cabinet. They're old, but they still shoot all right; Mr. Shea won a pig last Fourth of July in a shooting contest. The shells are there, too, and I know how to load them. I watched Mr. Shea do it."

"Guns are very dangerous for someone who's not used to them," I said slowly. For all that the sun was warm, there was a coldness in my limbs not accounted for by the chill of the bench on which I sat.

"I'm used to them," Ned informed me. "I always shot rabbits to eat, before I came to stay here. Before my Pa died and I had to go to work, we shot all our own meat. Once I even got a deer—sort of. I put the first shot into him, anyway. And I could show Chris—it's not hard to shoot a gun."

I had a notion my father would have been appalled at our casual discussion. But surely he would have been appalled, as well, at our situation, and he wasn't here to tell us what to do. We had to depend on ourselves—a slip of a girl, and two young boys.

"Well, maybe that's what we'll have to do. Have you posted, with guns. Not to shoot anyone," I added quickly, "but to keep them from doing any harm. Surely they wouldn't, if there were guns pointed at them."

Ames came back from the stables, skirting the spot where Annie had died. He glanced toward us, and I knew that we'd already spent too much time together in earnest conversation. It must not appear that we were plotting or no one would spring our trap.

"We'll talk more later. I'll come to your room this afternoon, right after lunch, we'll make up some excuse that sounds reasonable. Ned, you'll be responsible for getting the guns and the ammunition. You'll have to be very careful about that, make sure there's no one around. And don't get them too soon, or someone's sure to notice they're missing."

Ned shook his head. "Not likely, not from the sitting room, miss. Hardly anybody goes in there, except to dust. And since Annie"— a shadow passed over his face—"nobody's got time to dust. I heard Mrs. Dutton making a fuss over that. She wants to get another hired girl, but she doesn't think it'll be easy—not with two girls killed right here in our own back yard, so to speak."

We had to leave it at that. I didn't know whether I felt better or worse. I was only certain that I would feel *far* worse before I felt entirely better. The scheme we proposed was frightening, but not as frightening as the prospects we looked forward to if we didn't determine who it was who wished us ill.

18

The day passed as a sort of waking nightmare. I made plans, rejected them, speculated on "what-ifs" and "maybes." If Shea didn't leave, none of it would work. If Shea was the one I had to fear, we would gain nothing by elaborate planning unless he was tempted along with the others. And there had to be an opportunity for whoever the villain was to do me in, in a manner that might be thought an accident— or, like Anthea, suicide. Even someone as desperate and greedy as I knew my enemy to be would prefer not to face murder charges.

Unless, I had the sudden afterthought, it could be made to look as if Shea had killed me. To whichever of them it was, this would be an accomplishment, indeed; to be rid of both of us at once, Shea and I.

Shea had no relatives to whom his share of the estate would go; I had only Christopher. I did not let myself think what would happen to Christopher if my wild gamble turned out to be unsuccessful.

Shortly before noon my purchases were delivered from Mead's Department Store. At another time I would have been delighted with them. As it was, I only took the time to put them away.

This was done in Shea's closet, as there was no question of returning to the green room. The fabrics were lovely; I ran a hand over the rose-colored silk, wondering if I would ever wear it in happiness, perhaps going in to dinner on Shea's arm at some fabulous party. I smiled a little, ruefully, for I had never been to a real party.

I didn't hear Shea come in and was startled when he spoke.

"That's a beautiful color. You'll look lovely in it."

He was smiling, but there were lines of strain and fatigue in his face.

"I hope it's all right to put these things here—the shelves seem to be nearly empty. I'm afraid they'd take on the odor of smoke and burned paint if I put them in there . . ."

"Of course. I'll get my things out of here, move down to Uncle Alex's room and let you have this one to yourself." His smile, faint to begin with, faded completely. "I tried to make arrangements for us to move to the Vance Hotel immediately. But there are no suitable suites big enough for a couple and two young boys—we'll have to take Ned, too, won't we? The proprietor insists it will take at least two days to ready quarters for us. If you like we can go tonight, and take four single rooms, but it would mean a double move—we can do whatever you wish."

My pulse rate had speeded up. "I'm not in that much of a hurry to leave. Two or three days, it shouldn't make all that much difference."

"Not if we take precautions to keep you safe. I've spoken to Ned, too. Told him Christopher is not to be left alone except when he's in his room—and they're not to go off together without permission from either you or me."

I nodded, murmuring approval, but my mind was on that hotel suite. Would we, once there, be sharing a room at last? Or wasn't that part of his plan?

Shea stepped past me and gathered an armload of clothes from his wardrobe closet. "I'll take some of these out now. If I don't get around to it, you might ask Mrs. Dutton to make up the bed for me in the other room." The lines deepened around his mouth. "I ought to have moved into it immediately, so it wouldn't have been empty for anyone else to poke around in. Alex made that will, I'm convinced he did. Yet I can't for the life of me figure where he hid it."

My voice was small. "Is it so very important that we find that will? You have control of the mills now. Will it make so much difference?"

"There's no provision to speak of in the old will for Christopher," he said. "He's entitled to what the old man wanted him to have, and while he's a bright boy and getting around now, still, he'll need that

money, that share. And it's not fair to you to be left out, when he
intended that you should be a wealthy woman in your own right.
Besides, there are probably other things he intended to incorporate
into the will—he told me some of them, and they'd be to our advantage. Yes, we need the will. Only if one of them finds it first I'm afraid
it will know the quick touch of a match—maybe they've turned it up
already, for all we know."

He moved away, bearing more clothes than he could conveniently
handle. Some of them dropped, and he was unable to avoid stepping
on them before he could stop. There was a sort of crunching sound
under his weight, and he stopped, puzzled, to feel for whatever had
broken.

He brought up the object, surprisingly intact, and held it on his
palm. "Now where in hell did this come from? It must have been
in my pocket, but I don't remember ever seeing it before."

I stared, feeling the color recede from my face; there was no controlling my reaction and Shea saw it, his eyes avid with curiosity.

"Is it yours?"

I shook my head, fighting the constriction in my throat. "No."

"But you recognize it; you've seen it before?"

Surely there was genuine lack of knowledge in his eyes. I drew
a ragged breath.

"No. But I heard it described."

He was waiting, beginning to be apprehensive, perhaps, as well
as curious.

"The . . . the mother of the girl who was killed—Pearlie Grogan—
her mother was looking for a brooch the girl was wearing the night
she was killed. She thought the undertaker might have taken it."

Shea let the clothes slide out of his arm onto a chair. "Are you
sure?"

"I only know what the boys said, and Aunt Hesper. A cameo was
missing, with a dark red background and gold filigree around it."

His expletive was sharp and explicit. Not too long ago I would
have flinched from such strong language; at the moment, I understood too well to react at all.

He dropped the ornament onto the dresser, and then began going through the remaining pockets of his garments. After a moment
I moved to help him, but they were all empty except for a few scrib-
bled notes in one and some small coins in another.

Shea's jaw was jutting angrily as he moved to the wardrobe for another armload of belongings. He allowed me to go through these with cold fingers while he hauled out the items stored on the floor.

I found nothing, but Shea did.

At first I didn't realize what had brought forth a second and even stronger oath. It seemed an ordinary bundle of clothes, rolled up as if to put into the laundry; when the bundle was opened up for inspection it still meant nothing to me.

It was a man's shirt, very similar to the ones Shea commonly wore to work in the woods, of blue chambray. It was very dirty . . . but the stains on it were darker than ordinary soil would have caused, a dark brown that had made the fabric stiff . . .

Comprehension came as I raised incredulous eyes to meet Shea's. "Is it . . ."

"Blood. Yes, it's blood. On my shirt." His teeth came together so audibly that I wondered he didn't chip them. "Who was supposed to find this, I wonder? Of course if they'd found a bit of my watch chain at the scene of Annie's murder they might well have checked my closet, mightn't they? And while this didn't come from Annie—there was scarcely any blood except right around the wound—it could easily have come from Pearlie Grogan. They said the murderer must have gotten blood all over himself during the stabbing."

I couldn't have said whether the hand over my mouth was to control the nausea that rose through me or the small protesting sounds in my throat.

Shea was still speaking, his words grim. "Someone in this house is going to great lengths to incriminate me in one or all of these crimes. Well, I won't make myself available for any more 'clues.' I'll call Mrs. Dutton to pack; we'll take whatever rooms are open to us tonight; to the devil with waiting for a suite."

He left the clothes dumped in a heap in the chair; when he picked up the stiff and stained shirt I managed a whispered question.

"What are you going to do with it?"

"I'm going to burn it. It's my shirt—God only knows whose blood it is, there's no proving anything about that. But it won't go into the hands of the law as it was intended to do."

He rerolled it and stalked off, leaving the cameo brooch that must surely have belonged to Pearlie Grogan lying on the dresser.

What did I do now? Was it true that someone had planted these things, to be found as evidence against Shea? Or had he simply put them out of sight, not expecting them to be discovered, but improvising brilliantly for my benefit when the necessity arose?

If we were leaving tonight, would it be impossible to carry through with our plans?

For a moment the temptation surged through me: pack, and go with Shea. Trust him. Trust that once out of this house I would be safe with him.

Yet not to know for sure who it was who felt the need to eliminate me—could I bear to live that way, with doubts and suspicions, until perhaps eventually my enemy succeeded?

Everyone was there for the noon meal. The men had come in from the woods, as they often did, for the heavy meal of the day. It was all I could do to eat at all, but none of the others suffered from stunted appetites.

The time was uneventful, until Mrs. Dutton came to clear away our plates before the dessert. Then Shea raised his head and addressed her.

"I'd appreciate it if you'd help my wife to pack her belongings and mine; Ned will be able to handle Chris's things, I think. We'll be leaving this evening, after supper."

Did I imagine the electrified atmosphere as eating and conversation came to a halt? Without being obvious, I tried to scrutinize all their faces to ascertain reactions to this announcement. These revealed nothing, however, though I was sure the air crackled between us with unspoken words.

"This evening?" Mrs. Dutton echoed, astonished.

"We will be moving to a hotel. I may be late for supper; if I am, proceed without me. But whatever time it is when I get here, Ames can bring the wagon around for our belongings."

With a growing air of excitement I realized that Shea's announcement might well further our chances of success if I could put my plan into action, for it would be much more difficult to engineer "accidents" once we'd left the house. Anyone who wanted to harm me would want to do it quickly.

I packed in a burst of nervous energy, hoping that by the time we were ready to leave some of our questions would be answered. For a few minutes I reveled in the memory of that kiss between us, Shea and me—not the cool, chaste kisses, but the one that promised the love I dreamed of—and then there was no more time for dreaming.

If I were not to be taken out of this house, I must stage my incapacitating accident before Shea returned.

I contemplated the method of falling down the stairs. I had to make enough noise to bring someone running to the rescue, without doing any actual damage to myself. The last thing I wanted was to be actually incapacitated when confronting a killer.

I stood for a moment at the top of the stairs, heart thudding uncomfortably, before deciding that the real fall was out of the question. The thing to do was to drop something to make the noise, and then attempt to look as if I'd fallen with it.

That wasn't difficult to arrange, as I was supposedly packing to leave the house. It wouldn't be too odd for me to attempt to carry a satchel downstairs; I filled mine with various heavy items, including a number of books so that it would make a satisfying racket.

It didn't, upon my first attempt. I pushed it from the top of the stairs and it only went to the next step down. I retrieved it, inhaling deeply, and threw it.

It went end over end, the catch opening so that the contents were scattered on down the stairs below the landing; this resulted in enough commotion to bring several people running, almost before I was ready for them.

I hoped I was arranged in a convincing sprawl on the landing; I lay as if stunned, listening to Mrs. Dutton's shocked exclamations, and Hesper's more authoritative ones.

"Stop jabbering, and get Ames and Lawrie," Hesper ordered. "We'll have to get her upstairs. I hope it's safe to lift her. Are you able to move, Cecilia?"

My opportunities for play-acting had been few, but I did the best I could, speaking as if with an effort. "I think I've broken my ankle. It hurts dreadfully."

"Let's take a look at it." Hesper peeled back my skirt, exposing one perfectly normal foot. She tweaked it experimentally, and I gave a low moan.

"Can you wiggle it?"

I tried. "Yes, but it hurts." I willed myself to look pale. "My back hurts, too."

"You shouldn't have tried to carry that heavy thing," Mrs. Dutton said. "That's what Ned and Ames are for. Mr. Shea will be very upset with us all, he will, if you've hurt yourself."

"There's no reason why he should be upset with anyone but me.

I thought it would expedite matters if I brought down the smaller luggage myself . . . oh, my, I can't remember ever hurting so badly . . ." I doubled over, feigning agony, which was easier if they couldn't see my face.

"Ah, here's Ames and Mr. Lawrie. They'll get you up to bed, missus. Be careful, now, she's hurt her back, too."

I went limp, letting them take my full weight. They tried to stand me upright, with Hesper asking if my foot would bear my weight; I pretended to try it, then sagged, whimpering in a way that would have made my mother slap me had she been there.

"I'll take her," Lawrie said, and swept me up in his arms. He was surprisingly strong for a man who spent most of his time playing the organ and painting. I had a brief visual image of someone stabbing Pearlie and Annie—it had taken a strong arm to do that, but I couldn't afford to torment myself with such imaginings.

"We'd better send someone for the doctor," Lawrie said, depositing me upon Shea's bed. "There's no telling how serious it is."

I didn't want the doctor, but if they were to be convinced that I was indeed out of commission perhaps it was best to fetch him. He might be able to determine that I wasn't badly hurt, but I didn't think he could judge for certain whether or not I was in pain.

"Ned . . ." I said. "Please . . . I want Ned to run an errand for me."

"I'll send him up," Ames promised from the doorway. I think he was relieved that he hadn't had to strain his own back, getting me to bed.

The women hovered over me, once more inspecting my ankle. I lay with an arm across my face, trying to draw my mouth into lines of suffering.

"I think it's beginning to swell," Mrs. Dutton offered. "Broken or sprained, one."

"A cold cloth might help it," Hesper said. She was calm and practical. I moved my arm enough to look up at her through lowered lashes. If she felt any satisfaction at my predicament it wasn't evident, but she didn't show any sympathy, either. "I'll get her stocking off. Bring a basin and a cloth."

It was amazingly easy to convince them all of my suffering. A sharply indrawn breath when anyone touched the supposedly injured ankle was enough to do it. A cold cloth was applied to the ankle, another to my forehead.

"Here's Ned," Mrs. Dutton said. "What was it you was wanting him to do, missus?"

"I'd like to speak to him—alone," I said, and the tremulous note in my voice was not feigned, this time. We had begun to put our plan into motion; from now on the danger was real.

The others withdrew, I thought reluctantly. Ned approached the bed, his back to the door, and I saw that he was enjoying himself, which was more than I was.

"Yes, miss? You wanted me?"

I was sure they were there, listening outside, for they hadn't bothered to close the door; I lowered my voice so that it wouldn't carry, but said what we had planned, in case one of them had acute hearing.

"You know who Mr. Shea's lawyer is, don't you?"

"Yes, miss. Mr. Priddy." He spoke in a normal tone of voice, so that any listener would catch that much of the exchange; it ought to be intriguing.

I lowered my own tones even more. "I must see him. I have something important to give to him. Run and tell him. And Ned . . . don't mention to anyone what I've said."

Again he spoke in a normal voice, so that those in the hall could not fail to hear. "Yes, miss. I won't tell anyone."

I let my own volume increase. "It's important, so go at once."

"Yes, miss." Ned bobbed his head and was gone, leaving me lying there with the cloth nearly covering my eyes and my heart hammering so that I felt it must be shaking the bed.

Everything was now in motion. It remained to be seen what would evolve from it.

19

Ames returned after half an hour with the report that the doctor had gone out to Freshwater to deliver a baby. He'd gone for the new man, then, Dr. Henry, but he'd been called to some disaster at the docks.

"I left a message, but there's no telling when either of 'em will be back."

I groaned while suppressing my elation. Far easier to fool the people in this household than a doctor.

"Is it still extremely painful?" Hesper asked. There was a clinical detachment in her speech that would have chilled me had I really been suffering.

I clenched my teeth. "Yes. The cloth isn't helping very much. Isn't there anything else I can do?"

"Maybe some of them powders you have would help," Mrs. Dutton addressed Aunt Hesper. "Until the doctor can come. He'd probably prescribe sommat like that, wouldn't he?"

Hesper spoke thoughtfully. "He might, at that. I can bring them along, if you like, Cecilia."

"Anything. Anything, if it might help." I'd never had a broken bone or even a sprain that was severe enough to keep me from walking; I didn't know how far to go with my charade without risking overdoing it.

"Very well. I'll get them."

I had worried about how to make them believe I'd taken the powders without actually doing so. As it turned out, it was quite simple. The others had gone on about their business, and there was only Hesper left. She had mixed the potion for me, in a glass of water. I raised on one elbow, grimacing, and took a tentative sip, hoping there wouldn't be so much that the small amount would be dangerous.

My grimace deepened. "Oh, my. It doesn't taste very good, does it? I wonder—could I have just a glass of plain water, to wash away the taste?"

Hesper regarded me dispassionately for a moment, then nodded. "Why not? Try to get it all down quickly, though, before the medication settles to the bottom. It doesn't mix well, and it's harder to drink if it settles."

The moment she was out of the room I emptied the glass. There was no way I could do it without being caught up, except what I did: with a silent apology to Shea or whoever would have to deal with the carpet in this room after he was gone, I poured it between the mattress and the headboard. It made no sound, and I trusted that the carpet would absorb it without visible trace to anyone standing beside the bed.

I had my mouth worked into a pucker when Hesper returned with the water. "Get it all down, did you? It doesn't taste pleasant, but it will make you feel better shortly, I'm sure. Would you like me to pull the shades?"

I suppressed a shudder at the thought of being in a darkened room. "No, thank you. This is fine, the way it is."

"Very well. I won't be far away; I'm doing some mending in my room. If you need anything, you've only to call out."

I tried to remember what it had been like, when Christopher had been suffering so with his mangled and infected foot. How long had it taken for sedatives to take effect? How had he reacted to them?

Fortunately, I didn't have to do too much acting for a time, for they all went away and left me. It was difficult to lie still; the soggy cloths on forehead and ankle grew warm and unpleasant, but I left them where they were, pretending to sleep. When jumping nerves forced me to move, I moaned a little as if in discomfort, for I recalled that Christopher hadn't been comfortable even under the deepest sedation available.

The afternoon passed so slowly that I began to wish I'd waited until nearly time for the men to return home. Why had I subjected myself to this unnecessary time in bed, the prolonged pretense?

I heard Shea when he came in; Mrs. Dutton met him in the lower hall with the news of my fall. She hadn't finished her version of it before he was bounding up the stairs, hitting every second or third step.

"Jade?" He paused on the threshold, but only briefly. "Jade, are you asleep?"

It would be harder to fool Shea than the others; I knew that instinctively.

"Shea?" His name came oddly to my tongue; I gave a moment's thought to what it would be like to live intimately with this man, to speak his name in love and affection.

He crossed to me, lifting the soggy cloth from my face. "How badly are you hurt?"

I threw up an arm, partly to shield myself from his view, partly in a genuine shrinking from the light. "Hesper . . ." I said and because I was afraid he would see through my pretense, the tremor in my voice lent credence to my words. "She gave me something . . . it doesn't hurt quite so much . . . now."

I kept the folded arm over my face but was unable to resist sneaking a look at him from underneath it. If he betrayed anything but concern I couldn't tell it.

"Mrs. Dutton said the doctor hadn't been here yet. Where are you hurt, besides the ankle?" The ankle was examined, too, the limp cloth lifted. He didn't touch it, however, so I didn't have to produce a convincing moan.

"I twisted my back, I think. It's not bad, so long as I lie quietly."

"But you can't walk."

"No." I tried to sound drugged and wished I had a clearer recollection of how Chris had sounded when he was in pain. "I'm afraid . . . we'll have to wait . . . to move to the hotel."

I wanted to see his face, his reaction to this, but I thought it better to close my eyes and remain limp.

For a few seconds he didn't respond, and I wondered if he was suspicious of me. But why should he be, after all? I had made no protest at going with him when he suggested leaving this house; he had no way of guessing what I planned.

"I suppose you're right," he said finally, with reluctance. "Well, I'll see that you're safe; you'll be under guard every minute from now until we're able to leave."

My heart gave a convulsive leap. I had anticipated that he might feel this way, and I had to prevent him from sitting here with me himself.

"You can't sit up with me again," I protested. "Not when you have to be in the woods so early. Perhaps Ned would stay . . ."

"No, I can't stay with you during the evening. I have another appointment with Priddy, and I'm going to have to spend some time going over Uncle Alex's room again. That damned will has to be found. But I won't leave you alone."

It was a relief when he had gone. I found that I was perspiring freely, and my muscles ached from the strain of holding them in one position.

Shea didn't make it all the way to the head of the stairs before being intercepted by Aunt Hesper. I couldn't see them, but their voices came to me audibly enough through the open doorway.

"You won't be moving out tonight, after all." Was there a touch of satisfaction in Hesper's tone? Or did I only read my own suspicions into everyone else's behavior?

"No." Shea was short, curt.

"Poor child. She took a very bad fall. I'll sit with her for a time this evening, if you have to go out. If you like, of course."

"That won't be necessary. I'll make arrangements for her myself." He must have realized how he sounded, and good breeding asserted itself almost against his will. "But thank you for the offer."

I nearly forgot to close my eyes before Hesper reached my door; Shea's footsteps were receding down the stairs, and she walked very quietly for so large a woman. I sensed her bulk there in the doorway for a matter of a minute or so before she spoke.

"Shea?" I said his name weakly, as if roused from my painful stupor.

"No, it's Hesper. How are you feeling, my dear?"

"Not . . . well. I wonder . . . do you suppose I might . . . might have some of the sleeping medication again soon? And perhaps . . . some to take during the night, if the pain becomes too severe again?"

Were her eyes slightly narrowed, as if gauging my true condition?

"You can't take too much, you know. It's dangerous."

How ironic that she should speak to me of danger, when I was already taut with fear. Yet I must not show how aware I was of my own personal danger.

"But it's beginning to hurt again—surely it will be dreadful if I can't sleep all night with the pain of it!"

"Of course we'll give you enough so that you can sleep. I'll see to it," Hesper promised. "But it's a little too soon to give you another dose now, I'm afraid. Perhaps the doctor will come soon. If he doesn't, I'll look in on you a little later and bring you some more of the powder."

I lay in a sweat of apprehension when she had gone. Whom would Shea post as guard over me? If it were Ned, we had no problems. But anyone else could ruin everything. Anyone wanting to eliminate me wouldn't do so under the eye of a genuine guard. If I could get hold of some of the sleeping powder it might somehow be administered to an unwelcome protector along with his evening tea. Otherwise, I'd have to trust to the boys to lure him away from his post, and I was by no means certain that would be possible.

The hours passed, and I grew hungrier and hungrier, but there was no way to appease my appetite while remaining a convincing stretcher case. I longed for something to happen, anything, even while I dreaded whatever it might be.

I couldn't help speculating on what the method would be this time. An overdose of the sleeping medication? Smothering in the pillows, on the pretext that I had been too drugged to realize I'd turned into them? For it would be an accident, of course—unless Shea was once more to be implicated, so that he, as well as I, would be out of the picture in regard to the Robards fortune.

My imagination grew too vivid for comfort—another knife, plunged to the hilt into the hollow between my breasts, the crimson blood flowing across the sheets and soaking into the mattress—I gave a strangled cry and pushed aside the cloth on my eyes, staring rather wildly around the room as if my attacker might even now be hovering over me, blade ready.

"Missus? You all right?"

The housekeeper stood in the doorway, then hurried across the room to my side. "Ah, poor girl, the pain's so great it's making you sweat great drops, it is. I'll see Mrs. Hesper, she must have some more of the medicine for you. It's a wonder the doctor hasn't come by this time. I thought I heard the front door a minute ago and was going down to see who it was, but the bell didn't ring, come to think of it, so it must be someone in the family."

I fell back against the pillow, gasping as if the mental image had been real. How was I going to stand it for hours, staked out this way, until the scheme came to fruition?

"What's the matter?" Hesper must have been listening from her own room, for she appeared as soon as Mrs. Dutton finished speaking.

"Ah, it must be very painful. See, she's sweating so she's soaked the bed and it's standing on her face as if it were hot in the room instead of chill!"

My nervousness had the positive effect, then, of convincing them of my genuine distress. They insisted upon changing my bedding, and getting me out of my clothes into a fresh nightgown, which did indeed feel better, but I felt more helpless that way. It was as if in depriving me of my clothes I was deprived, also, of some of my strength and wits.

"There, now, isn't that better? Do you think it's too soon to give her some more of the powder, missus? Since the doctor hasn't come?"

Hesper regarded me in a seemingly cold-blooded way, but she assented easily enough. "Yes, certainly. I'll prepare enough to keep her asleep for the night, hopefully. Who's there?" She spoke sharply when there was a hesitant rap on the door.

Mrs. Dutton opened it at Ned's identifying voice. He looked past the women to me with a worried air.

"I spoke to Mr. . . . to him, missus. But he can't come before morning, he said. His wife's sick, she is, and he can't leave her."

I had no doubt that both women knew who was being referred to. I had sent an urgent message to the lawyer Shea had hired, and now they knew I couldn't communicate with him before this night was over.

I was not an actress, but I was frightened; the trembling of my hands on the edge of the coverlet they drew over me was enough to convince them, I thought, of my distress at this "news."

"Is there anything you'd like, missus?" the housekeeper asked. "I can't be up and down the stairs a dozen times, but if you'd be wanting a cup of tea or the like, I'd bring it on my way up to bed."

"Tea . . . yes, maybe I could manage some tea," I murmured. I would have dearly liked a thick slice of bread and butter to go with it, although in truth it might not have stayed down, nervous as I was.

"I'll bring along the sleeping medication," Hesper added, and as they turned to go I heard her say sharply to someone outside my door, "What do you want?"

"Mr. Shea said I was to sit here in front of her door . . . the young missus." I thought, from Ames's tone, that he was none too happy about that, as why should he have been? After working all day in and around the stables, he felt he'd earned a night's rest, not another lengthy shift.

"Sit . . . ? Whatever for?" Hesper demanded.

"So that no one bothers her, he said." The old man's tone was stoic.

Hesper made an exasperated sound. "Why should anyone bother her, for pity's sake? I'm going to give her something so she can sleep— and then there's no reason why we shouldn't all do the same thing ourselves."

"You try telling that to Mr. Shea," Ames said. "I'll be needing a chair. He said a straight one, so that I don't doze off."

I exchanged a telling glance with the boy at the foot of the bed. Ned knew, as well as I did, that no trap was going to be sprung with Ames sitting guard outside the door.

"I'll see what I can do," Ned muttered, and fled the room, leaving me with prayers that were little more than a wordless jumble.

I had feared that Hesper would once more mix the sleeping potion herself, and insist upon watching me drink it, but she didn't. She brought the powder in a packet, placing it carefully with the glass and pitcher of water on the night stand.

She demonstrated the dosage. "This much . . . no more, or you might not wake up for days," she cautioned. "If you take some now that should see you through the night. If you wake very early and are still in pain, you might take another dose, but not before dawn."

I nodded. "Yes. Thank you. I'll . . . I'll wait until I've drunk my tea, I think."

And then she was gone, and I heard Ames settling himself in the hallway with a long sigh.

It wasn't Mrs. Dutton who came back with my tea but Lawrie. He peeked in at me cautiously, as if I might be contagious.

"Cecilia? Do you want some tea?"

By this time it was no effort to look wan; I felt that way, taut to the point of screaming yet drained of strength, too. I motioned with a listless hand to the night stand. "Just put it down there, please."

Lawrie moved quietly across the room to follow my directions. "Mrs. Dutton sent up the pot, in case you want more than one cup. Are you sure you don't want something to eat, as well?"

"No. I don't think I could keep it down."

This was true, too; my stomach was in a tight, hard knot and an occasional wave of nausea swept over me. I could almost believe I really was ill.

"Shall I pour out a cup for you?" Lawrie's voice was low and pleasant; under other circumstances I would have appreciated his concern.

"Yes, please. And I think . . . would you leave the hall door open when you go? So that a little light comes in?"

"Yes, certainly. Ames has only a lamp beside him; the gas lights have been turned off, so that probably won't be too much light for you, will it?"

I assured him that it would not, and he left me there. Although I was covered I felt very cold. Perhaps the tea would help.

Mrs. Dutton had sent me a delicate china cup and saucer; the heat of the beverage was welcome through it, and for a moment, propped on an elbow, I savored that, warming my hands.

The first sip stopped me as the nausea rose again. It was very sweet—the housekeeper knew I liked my tea sweet and I thought she'd put in honey—but there was too much of it. Disappointed, I replaced the cup in the saucer, thinking that until this night was over my stomach would probably reject anything I offered it.

Outside in the hallway, the chair creaked as Ames shifted his weight and cleared his throat.

Immediately, I forgot my own stomach. If Ames could be per-suaded to drink some tea—with a dose of Hesper's powder in it—he ought to fall soundly enough asleep to convince anyone that he was no obstacle to any action they might plan.

My hand was almost steady as I measured out the dose Hesper had told me, hesitated, then added half again as much more to the amount in my palm, and dumped it into the tea, stirring it carefully so as not to make any noise with the spoon.

Then I called to the man in the hall. "Ames?"

He was up at once, though moving slowly; he stood silhouetted in the doorway, his shoulders giving mute evidence of his fatigue. I felt a moment of compunction at what I was about to do to him, but, after all, he did need the sleep.

"Yes, missus?"

"I find I can't drink the tea, after all. I wonder if you'd like some of it? It has honey in it, so it's rather sweet. . . ."

"A cup of tea would set well, at that," Ames said, pleased, and I watched as he stood and drank it, after carefully carrying it out of my bedroom. "I'll just put the cup down here beside me," he said, "so's not to disturb you again, missus."

I heard the gentle rattle of cup in saucer when he had finished, heard the sigh of satisfaction, and held my breath, wondering how long it would take him to succumb to the sleeping medication.

20

The storm broke with a rattling of palm fronds outside my window, followed at once by driving rain. Somehow, although I had never given much thought to storms except when at sea, this one was fright-ening. I realized why when I heard someone speaking to Ames in the hall. It covered all the smaller sounds within the building: foot-steps, whispers, opening and closing doors were drowned in the fury of the elements. And this at a time when I lay waiting a potential killer—no, he *had* killed, at least twice—and was straining to hear the slightest sound that might indicate our trap was being sprung.

I raised on an elbow, peering into the semi-darkened hallway where the small pool of light from a shaded lamp cast a bright circle on the floor at Ames's feet.

There were other feet there, a man's boots—Edward's, I thought, from the size of them.

In the brief lull between gusts of wind, I heard his words clearly. ". . . for everybody. It's going to be a bad night."

"Aye, and that it is," Ames agreed. "But I've already had some tea—the missus gave me a cup of hers."

The windows rattled, the palms brushed the side of the house as if trying to pry it apart, and I lost a few words. Then, "Well, maybe another cup. It might keep me awake. He'll have my scalp if he finds me asleep when he comes in, but it's hard for a man . . ."

Edward, carrying tea around to everyone in the house, even the servants? It seemed an unlikely task for him, although his mother might have commanded the service. The brandy bottle, kept to himself, was more Edward's style.

When Edward was gone, moving toward the back of the house and his mother's and Lawrie's rooms, there was only silence. If one could call it silence when the wind swept in off the sea, cold and sharp as the knives that had struck down two young women, working its way through every crack. The curtains moved as if by ghostly fingers . . . I brought myself up short.

That was too imaginative, by far, and I couldn't allow myself to get any more worked up than I already was. I wished I were dressed . . . I would feel better with my clothes on, better prepared to cope with whatever was going to happen, I thought. If anything was going to happen.

It would not, of course, while the old man sat awake at my door. What if the sleeping powder I had given him was not enough? What if he didn't fall asleep at all? Or what if I'd given him too much, and he never woke up again? Hesper had said the stuff was dangerous . . .

How long would Shea be gone? This was another business discussion with the lawyer, but on such a night he would surely try to come home as soon as he could. There would be no hearing the sounds of a horse, or the creaking of wheels and springs on a carriage—not even footsteps on the stairs would carry to my ears except during one of those momentary lulls in the storm.

Where were Chris and Ned? They were supposed to get up here and hide themselves as soon as they could, with Ned creating a diversion if necessary to draw the old man from his post. I wasn't at all sure of the boy's ingenuity if Ames resisted; he hadn't Chris's inventive mind. But Chris couldn't come up here on crutches without creating more of a commotion than we wanted. And Ames might well refuse to go anywhere, for anything—in *his* shoes, I shouldn't have wanted to face Shea's wrath for a fault in judgment.

In the hall Ames cursed under his breath. When Ned spoke, he was so close that I jumped, and it seemed that even Ames hadn't heard him coming.

"Is there something the matter?"

"My God! Make a little noise when you come up on a man!" Ames said. "I think drinking that tea was a mistake; it's making me sleepy, not keeping me awake! I've been up since before six this morning; it's too much to ask of a man to stay up all night, as well."

"It's not really all night, is it? Only until Mr. Shea gets back?" Ned asked.

"Aye, only until he gets back! And you know the sort of hours that one keeps! Two in the morning, and nearly time for me to be getting up again, more than like!"

"Maybe I could spell you," Ned offered. "I wouldn't mind."

"He'd kill me if anything happened while I was away from this door," Ames said. "Fillet me, like one of them fish off the docks! He told me so!"

"Well, if you're feeling sleepy, maybe it would be a good idea to take a short nap—or at least a walk around, to get your blood stirring again," Ned persisted. "It's not late—not near late enough for Mr. Shea to be coming home. I guess everybody's gone to bed because it's such a nasty night and there's nothing much to do, but it isn't even ten yet. When did Mr. Shea ever come home by ten?"

"Never, that I recollect." The chair creaked when Ames got out of it. "All right, you stay here while I go downstairs and see if I can rustle up some coffee—that's better than tea for staying awake. I'm so sleepy I feel like I'll die if I don't do something. Mind, you don't move from that chair until I get back, because whatever Mr. Shea does to me, I'll do to *you* twice over!"

"I'll stay right here," Ned promised.

I watched as Ames staggered toward the head of the stairs—and staggered was the word, for he nearly fell, reaching out a hand for a banister to save himself, swearing more loudly this time.

"Don't know what's the matter with me," he said in a thick voice, and then he was gone, the sounds of his descent lost in the buffeting wind.

"Miss?"

Ned stood on the threshold of my room—Shea's room—peering into the darkness.

"I'm here. Where's Chris?"

"Waiting for Ames to get out of the way. He's hiding in the music room; he'll come up as soon as we're sure it's safe. I think everybody else has gone to bed. The lights don't show, anyway. I thought maybe you were sleeping."

I strangled on a small laugh. "Not likely! Right now I wonder if I'll ever sleep again!"

Ned nodded, but I don't think he was as nervous as I was. He'd caught a little of Chris's anticipation of an "adventure," and he, after all, was not the staked-out sacrifice. He pulled away suddenly, listening.

"I think he fell. Should I go see?"

"Yes." It was all I could do to restrain myself, to stay in bed, shivering in spite of ample covers, while Ned went down the stairs. It seemed forever before he returned, and this time he had Chris with him. They had managed the stairs with far less noise than I'd thought possible.

"He's passed out, as if he's drunk," Chris greeted me. "Ned got him onto the sofa in the parlor, so he should sleep it off there."

"He drank my tea. I hope I didn't put too much of the sleeping powder into it. Are you sure he was breathing all right?"

The boys giggled a little. "He was snoring loud enough to hear him out in the hall," Chris said. "See what I've got, Sissy."

I stared at the pistol in his hand. It wasn't large, but it looked as deadly as I knew it was. It ought to have been reassuring, knowing that I was now protected by a gun, even in the hands of a young boy; it made me more uncertain than I'd been before.

"You don't know how to shoot it," I said.

"I showed him how, miss," Ned told me. "It's not hard. You just squeeze the trigger there. It'll stop anybody who has any bad ideas, don't you worry about that."

"Be very careful with it," was all I could think of to say. Chris gave me a look of controlled disgust.

"What do we do now, miss—missus?" Ned asked.

"You get out of sight, and I pretend to be asleep," I told him in the firmest tone I could muster. "Chris in the wardrobe there—and you in the next room."

Chris tucked his crutches out of sight inside the big wardrobe;

there was plenty of room, since Shea had taken away his belongings and I had so few to replace them. Ned arranged some of the spare bedding on the floor of it so that Chris could sit comfortably, the pistol at the ready in his lap. And then Ned pushed the door almost shut; it wouldn't be noticed that it was ajar unless there was far more light in the room than I expected there would be.

It was close in the wardrobe, but decently warm. Ned had the worst place to hide, in the room next door, because the smell of burned paint and fabrics was so strong, and a window had been left open to dissipate the odors, so that the temperature was very low. We agreed that it was only sensible to close the window, since the rain was sweeping in on the floor, but he still needed a coat. He had the mate to Chris's pistol, and he demonstrated for me that it was loaded. He would conceal himself under the robe thrown over one of the brocaded chairs; he was far enough to one side to be out of sight if anyone should enter my room through this one, and he sat on a line with the crack in the doorway so that he could observe the foot of my bed.

"Don't you worry," Ned assured me. "If anybody tries anything, we'll put a stop to it in a hurry."

The entire scheme seemed far more risky now than it had earlier, in the daylight. Two young boys, inexperienced with guns—and I, totally without a weapon of any sort.

For a time the house was silent, with only an occasional rattling window to bring my heart into my throat, and then gradually the wind dropped and there was only the steady thrumming of the rain. As there was a third floor above us, I didn't hear the rain on the roof, but it continued to slash at the windows in an audible way.

After a time I came to hate the clock on the landing. It was so long between the quarter hours, and while it was chiming anyone could have been doing anything and I wouldn't have heard them. I remembered thinking that the clock must have covered the sound of a door opening and closing, the night poor Pearlie Grogan had left this house.

A stirring somewhere in the darkness brought the hair up on the back of my neck until Chris said, "Sissy? How much longer do you think it will be?"

Annoyed because of my fear, I spoke with some sharpness. "How do I know? Nobody will come until they're sure everyone's asleep. Maybe not until three or four o'clock in the morning."

"No, they won't wait that long, will they? Because Shea will be back before then. And when he finds out Ames is gone—well, he won't leave you alone."

"Nobody will come if they hear us talking," I reminded.

"But, Sissy, I don't think I can wait that long. I have to go to the bathroom."

It was a struggle to keep my voice from rising. "Christopher! Why didn't you think of that before you came upstairs? You can't go clumping down the hall . . . everybody would hear your crutches!"

"I did think of it—but I guess it was that tea we drank. Mrs. Dutton said there was plenty for everybody, and it was fixed with lots of honey, the way I like it. I'm just not used to drinking so much in the evening."

At first the alarm was only a vague stirring. "Tea—did you both drink tea? You and Ned?"

"Yes. I guess everybody had some."

I had a brief mental image of old Ames, snoring off a dose of sleeping medication. Edward, uncharacteristically, had brought up tea to Ames, too.

"I'm going to have to go, Sissy."

Outside, something banged in the wind. I held my breath, waiting to hear sounds of someone entering the house, but there was nothing. I kept my voice low, but its intensity carried to Chris without difficulty.

"You can't possibly go down the hall to the bathroom. They'd hear you."

"All right. I'll go in the green room." I could make out his movements as he maneuvered out of the wardrobe and groped for his crutches; I thought it better not to ask exactly how he intended to manage. I sat up, once more bathed in cold perspiration, eyes on the dimly lighted rectangle of the hall doorway, straining to hear approaching footsteps, until Chris came back.

Halfway into his hiding place, he yawned loudly. "I'm getting so sleepy—what time is it, anyway?"

"Quarter past eleven. Chris, who made the tea?"

"Mrs. Dutton, I guess. She's the one said we could all have some."

"Was anyone else there? In the kitchen, when she made it, or just afterward?"

"Practically everybody. Aunt Hesper was there, fussing about cups that had to be rewashed before she'd use them—and Lawrie and Edward. And Ned and me, of course."

I didn't ask him if anyone had had an opportunity to put anything into the tea. If it had been drugged—as I had drugged poor Ames—there was little we could do about it now. But the thought of being alone, while my "protectors" also slid into that deep and unnatural sleep, was terrifying.

The clock chimed the half-hour. Somewhere deep within the house I thought I heard a door open, but even though the sounds of the storm were subdued I couldn't be certain. Surely if anyone were going to do anything it would be soon; they couldn't count on Shea being away much longer.

Unless, of course, it was Shea I had to fear.

I put that thought firmly away from me. I wouldn't believe it was Shea, I wouldn't even consider such a possibility.

There was a thudding from the wardrobe.

"Chris?"

My whisper hung unanswered in the air. I moved to slip out of bed, because if my brother had fallen asleep it was safe to assume that Ned was asleep as well; in that case, all I could do was confiscate one of the pistols for whatever good I might do with it.

And then I stopped, one bare foot brushing the carpet, because there was someone in the hallway.

Even as I sat, respiratory system paralyzed and heart beginning to pound so that it interfered with my hearing, the light in the hall went out.

21

For long moments there was only the silence, intensified by the rain on the windows and the blood thundering in my ears.

I heard the foot on a creaking board—or perhaps a careless toe had encountered the chair Ames had left beside my door. I knew in that moment that this had been a wild, foolish thing to do; even had I been sure both boys were awake and ready to help me, it was too dangerous, too much of a risk.

Yet I had taken it, and now there was no retreat, nowhere to hide. I wished desperately that I had dressed, which was foolish, too, no doubt. How would the fact that I wore petticoats and a dress rather than a shabby nightgown protect me from a would-be murderer?

I sensed rather than saw him enter the room. The light had seemed very dim, but once it was gone the darkness was so absolute, at least for the first few minutes, that I might have been struck blind. Yet I knew someone had come into the room and was listening as I listened.

Listening . . . for my regular, drugged breathing? I ought to be trying to simulate that small sound, but I could not. The breath caught in my chest was painful, and there was no way I could control it. Still, perhaps the storm, dying as it was, would cover my jagged inhalation.

I don't know whether my eyes were beginning to adjust to the lack of light, or whether it was still a matter of instinct, but I was certain the intruder now stood beside my bed, too far away to touch me, but much too close for comfort.

Might I have a chance of running for it, dashing not toward the hall but for the green room? That would give me precious seconds in which to scream—to scream for my life, with the prayer that someone—anyone—would come before the intruder could reach me.

The trouble was, I couldn't see well enough to be sure exactly where that door was—and I knew there would be a faint creaking of bedsprings if I moved, telegraphing the fact that I wasn't asleep.

The form bent over the bed . . . yes, I could see now, a little . . . and I heard the brush of fabric against fabric, and the controlled breathing. So close . . . so close he must surely hear my own ragged and painful respirations, too.

I wished now I had left a light burning. To be sure, it would have made it more difficult, since I would have had to feign sleep more carefully than I had done. But now I would be able to see who it was who bent over me, whose hands groped among the bedclothes for me.

I felt the sudden desperate conviction that should those hands find me, while the identity of the intruder remained unknown, I would suffer an attack as fatal as Grandfather's had been.

It was this conviction which drove me out of the bed, to stand shivering and uncertain of what to do next.

I sensed the sudden immobility of my enemy, and then I heard the deliberate motions as matches were sought and found on the night stand, the chimney lifted from the kerosene lamp.

Could I have run away while the lamp was being lit? I don't think so. My enemy was closer to the door than I, and there was no such thing as moving without sound. As if the weather, too, wished me ill, the storm had died away, leaving only the dripping eaves and my own harsh breathing to fill the silence.

The match flared. The figure beyond it loomed large and dark, and then the wick caught the flame, and the chimney was set over it—as neatly as if we were come together in the parlor for an evening visit.

Hesper set the lamp back on the night table; it cast her face into bold relief and sharp shadows, and though I had thought it would be less terrifying to look upon the enemy than on the unknown, it wasn't true.

Because Hesper had come here to kill me, and she still intended to do it. It showed in her face, in the deep-set dark eyes that raked across my slight, shivering figure.

"You should have drunk the tea," she said.

The tea. Yes, of course, I'd known that, too, hadn't I? That the tea had been prepared for all of us so that all would sleep.

"It would have been easier, all around," she said.

If Christopher and Ned were asleep behind their respective doors, as I was sure they were, no weapons would be brought to my aid. I weighed the possibilities of reaching the one that Christopher had and decided the chances were slight.

"Why?" I asked, and was amazed that I sounded as normal as I did.

"You should have stayed in China," she said, and perhaps that was an oblique answer, perhaps she thought it covered everything.

Hesper, I thought. Not Shea. I knew, now that it was too late, that I could have told Shea. It could have been Shea hiding in the other room, ready to rescue me—Shea, who would have known better than to drink the tea with the honey and the drug mixed into it.

She had brought a pillow with her. A large, fat pillow. It was obvious what she'd meant to do with it.

She was watching me like some great bird of prey, ready to swoop down on me and sink powerful talons into me. If I screamed, would anyone come? Or had they all drunk the drugged tea, so that a scream would be no more than a restless moment in some distorted dream?

The clock on the landing chimed. She nodded a little. "Oh, yes. He'll be coming soon. But it will be too late. You will be dead, and everyone else in the house will be asleep—drugged the way he left them, very cleverly, with sleeping powder mixed into the very tea itself, knowing we'd all be drinking of it on a night like this—and when they find you they'll also discover that *he* did it—and then we'll be rid of the two of you."

"You killed Annie . . ." I said slowly, picturing those strong, capable hands wielding that heavy knife.

A spasm of distaste twisted her mouth. "Annie. Never knew when she was well off, that girl. A troublemaker. As if Edward would have married her—a common serving girl! I didn't know it was Annie . . . I was waiting for you, and the foolish girl wore your gown . . . but it doesn't matter. She thought she had some claim on my son, but I'd never have let him marry her. He ought to have used more finesse . . . it would have all come right, if you'd married Edward. All this would have been unnecessary. We earned the Robards fortune, and we're entitled to it. Alex had no right to leave any of it to you . . . a girl he'd never even seen! I spent years in this house . . . years! . . . waiting on that nasty old man, hand and foot, suffering his slights and rebuffs, holding my tongue when he was unreasonable and cruel. I earned it, and I mean to have it."

I ran my tongue over dry lips. "Your sons will be rich men. You'll always have plenty of money, a place to live."

"A place to live! Is that what you think is sufficient reward for what I've been subjected to since my husband died? *He* ought to have had a share in the mills, but no, they all belonged to Alexander. And my sons have a pittance compared to Shea—he has the control of everything!"

A slight froth glistened on her lips as she spoke. "No, I won't leave it that way. It's not fair, and I won't settle for that. My sons are weak, and foolish, and they'll go through what they have and leave me with nothing. But with you and Shea out of the way, there should be enough for me . . . this house, for one thing. They'll let me have this house."

"You can't hope to get away with it," I told her, with more hope than conviction. "Shea is with the lawyer; they know he isn't here, drugging people and . . . and killing them."

Hesper did a dreadful thing then. She smiled. I had never imagined such wicked amusement, and I couldn't doubt that it was genuine.

"The drugging was done before he left the house, knowing we

would drink the tea. And killing takes only a few minutes. With all of us insensible, who else will have been able to do it?"

My ears ached, listening for the sound of the front door, for footsteps on the stairs, for a voice—Shea's voice—and I prayed that he would come soon, and that I could keep her talking, rather than acting, until he did so.

Not that she was misled by my feeble attempts to keep her at bay. She was simply so sure of herself that she wasn't worried about it.

"I meant to simply smother you," she said in a conversational tone. "So easy, if you'd been sleeping. But now maybe I'll have to do it another way. There's so much blood with a knife, but I brought it, just in case I needed it."

She withdrew it from one of her voluminous sleeves and I stared, mesmerized by the gleaming blade. It was smaller than the one that had been used on poor Annie, but quite large enough to do the job. Breathing was so difficult that for a time it would be suspended, and then I would suck in a ragged and painful breath that made my chest heave as if in convulsions.

"A little blood on Shea's clothing . . . not all that difficult to arrange, really . . . chicken blood does as well as human . . . and I think the authorities will be convinced. Especially since they won't be able to wake any of us before late tomorrow. I've taken it often enough myself to know how the drug affects me, and the others are genuinely in a stupor by this time."

"You're mad." The words were little more than a whisper.

She shook her head. "No. Not mad. Determined, and deserving. I've earned far more than Alexander was willing to give, even when there was so much, plenty to go around. He didn't leave me a thing directly. Not a thing. But I'll have it anyway."

She began to move, then, toward the foot of the bed, preparatory to rounding it in my direction. I was scarcely aware of backing away, moving at the same slow speed, in the direction of the wardrobe.

I groped in desperation for something more to distract, to delay her. Where was Shea? Why didn't he come? Could even Shea handle this woman, armed as she was with a knife?

"Pearlie . . . Pearlie Grogan. You killed her, too. Why did you have to kill Pearlie?"

She didn't stop moving, but she continued to speak. "She was a fool. Only a fool believes a rich man will marry her when she is a nobody, no more than a town tramp. She wanted Edward, and when she found out he meant to have you, instead, she was very angry. She sent him a note . . . a badly written, misspelled note . . . demanding a meeting, demanding that he keep his promise to her. As if she had any right to demand anything of him, the slut. I really had no intention of killing her, to begin with. I only met her to convince her that she would be wiser to remain silent than to come to you with her wild tales. But she was so unreasonable there was nothing else for me to do." Her shoulders flexed in a shrug, as if Pearlie Grogan's life had been of no consequence. "Just as there is nothing more for me to do now . . . except to kill you, and make everyone believe Shea has done it."

"You'll never make anyone believe it was Shea!"

"Oh, I think I will. Many people think he killed Anthea. And a lot of people don't like him because he's a hard man. They would be delighted to believe that he killed you as well; they'd like to see him brought down."

She raised the knife purposefully, and I knew that there would be no more delay. Hesper meant to do exactly what she had outlined to me. The lamplight glittered off the slender blade, and I stumbled away from it, only realizing as I reached the wardrobe that if she found Christopher there, helpless, his fate would be the same as mine.

I veered, then, toward the connecting door with the green room, in a desperate effort to reach the pistol Ned had.

I knew at once that I couldn't make it; Hesper was as close to it as I, she was armed, and she was filled with a cold and deadly determination.

There was only one direction left for me to go: across the bed. I glimpsed her face, unalarmed because she knew that on foot, on the floor, she could outmaneuver me. She didn't realize that I wasn't trying for the doorway into the hall, but for the lamp.

I threw it, full at her, and saw her expression change as the oil spilled out across the front of her dressing gown. Quicker than the eye could follow, the flames raced up her sleeves; as she threw up her arms in a frantic effort to escape, her face was wreathed in fire like some demon in hell.

Only as the flames licked out at the bedclothes and seemed to spread instantly to curtains beyond did I realize what I had done.

I had stopped Hesper, but I had fired a house full of heavily drugged people. And I was alone to try to save them.

22

If there was ever a moment when sanity threatened to leave me, that was it.

Hesper was screaming; she had dropped the knife and run toward the door, trailing fire behind her, beating at her garments, which were loose and flowing and fully conducive to burning.

The bed was smoldering, and where the lamp had landed on the carpet a pool of kerosene blazed brightly, illuminating the room in a nightmare scene.

I jerked smoking quilts from the bed and tried to beat out the flames, but there was too much spilled fuel; the quilts soaked it up and blazed the brighter for it.

I ceased my feeble attempt to fight the fire. I couldn't do it alone, and I had no idea where the hoses were kept or hooked up. Already there was far more than could be quenched by a few bucketfuls of water. I had to try to get the others out of the house before the entire thing went up.

I stepped backward, and collided with a solid body. Even as the scream rose in my throat, I recognized the hands that swept me away from the fire.

Shea had finally come.

There were three of them, besides Shea, and for a time I was too confused to comprehend their presence or determine how they had come to be here.

I shouted to Shea that Christopher was in the wardrobe; he was grim-faced, but left me to rescue my brother, who was soundly asleep in the nest of blankets there. I was frantic to get him outside, but someone spoke to me, soothing, reassuring.

"The house isn't going to go, Mrs. Robards. We'll have it out in a jiffy; just you stay out there, out of the way, with the lad. Just a little water, that's all we need."

A little water. An impossibility for me. To four able-bodied men, it was a matter of minutes' work to bring things under control. Granted, the room was a shambles, every bit as bad as the green room next door, but except for a little smoke damage on the hall ceilings nothing else was much disturbed.

Not until it was all over did Shea turn to me, opening his arms; I moved into them as if I had never belonged anywhere else.

"It was Hesper," I began, opening parched lips, but he only drew me close.

"You don't have to tell me. I heard it all," he said, and rested a cheek against my head.

"You gave us a bad minute or two, though, throwing that lamp," another voice said cheerfully. After a moment I realized who he was: the constable. The lawyer, Priddy, was there, as well as the constable's assistant. "We weren't prepared for that. We didn't want to step in too soon, not before we'd heard all she had to say and were sure of our ground."

I drew back a little from Shea's embrace to look into his face. "I don't understand. Where were you?"

The other men were smiling somewhat, but there was no smile on Shea's lips. "In the green room. Listening."

All the time I had been rigid with fear? All the time I had been waiting to feel the chill of that steel blade in my chest? Shea had been here?

He must have read some of this in my face.

"You should have told me what you were planning." Perhaps he read the answer to that, too, for he didn't press the point. "It's a good thing I guessed what was going on. I was sure you weren't badly hurt once I'd taken a good look at you. And the boys were too excited over something to conceal it. It took me a time to figure it out, and since you hadn't seen fit to confide in me"—there was no censure there that I could read—"I decided to let you play it out, your own way. If there was a killer in this house, the sooner he was unmasked the better. And the more witnesses, the better." He gestured with a grimy hand at the other men.

"He came to me with an incredible story," the constable told me. "I couldn't believe it, at first—putting evidence at the scene of a murder to implicate someone else in his own family—we don't have much of that sort of crime in Eureka. But he convinced me that it couldn't hurt to come along and see what happened here tonight."

He shook his head wonderingly. "Finding everyone drugged, asleep, gave us our first clue that we were on the right path, so to speak. Not a normal state of affairs, certainly. You did very well, Mrs. Robards, in drawing the truth out of the woman."

I remembered her then. "Hesper—her garments were burning . . . !"

"She'd have gone to the bathroom, for water," Priddy suggested, but Shea was already moving down the hall.

He didn't let me follow him into the room; after seeing his face, I made no attempt to do so.

"I don't know if she was seriously burned. I'd say not, although it must have been very painful."

"Is she dead?" The constable stepped to the doorway, then vanished inside, out of my sight.

"No, but she's unconscious," Shea said, for the benefit of the rest of us. "She must have had the devil of a quantity of that sleeping stuff, the way she spread it around tonight. I hope the others will all come out of it; I'll be very surprised if *she* does. She wouldn't want to."

"Well, we've got our work cut out for us," the assistant constable said briskly. "We'd better get a doctor over to look at all these people, see if anything needs to be done for them. I suspect, though, it's simply a matter of letting them all sleep it out. Shall we take the boy downstairs, put him into his own bed, then?"

"Yes, please. And Ned, too—he's in the green room."

"Sleeping like a babe," the lawyer confirmed. "Too bad you didn't think to ask her one more thing, Mrs. Robards." At my questioning look, he added, "About the will. If there was another one. If she found it."

"We've stripped Uncle Alex's room," Shea told him. "Everything but the paper off the walls. If he wrote one, it had to be there, because he didn't leave the room, and nothing was taken out of there before we began to search. So either they found it and destroyed it— or he didn't finish one, after all."

"You may have to settle for the old will, then," Priddy told him. "We can try for a better court decision than that, but without the will itself—well, it's unlikely we'll get far, even after what's happened here, tonight. It was only Hesper Robards herself; there's no evidence either of her sons was involved in any of the dirtiness."

My attention had caught, somewhere back, on Shea's words. Unconscious of my disheveled state, unaware even that I was shivering with cold in spite of Shea's coat thrown around me, I drew the conclusion out of the back of my mind.

"Shea . . . there was one thing taken out of Grandfather's room."

The men fell silent, staring at me.

"And what was that, Jade?"

"The figurine I brought him from China. It was a puzzle . . . it comes apart, somehow, although none of us had found its secret. Grandfather loved puzzles. Perhaps"—and excitement began to grow within me—"perhaps he found out how to open it . . . perhaps he hid the will there, thinking we would attempt to solve the puzzle, too."

"I'm not a bad hand at puzzles," the assistant constable said, and when I brought the jade figurine and put it into his hands he examined it closely, touching, prying, twisting, absorbed in the task.

"I still don't understand everything," I said. "You left the house, and I listened so carefully for your return—how did four of you get upstairs and into the green room without our hearing you?"

"We'd been there for some time, Priddy and I," Shea said, his mouth softening. "The others were checking the rest of the house, but I didn't want to let you out of my sight long enough to help them. We came in through the window—luckily it was open, and that didn't make any noise. We brought the tall ladders from the fire department —as a matter of fact, there's a fire wagon down in the side yard, if we'd needed it. There was no other way to get inside without being seen and heard. It was a wet and nasty business, and we've been sitting around in damp clothes for hours, now, cramped together in the wardrobe closet. We'll probably all have pneumonia tomorrow." His slight smile belied any worry on this score, however. "You gave us a bad few minutes when it looked as if young Ned might try to hide himself in the closet with us."

"Aha! And that does it!"

We turned to see that the jade figurine had fallen before the cleverness of the assistant constable. He held the head aloft, triumphant.

"And there's the will," Priddy said softly. "Well, that should do it all up nicely."

There was more, of course. The doctor came to check on everyone in the house, all of whom were pronounced to be sleeping soundly but not dangerously, so far as the doctor could tell.

Hesper, at that time, seemed no different than the rest, but we all knew; she had taken everything that was left of the sleeping powder, and there had been far more than I had put into poor Ames's tea. She was put into her own bed and the doctor shook his head over her.

Christopher, to my relief, roused slightly as we were putting him to bed; his eyelids fluttered, and he murmured, "Sissy?" until I spoke to him.

"Christopher will be all right," I said aloud.

"And you, Jade? Will you be all right?"

I turned to look into Shea's dark and sober eyes.

"We can't leave this house tonight. Not until"—I gestured at the sleeping boy before us—"everyone wakes up."

"No," he agreed.

"There's only one room left that's fit to sleep in. Grandfather's room."

He waited a few seconds more, and I knew that it was up to me to make the decision. He was not going to force me into it.

"Shea, let's go up to bed."

He smiled then, and swept me up into his arms so that his coat fell off my shoulders onto the floor.

When he bent his head to kiss me I knew that my worries about a passionless marriage were groundless. I closed my eyes and let him carry me up the stairs. Tomorrow we would leave this house, and until our own could be built we would be homeless, but it didn't matter.

From now on my home would be within the circle of these arms.